AFTER
THE HORSES

AFTER THE HORSES

A Dan Sharp Mystery

Jeffrey Round

DUNDURN
TORONTO

Editor: Shannon Whibbs
Design: Courtney Horner
Cover Design: Laura Boyle
Front Cover Image: © Olivier Le Queinec
Author Photo: © Don McNeill
Printer: Webcom

Library and Archives Canada Cataloguing in Publication

Round, Jeffrey, author
        After the horses / Jeffrey Round.

(A Dan Sharp mystery)
Issued in print and electronic formats.
ISBN 978-1-4597-3131-8 (pbk.).--ISBN 978-1-4597-3132-5 (pdf).--
ISBN 978-1-4597-3133-2 (epub)

        I. Title. II. Series: Round, Jeffrey. Dan Sharp mystery.

PS8585.O84929A64 2015   C813'.54   C2015-901268-6
                                              C2015-901269-4

1   2   3   4   5   19   18   17   16   15

We acknowledge the support of the **Canada Council for the Arts** and the **Ontario Arts Council** for our publishing program. We also acknowledge the financial support of the **Government of Canada** through the **Canada Book Fund** and **Livres Canada Books**, and the **Government of Ontario** through the **Ontario Book Publishing Tax Credit** and the **Ontario Media Development Corporation.**

Care has been taken to trace the ownership of copyright material used in this book. The author and the publisher welcome any information enabling them to rectify any references or credits in subsequent editions.

                                                    J. Kirk Howard, President

The publisher is not responsible for websites or their content unless they are owned by the publisher.

VISIT US AT
Dundurn.com | @dundurnpress | Facebook.com/dundurnpress | Pinterest.com/dundurnpress

Dundurn
3 Church Street, Suite 500
Toronto, Ontario, Canada
M5E 1M2

For Red Cruz, a great companion

And for Felice Picano, Andrew Holleran, and Edmund White, great pathfinders

"Why lock the barn door after the horses have bolted?"
— ENGLISH IDIOM

Contents

Prologue

Toronto — 2011
Immigrants

Her breath came out in white slashes. February was a hateful month, inhuman and frozen over. She was late and not for the first time. It wasn't her fault, but that wouldn't matter to him. She willed her feet to hurry, watching warily for ice. No good falling and breaking her neck on top of everything else. His words came back to her in the crisp, precise tones of someone who had learned English as a second language: *I need punctual help, Irma. I don't appreciate dawdlers, even if you're just cleaning my toilet. I expect you to be on time. Please don't let it happen again.*

Please. He'd said *please* at least.

What he hadn't said was what would happen if she showed up late again, though she had a sinking feeling she was about to find out. He was a wicked man. There were no warm feelings, no acts of kindness stirring in his depths. A snowman planted in one of the yards reminded her of his tiny eyes and bleak, humourless gaze. Yuri Malevski.

"Bloody Macedonians — hard as rock!" she swore under her breath.

She would beg, if it came to that. She would remind him she was honest. Nothing had gone missing by her hand in the two years she'd worked for him. Everyone knew stories about the help who stole and pillaged, taking what wasn't rightly theirs. She would never steal so long as she had food to eat and a roof over her head. She was poor, not desperate.

It was the same from house to house. She scrubbed toilets, mopped floors, and wiped the children's bums, all without question. She walked pets and toted empty liquor bottles quietly out the back door so the neighbours wouldn't see. There was no end to the services she provided. The women were the worst. They expected perfection: floors you could eat off, countertops you could see your reflection in, toilets you could drink from. She wondered that some of them didn't ask her to screw their husbands to save them the bother.

They all took advantage. *No papers, Irma? Tsk-tsk. Here's what we will pay you, then.* What choice did she have? They might be surprised to know she'd grown up with finery. As a girl, she had ball gowns and jewellery and cut flowers in the house. Back home she'd had manners and once — *once!* — she'd been beautiful. Then time caught up with her. She wasn't young anymore. Even her hands were pitiful to look at now.

Everywhere she went, they wanted something from her. This one especially, with his parties and the boys coming and going at all hours in all states of dress and inebriation and god knows what else. The tales she could tell, if she had the chance. He was almost like a woman himself! Fancy clothes and expensive haircuts and all the trappings. He once told her how much he'd paid to have his hair done. She was shocked! It was more than he gave her for an afternoon's wages.

No wonder everyone took from him. Boys he met god knows where, eating his food and drinking his alcohol. Because he let them! He just laughed. And then there was that dreadful one she'd run into early one morning, neither man nor woman. She could hardly countenance that.

"Filth. Depravity."

She spat the words like stones then looked around to see if anyone had seen her talking to herself. No one had noticed.

Yes, the stories she could tell. There were drugs in that house and worse. Oh, far worse! She couldn't choose her employers, but she could pray for their salvation. It was her duty. God's little test. She had the pamphlets in her purse. She would leave another one on the counter today. Maybe one day he would read it.

She turned the corner onto Beatty Avenue, counting the steps to the grey monolith. The house loomed. Stone, built in the last century, with three separate chimneys. Necessary, no doubt, back in the day when people heated everything with coal and the rich had servants to stoke their fires. She shivered, grateful at least that she lived in the present age. It was hard being poor today, never mind in centuries past.

She let herself in the iron gates and pulled them closed, trudging along the path like a dwarf approaching a giant's castle. Yesterday's snow lay undisturbed. No one had shovelled or swept the drive. If Yuri Bloody Malevski was so proud of his yard, he might pay one of those boys to clear the way. Or get them to do it for free for all the parties he threw.

She gripped the railing with a gloved hand and hauled herself up. The door was double-locked from inside. Strange, because that only happened when her boss went out of town. He'd texted her a new entry code the previous day, but he hadn't said anything about being away. He was a stickler for security, having been burgled twice. She knew that because he made a point of telling her. His home was full of valuables: artwork, rare books, carpets, antique table settings. The sort of things you found in the best residences in Europe. All the doors and windows were alarmed. He made sure she knew that, too.

She stepped back and looked up at the house. Dark and unwelcoming, that was how she always saw it. The windows were uniformly large, but darkness showed behind them all, even in daytime. A devil's house. It made her shiver. There was nothing for it but to go all the way around back.

She stepped off the porch, the snow already over the tops of her boots. Drifts like white waves curled and froze mid-air. The storm had blanketed the yard. No footsteps showed here, either. She pulled open the rickety screen door, checking her phone for the new code. He was always changing it then changing it back again. At least this time he remembered to tell her. Once he forgot to let her know. She'd showed up and couldn't get in until he returned in his big blue Mercedes. Fine for him to make mistakes!

She punched in the numbers. A red light turned to green. The latch clicked and she pulled hard. The door crackled from the cold. Then she was inside, a beep registering her entry. She had twenty seconds to re-enter the code and shut off the alarm or she'd have security swarming over the premises. Or so he said. Maybe one day she'd let it go off and see what happened. What could they do? She re-entered the numbers and the beeping stopped.

Safe.

Inside, all was silent. She hoped she wouldn't find naked bodies lying on the sofas and spare beds. It wouldn't be the first time. Sin and abomination. Sodom and Gomorrah. God's wrath on the sinful.

A quick glance told her the place was tidy. Maybe the boy, Santiago, was back. He was one of the few who bothered to lift a hand around the place. An illegal like her, he once said she reminded him of his mother. Sometimes he slipped her an extra twenty for her hard work. Malevski had taunted the poor boy by dangling citizenship in front of him, getting his hopes up. Men marrying men, imagine that! It was a crazy country she'd come to. But then they'd argued and he'd been out of favour for the past few weeks.

If not Santiago, then maybe it was that other boy who lived under the stairs. The one with the pale makeup, his face like a vampire's. There was something not quite right about him. She didn't like to be alone in the house when he was up there in that little room. She'd read his diary once, just a few lines: *Dear Darkness, I want to die.* Terrible!

She set her purse on a table in the hall then took off her gloves and coat, laying them over the big blue chair. It was cold. That was Malevski saving money on the heating bills again, no doubt. She flicked the thermostat and heard the furnace starting up.

Still no sign of her boss. If he was going to fire her for being late, surely he'd have been there to meet her when she arrived. Or maybe he intended to let her finish her day's work then give her the sack without pay. It wasn't as though she could complain to anyone.

The kitchen was dirtiest. The remains of a meal lay in the sink. She put on gloves and soaked the dishes, making sure the water was extra hot. The food was caked on and hardened. Italian? Lasagna, maybe. There was something sticky on the floor and a spray of dried sauce across one of the cupboard doors.

That was the worst of it. The dining room hadn't been used since her last visit. A little dust only. Once again she wiped down all the surfaces, wringing the rags out, the water left clean in the pail. When she finished, she took the pamphlet from her purse and carried it to the long dining table. She always left one behind for him, but he never said anything. Someday he would read them.

She stopped abruptly. There he was already, the same pamphlet propped against the silver candlestick holders. Jesus with his purple heart staring back at her.

"Make him repent his wickedness!" she hissed, crossing herself.

She stopped for a moment to listen. Irma was used to being in empty houses, but this one gave her the creeps. She wondered if the strange boy was upstairs in his little room. Fortunately, he never asked her to clean it. He was rather neat in that regard, and kept the place spotless. Once, she asked if he would like her to wash the floor. *I'm entirely capable*, he told her. She wasn't sure about that, but didn't bother to contradict him.

A phone rang in another room, echoing through the place until an answering machine picked up. "This is Yuri Malevski," came her boss's voice with its distinctive pronunciation before clicking over to record.

Irma listened, thinking he might be trying to reach her. Perhaps he got delayed somewhere because of the snow and wanted to give her special instructions. But it wasn't him. It was his accountant saying he was still out of town and confirming Saturday's meeting.

The call ended. Almost immediately, it rang again. This time it was a florist saying he'd attempted a delivery on Tuesday, but hadn't been able to use the entry code he'd been given. He was unwilling to leave the flowers because of the cold and left a number to reschedule. So it wasn't just her. Yuri Malevski forgot to give the code to others, too.

She paused with the dust rag to listen for sounds from upstairs. For all she knew, he could still be lying in bed. He expected her to get to his house by eight in the morning, while he idled away the day. He probably hadn't any idea how horrific the weather was outside. And why would he? When he went out, he simply stepped into his car and zoomed off without feeling a thing. Life was easy for some.

She rinsed out her washcloths and emptied the bucket into the kitchen sink before going back out to the hall. The place was finally beginning to warm up.

It was the flowers that gave her pause.

She'd always thought it a marvel how you could be in the depths of darkness in that mausoleum, and then step through a doorway where all was light and airy, the windows stretching up twenty feet. Now petals lay curled and withered on the conservatory floor. He'd always been fastidious about his plants. *Never touch my orchids*, he told her when she asked if he wanted her to water them. *They're particular.* Just like you, she wanted to say, but held her tongue. They required three ice cubes per pot, once a week, he explained. He preferred to do it himself.

Ice cubes!

They didn't even grow in soil, just absorbent material that retained water after the ice melted. Now, looking over the petals strewn across the floor, she saw that nearly all the flowers had dropped. How could he not have noticed? Not that she cared. She disliked orchids. They were sinister. The leaves were waxy, the petals cool to touch like the flesh of the dead. One or two had kept their flowers, the blossoms curling around the centres as though shielding a tiny throne. They looked as if they concealed something evil, like in those horror movies where creatures emerged from things when people turned their backs on them.

He'd given her a tour the first day she came to work for him. Some of them cost a great deal of money, he told her. They'd been imported from far-off lands. She wasn't sure if he said it to impress her or to make her wary of touching them when he wasn't around. *The name comes from the Greek* orchis, he'd informed her in his precise English. *Why is that?* she'd asked in all innocence. He'd smiled his cruel smile and pulled one from its pot. Orchis *means testicle, you see.* There, dangling before her, were twin tubers looking for all the world like a man's privates.

Wickedness!

He laughed to see her blush and cross herself. *Ah, Irma! You're so innocent,* he told her, then turned back to his flowers.

But here they were now, fallen at her feet. She went to the pantry to retrieve the vacuum, sitting it upright while she trailed the long black cord to the wall and inserted the plug. The whirring noise was comforting. The blossoms were gone inside a minute. She just hoped he wouldn't blame her for the damage.

She closed the door on the plants and lugged the vacuum to the foot of the stairs. Carrying it up was always a chore. Of course, he was too cheap to get a second one for upstairs. She stopped to rest a moment before continuing. Then she saw the stains. Like the ones in the kitchen, only darker. First on one stair and then another higher up.

"God in heaven!"

She left the vacuum at the foot of the stairs. Her hands shook as she continued upward. Dead flowers and a house in the deep freeze. Yes, there was evil in this place.

She felt it in her bones, and her bones were never wrong.

One

Izakaya

"Just talk to the guy, would you?"

Dan rolled his eyes. "I can't get involved. This is police business."

There was a pause followed by the telltale sound of a match being struck on the other end of the phone. *Any excuse for nicotine*, Dan thought. *Where the hell does he get actual matches these days?*

Donny was using his Reasoning with a Child voice: "No one's asking you to get involved. He just wants your candid opinion. I know he would very much appreciate it."

Dan sighed. It was no good arguing; he was useless at evasion. Drive the truck straight down the freeway, none of this mucking about in back alleyways stuff. That was his style.

"All right," he conceded. "I'll talk to him."

"Thank you."

"As a favour to you — no other reason."

"So in other words, I owe you."

"In other words, you owe me *again*."

There was a breathy, pack-a-day chortle. "Let me know when you want to collect."

"Oh, I will. Don't worry."

In any conversation with Donny, the smooth exhale of a well-smoked cigarette was a familiar sound. Being asked to participate in a case that had all the markings of a police-only investigation was not. If anything, Donny was the one to urge caution, advising Dan to keep a low profile on risky undertakings, but here he was encouraging Dan to step directly into the ring.

"So who is he again?"

"You remember Charles?"

"Sort of. Well, no. Not really."

"He's the lawyer I dated briefly after Jorge the Argentine soccer player."

"Jorge I remember. Oh, yeah. The legs."

"Right. Getting back to Charles."

"Sorry. No facial here. Remind me."

"Good looking. White. Square jaw and all that. Probably not exotic enough for you, that's why you don't recall him. Anyway, Charles started dating this guy, Lionel. An accountant. Also very good-looking. They're the perfect couple. They had the most spectacular wedding on their penthouse balcony in Radio City a couple years ago. It was big enough to hold a hundred people. They're both very successful, lots of money between them. And believe me when I say they lack for nothing."

"Oh, I believe you."

"Good. So when I say that Charles was panicked, you'll understand why I thought of you. Guys like that normally don't even sweat when they play handball, but Charles is an absolute mess. He wouldn't even talk about it on the phone. Insisted we meet in person. With all his connections, he couldn't think of anyone to call, so I mentioned you." Pause, with intent. "I sort of offered your services."

"Nice touch. So what exactly is the problem?"

"I don't know."

"Not helpful. Are you saying he wouldn't tell you?"

"He was too *afraid* to tell me. All I know is it has something to do with the murder of Yuri Malevski, owner of the Saddle and Bridle."

"The country-and-western bar on Richmond?"

"That's the one. They're a rough crowd to look at, but mostly pussycats when you meet them. They host the Mr. Leather Contest when it's in town."

"I heard they closed after the murder."

"They did. Yuri was killed at his home in Parkdale, but the bar's been locked up ever since. Apparently the police are looking for evidence of immigration scams, not to mention the usual narcotics aspect and anything else that comes to light. They think Yuri was running all that through the bar."

"I'm sure they'll be thorough, since it was a gay bar."

"There was also a rumour Yuri was making payoffs to someone, so they'll be looking for that, too."

"Payoffs for what?"

"Ah." Dan heard a sharp intake of breath as the cigarette swung into action. "That I do not know.

For the answer, we must consult Charles. The reservation's in an hour."

The place was packed. Fifteen years earlier, Toronto had barely heard of sushi. When you could find the stuff, it was priced to the hilt. Now it was *de rigueur* at cocktail hour in all the stylish homes and there was an *izakaya* — or sake house — on every other corner. From feeling squeamish about raw fish and squiggly things on their plates to becoming connoisseurs in a decade and a half, Torontonians had made the leap and landed solidly on both feet.

Dan sipped his soda water and looked across at Charles the lawyer as he deftly scissored a maki roll with chopsticks and lifted it to his mouth. He was, Dan noted, expertly groomed and outfitted in the image of a successful man. His moustache looked hand-manicured. Donny was right, however. Despite being textbook-handsome, Charles wasn't exotic enough for Dan's recall. He'd met a thousand Charleses in his time, each indistinguishable from the next. In his opinion, they put more emphasis on their couture and professional alliances than anything that might reasonably be called a personality. Still, he reminded himself, it wasn't their fault. They were programmed by their upbringings and choice of career. But *this* Charles at least was passionate about something: his husband's security.

"He doesn't actually know I'm here," he confided to Dan.

"Lionel's a very private guy," Donny seconded.

"Even more than me," Charles said, smiling broadly. "And I'm the lawyer in the family."

"How do you think he'd feel if he knew you were discussing his private matters without his knowledge?" Dan asked.

Charles leaned in. "I'm counting on your discretion, Dan. If he felt you were on his side, or at the very least that you wouldn't say anything about this to anyone else, I'm sure he'd be fine about it."

A lawyer's answer.

"And if I were meeting him to discuss your private concerns, how would you feel?"

Charles looked uncomfortable for a millisecond then smiled his winning smile again. His eyes floated lightly over Dan's chest. "I'd be fine knowing I was in your capable hands."

Dan caught the flirtation under the remark, but let it pass. "Then let's talk," he said.

Donny relaxed visibly and leaned back. Maybe, just maybe, his best friend was not going to be the uptight prude he so often proved. Dan didn't like to disappoint Donny, but he wouldn't step outside the bounds of his profession without good reason. Having an attractive lawyer for an ex-boyfriend did not constitute good reasoning to Dan's thinking.

Charles looked at Dan. "When we spoke, Donald assured me this would be kept in strict confidence."

Dan shot a glance at Donny: *Donald?*

Charles continued. "When I told him why I was concerned, he explained that you might be the best person to turn to, all things considered."

"All things considered?" Dan said.

Charles's smile crumpled. "Sorry, I wasn't … when you hear what I'm about to tell you, I think you'll understand my hesitation."

"Okay. Shoot."

"As Donald has told you, Lionel was chief accountant for a bar called the Saddle and Bridle."

"I'm familiar with it," Dan said.

"Then you will know that the owner, Yuri Malevski, was found murdered a couple of months ago."

"Yes. I'd heard."

"Lionel was also Yuri's *personal* accountant."

Charles paused. It seemed a cue for something.

Dan cocked his head to encourage him to continue. "And?"

"Well …" Charles blinked and smiled again. It seemed to be his default when all else failed.

The penny dropped. "And being Yuri's personal accountant required a certain amount of *discretion* on Lionel's part," Dan suggested.

Charles nodded and turned to Donny. "This guy's good," he said.

Dan got the message: saying things for Charles meant he did not have to make any potentially incriminating statements himself.

"Which is why Lionel is reluctant to talk to anyone," Dan went on, half guessing. "But surely the police have already questioned him about the murder?"

Charles's expression turned grave. "They did. Lionel is afraid because of what he knows. When Yuri didn't show up at their last meeting —"

"Sorry, when was this?" Dan interrupted.

"Two months ago. Right after we got back from Mexico. Lionel and Yuri were scheduled to meet the day after we returned. It was a Saturday. February twelfth, to be exact. Yuri called on Tuesday and left a message while we were away on a jungle tour. Lionel didn't get it till Thursday. When he called back, the mailbox was full, so he left a message on Yuri's home phone."

"And Yuri was a no-show on Saturday. What happened?"

"Lionel called Yuri's cell a couple of times in the morning, but there was no answer. He showed up at the bar for their meeting, but no one had seen Yuri. So Lionel tried his home. Still nothing. Nor had there been any further communication from Yuri saying he wanted to postpone the meeting. It was a monthly affair, so Yuri always knew in advance when he needed to change the date. Anyway, when Yuri didn't show up, Lionel started to worry that something had happened to him."

"Why?"

Charles shrugged. "He knew Yuri's lifestyle: sketchy friends, drug users, and rent boys. You name it — if it was dirty, Yuri was into it."

Dan nodded. "What did Lionel do next?"

"He called a few friends and business associates, including one of the bar managers who was off duty that day. Turns out no one had heard from Yuri for several days, in fact. They went over to the house and found the front door was double-locked and that he'd changed the entry code. That was odd, too, since Yuri always told Lionel when he changed the code. But this time he hadn't."

"Who found him?" Dan interjected.

"The bar manager called the police, who called the security company and got them to let them in. They found Yuri murdered in his bed. They've questioned a lot of people, but they haven't named any suspects yet."

Dan took this in. "So who do you think did it?"

Charles looked uncomfortable and turned to Donny again.

"Tell him," Donny urged.

Charles clasped his hands. Dan resisted the urge to tell him to stop using over-obvious court tactics and get on with the story.

Charles nodded, as though trying to convince himself. "Lionel thinks the police did it and will try to cover things up."

"Why?"

Donny leaned forward like a spectator at a hanging waiting for the trap door to open.

"Blackmail," Charles said.

Dan blinked. "Blackmail?"

"Payoff money. Call it what you want."

"Payoff for what? To whom?"

Charles looked to Donny. For the first time there was a glimmer of doubt in his eyes. He turned back to Dan. "Surely you've heard of bar payoffs? The owners pay the police for overlooking certain violations. Overcrowding and whatnot. A regular payoff ensures your bar is not visited on certain nights of the week, that sort of thing."

Dan looked sceptically at him over the table. "And Lionel thinks that's why Yuri was killed? For bar payoffs?"

Charles looked deflated. "Yes."

"Did Yuri pay them?"

"Lionel said he paid them for a while, but then he stopped paying them. That's what the problem was."

Dan studied the two faces watching him as though he could see clearly beneath the surface of what seemed to him a very slight mystery.

"Then why not bust him or fine the bar? Why kill him? They're police, not hired assassins."

Charles seemed at a loss for words.

"Maybe to send a message?" Donny suggested.

Dan gave him a jaundiced look. "That's all very colourful. You back on Netflix again?"

Charles studied him. "You don't think it likely?"

Dan shrugged. "All I'm saying is it sounds too much like shoddy TV. Who would they kill next? Every bar owner who put a stop payment on their blackmail cheques?" Dan let Charles squirm a bit before he continued. "Who else might have wanted Yuri dead? Did he have a quarrel with anyone? As you said, he was into questionable things. Maybe he pissed off the wrong person."

Charles leaned back. "You're right. There was an ex-boyfriend. He gets a checkmark in both boxes: drugs and immigration. He also knew about the payments to the police."

"An ex-boyfriend? What's his name?"

"Santiago Suárez. They had a big messy break-up not long before Yuri was killed. If I were a cop, he'd be my first choice in a suspects line-up."

"Then you should have a chat with him," Dan suggested. "Or better yet, let the police do it."

Charles shrugged. "We would, but we don't think he'd talk to us."

Donny was staring at him. Dan felt that sense of futility again that said he wasn't going to be able to avoid whatever Donny was about to ask.

He turned to face him. "What?"

"*You* could ask him," Donny said at last.

"That would be interfering in police business. Why would he have any reason to talk to me?"

"Because he's an illegal. He won't go to the police, because they'll throw him out of the country. You could threaten him with exposure if he won't talk to you."

Dan shook his head. "You want me to threaten him? What TV series is this coming from? Since when do you encourage me to be a hard-ass and go around interfering in things that are not my province and threatening illegal aliens?"

Donny shrugged. "It was just a thought."

"I'll say," Dan said.

"There's another problem," Charles said. "We can't find him."

"You don't know where he is?"

Charles shook his head. "Nobody's seen him since we got back from Mexico. What if I paid you to look for him and then let me decide if I want to talk to him?"

Dan looked off for a moment, his training kicking in. "He could be in a million different places. If he thought the inquiry might implicate him in a murder, he very likely absconded back to … where is he from?"

"Cuba," Charles supplied.

"Cuba. Hmm. Maybe not then. You don't willingly go back to Cuba, from what I hear." He considered. "Well, he'd go wherever Cuban expats go. Maybe there's an enclave in Montreal, for all we know. Did he have money?"

"Not his own," Charles said. "He was living off Yuri."

"Maybe he killed Yuri and stole the money," Donny suggested, looking more than a little excited by the thought.

"You should be the sleuth," Dan told him.

"Thanks, but I'll stick to fashion."

Dan turned to Charles. "Give me some addresses and maybe a few phone numbers. Whatever you have."

He copied the information in a small notebook.

"You'll look into it?" Charles asked hopefully.

Their waiter passed by with a flirtatious smile. Charles palmed him a JP Morgan Palladium credit card. *Private bank and an extremely high spending threshold*, Dan noted. The waiter registered the card for a mere second before resuming his expression of unruffled winsomeness.

"I'll ask around," Dan said. "But I can't promise anything."

"Whatever the cost, Lionel and I will pay. Just let us know what it's worth to you."

Dan stood, marvelling again at the tendency of men to think their clothes and credit cards were anything like indicators of their true worth.

Two

Tall in the Saddle

The sun threw long shadows as Dan left the sake house and headed down the stairs. He passed a skinhead seated on the bottom step beside a mangy dog, some ersatz version of a pit bull. The kid's boots reminded Dan of the Doc Martens of his youth, except these looked far more pricey. Make-believe punk. Someone born three decades too late trying to be the person he imagined himself to be. How do you liberate your inner anarchist? You could change your outer self, but not your internal reality. Dan dropped a loonie in his outstretched palm and walked on.

Richmond Street lay a good fifteen minutes south. For years he'd never been able to recall which of the one-way streets between King and Queen was which, until someone told him the city planner's secret: boy-girl-boy-girl. King, Adelaide, Richmond, Queen. That cemented it for him.

He passed Massey Hall, that gloomy, neo-classical tribute to Canada's premier family of days gone by.

Back when Dan was growing up amidst Northern Ontario's mining industry sprawl, the joke went that Canada had no social classes, just the masses and the Masseys. All that was long gone. In these days of rampant consumerism, the country's social compact had splintered beyond any chance of reunification. Dan thought the old system highly preferable.

The Saddle — or more correctly the Saddle and Bridle, as it was christened — had opened at the outset of the first AIDS decade. Back then it catered to a generation of gay men who felt they'd found themselves at last, only to discover that in finding themselves many would lose their lives and their friends far too early and in extremely unpleasant ways. The ugliness of the disease in its early years could not be overstated, before drug cocktails and therapies commuted a death decree into a life sentence, albeit one with no foreseeable chance of pardon.

Nevertheless, the bar thrived, becoming one of Toronto's pre-eminent dance clubs, changing hands and owners several times along the way before ending up in the clutches of one Yuri Malevski, a Macedonian immigrant who had come to Canada seeking freedom from discrimination in the Old World. Malevski happily embraced all that was forward-thinking about his adopted home, even while a fearsome virus was decimating his community in ways far more atrocious than even the worst politicians and religious fanatics had been capable of devising.

Like nearly everyone else in the gaybourhood, Dan had heard of the murdered nightclub owner. Who hadn't? Over the years, Malevski's reputation grew. He was praised for being a hard-working community entrepreneur, a generous AIDS-charity benefactor, even while rumours proliferated about the deteriorating physical condition of the bar as well as its notorious after-hours activities. And the band played on. Few blamed Malevski for what happened behind the scenes in his club. Drug use was rampant, and, despite the risks it entailed, sex had become a free-for-all. One pair of eyes could not be everywhere, they said. Not his place to try and stop it, they said. This was back in the days when the gay community was still reinventing itself, looking for greater acceptance from the world at large as it transformed from social pariah to business success. Who would dare to interfere?

The old millennium ended and another began. All the while, the club thrived. Malevski became a solid part of the establishment, entrenching himself in the bedrock of the community. Then the murder happened. It was a shock to many, but not to all. The real bombshell was the way his reputation got served up to public censor. It was messy, semen-splattered news of the coarsest sort: a rich pervert — who entertained hustlers, drug dealers, drag queens, and transsexuals — found murdered in his luxury home. The media feasted on it. What newspaper wouldn't splash it across their front pages, wringing every last cent from a curiosity-starved public? Strangely, in all this, the police were unusually reticent, treating it as an everyday incident, a run-of-the-mill murder rather than the sensational headline material it was proving. That in itself, Dan thought, made it noteworthy. Why downplay the case when publicity might help catch a killer? Still, chasing illegal Cuban boyfriends and other potential murderers wasn't his thing. Let someone else be heroic — the Dan Sharps of this world needed to be practical.

He passed a muffin shop, letting his eyes roam over the display while noting a dozen ways to flavour something he didn't particularly want before deciding he didn't actually need another sugar high. He pictured Donny's fingers tapping restlessly on the counter whenever he ran out of cigarettes. If he wanted to criticize his friend's bad habits, it wouldn't do to have too many of his own.

Dan found the Saddle and Bridle looking as forlorn and neglected as a cast-off lover. Sheets of bare plywood covered the windows. Concert posters had been pasted over the exterior like a second skin. From outside, it appeared to be little more than an overgrown, neo-gothic pub, heavy on the brickwork. Passing by on the street, you might not even register the nature of its clientele unless you stopped to consider the giant mural of two moustachioed men seated together on a black stallion, their smiles gleaming three storeys above the parking lot. Inside told a different tale. The walls were covered with far more revealing artwork of men in various states of undress and sexual postures — nothing extraordinary for a gay bar, though Dan recalled a rumour the place contained a labyrinthine basement suitable for torture, long-term imprisonment, and the deepest, darkest acts of fetishistic carnality, all just waiting for Vlad the Impaler to return.

He skirted the building, trying first the front then the back door. Both were locked. He was about to step aside and be on his way when he heard a staccato tapping from within.

A dim recollection surfaced through the bric-a-brac of memory: himself as a twenty-something club-goer, right before he became a dad and his social life virtually ended overnight, having just had a pass made at him by a drunk whose hands wouldn't accept "no" for an answer. He'd been upstairs in a corral-like area, surrounded by cowboys-in-drag with their chaps and spurs and Stetsons. This particular wrangler had a lasso strapped to his belt, though he'd looked too inebriated to use it even if he wanted to.

Freeing himself from the man's insistent pawing, Dan pushed his way through a maze of black-lit rooms and out a private exit leading to a back alley fire escape. At the bottom, he passed a trellised garden where a clutch of drag queens slinked about, cocktails in hand, before making good his escape onto the street. It was months before he returned.

Looking up now, Dan saw the fire escape, smiling to find it intact after all those years. It touched ground in the back alley where he'd ended his youthful adventure. A quick climb up a rickety set of stairs and the exit door opened at his touch.

He stepped in and looked around. There was no one about, and therefore no one to see him doing something he shouldn't be doing. It wouldn't be the first time he'd overstepped his bounds and trespassed in order to get a firsthand look at something that conspired to keep him out.

Inside the bar, chaos reigned: floors ripped up, ceiling tiles missing, walls in a shambles. The police had done their worst, tearing the place apart and tossing things aside in search of evidence of the nefarious intrigues that had gone on in the after hours. There was no respect for the recently deceased, it seemed. *What is a man remembered for?* Dan wondered. *The good things he does in his life, the legacy he leaves behind, or for whether he partied to excess once in a while?* Yuri Malevski had done favours for the gay community, but he'd also been the sort of man whose life harboured dark secrets. Nothing new in the annals of time, but clearly whoever had been through the bar in the days since his death had found little about him to honour.

Dan glanced around. There, behind what was once a very busy martini bar, lay the entrance to the rumoured dungeons of debauchery and sexual abandon. He tripped the latch and opened the door. Steps led down into darkness, but the lights still worked when he flipped the switch, illuminating a swath of wooden stairs descending to who knew where. He followed, wary of broken boards and slippery footing. It wouldn't do to twist an ankle while trespassing.

At the bottom lay an overturned burlap bag with grain spilling from a tear in its side. A large rat waddled away at Dan's approach. Cartons of empties were stacked along one wall, the wooden shelves old and dusty. The entire space was no more than twenty by twenty feet. No whips, chains, or manacles, no implements of torture anywhere in sight, just a dusty, neglected storage space. Poor Vlad.

Dan heard a series of staccato cries from above. He stuck his head through the door and looked cautiously around. Then it dawned on him: hammers and nails, saws and drills. Some sort of restoration work was being done here, probably in preparation for selling the building. In fact, the place had always been a dump whenever he'd come by as a patron over the years. As a twenty-something with a fondness for alcohol but a disdain for dancing, he'd worried over the thump-thumping of the dance floor above while he sat at the downstairs bar nursing a Scotch. It turned out it wasn't the dancing he should have been concerned about once his drinking took on the force of a hurricane in his life, but in any case he recalled being there the night the place threatened to collapse. He'd been on his third Scotch when something plopped into his glass. He looked up as a fine dusting of plaster fell down around his ears. Many had predicted the bar would literally cave in one day, and that night it came close. Not surprisingly, it stayed closed for a month after that, probably just in time before someone met their death there. As it turned out, the death hadn't happened on the premises after all.

As he crept forward, the cries reached a crescendo before stopping abruptly, a final cry echoing in the air. Was he too late to prevent an assault? The sound had come from the room right ahead of him.

He knelt and peered around a corner, finding himself privy to the ultimate gay voyeuristic scenario. Two hardy specimens of manhood, coveralls and T-shirts discarded on the floor but hard hats still adorning their crowns, were having a go at the old heave-ho.

Dan stared at the supple musculature being given a solid workout, barely suppressing a laugh. A decade earlier he might have asked to join them. Now, he was a middle-aged man with a teenaged son and a reputation to uphold, as boring as that might make him. Still, a little lust in the afternoon never hurt. Nice work if you could get it.

Three

Fathers and Sons

Dan drove to the Annex and pulled up the drive of an ivy-covered stone house. Kendra waved from the kitchen window.

"Come in," she called. "I'm making *ma'amoul*!"

She set a plate of sugar-dusted cookies on the table. He looked her over, this woman from another culture who also happened to be the mother of his son. An unforeseen occurrence, the consequence of a single date brought about by a crush on her highly attractive brother. Dan seldom thought about it now, it seemed ancient history. The fact was it had happened and turned out for the best all around, though there'd never been any question of their becoming a couple in the traditional sense. Neither wanted it then and it would serve no purpose now. They simply shared in raising the child they produced.

He bit into a cookie. A flavourful wash of warm oranges and dates flooded his mouth.

"Mmm ... fantastic!"

She smiled. "You always say that."

"Only because it's true." He popped in the remainder and wiped the powder from his fingers.

Kendra gave him a sideways glance. "You need to talk to Ked," she told him. "He's thinking of turning down his acceptance to UBC because of you."

It was always straight to business with her.

Dan sighed. "I didn't even know he was accepted. Why doesn't he tell me these things?"

"He probably doesn't want to worry you."

"Worry me about what?"

She gave him a rueful look. "He thinks you need him here. He's afraid of abandoning you by going off to school."

Dan shook his head. In light of their relationship, it made sense. Ked had always lived with him. They'd formed a bond against the world, making them a fully functioning unit, though perhaps it was unfair to both of them. For one thing, it kept Dan's desire for a partner at bay with the excuse that his son needed him more, but that excuse was officially due to end when Ked went away to university. *If* he went.

Over the past few months he'd tried pushing Ked away gently, but recently he'd sensed resentment because of it. It would be hard to explain his actions to his son, especially since they were deliberate on Dan's part.

He looked at Kendra. "What do you think?"

"I think he should go where he can get the best training, naturally. The University of British Columbia is the best for his field." She waited. "I've got enough money to help him out, wherever he wants to go."

Dan nodded. "I've got some, but not as much as he'll need."

Her jaw line was set. "Then it's good he's got two parents."

Dan smiled. "I'll say. In the meantime, what do you think I should say to him? Should I let him know you've told me this?"

"Don't let him know we've been conspiring against him — that's how he'll see it, anyway. Just ask him what his plans are. He'll tell you when he's ready."

She pushed the plate forward and smiled when he grabbed another cookie: men were all children under the skin. They worked best on reward and punishment.

"How's Domingo?" she asked.

Dan's look darkened. An old friend, a recurrence of cancer. He preferred not to dwell on it. "I don't like it. We talk a few times a week, but it sounds like she's resigned."

Kendra shook her head. "I'm so sorry to hear that. It's never good when the patient stops fighting. Did she decide to do the chemo at least?"

"Yes, but I gather this next round is the last, if she makes it. She seems to think there's no use. She just wants to enjoy whatever time she has left rather than turn it into some heroic struggle."

"I'm sorry, Dan. I know she means a lot to you. Just be there for her."

"I will. For now, she's getting the best help she can. That's what counts."

His cell rang as he pulled up in front of his house. It was

Donny. He'd held out longer than Dan expected. Friends for more than a decade, Donny had been a constant in Dan's life, the still point around which his compass revolved. When Dan had passed off a street youth for temporary shelter to Donny several years earlier, the pair had become a family unit: black father and white son. In Dan's opinion, Donny had never seemed so suited to anything as he had to fatherhood, however convulsively it had begun. It had also seemed to put them on par again, both of them friends as well as fathers.

"You didn't like him."

"Is that a question?"

"No, I could tell. You weren't warm to him."

"Do lawyers do 'warm'? I thought they were all cold-blooded."

"Primarily, yes, but this one is a little different."

"Because you dated him once?"

"I'm telling you, Charles is a nice guy."

Dan wasn't about to let him off the hook easily. "Fine, but I dislike the breed on principle."

Donny spluttered. "He's a lawyer, yes, but a lawyer who has never done anything to you!"

"Yeah, but he would for money."

A long pause ensued. Dan glanced up and down the tree-lined street in Leslieville that he called home. Calm, peaceful. If it hadn't been for that, he might not have been able to endure the city for as long as he had. It was here he'd given his son the sort of childhood that he, Dan, had never had.

"So will you take the case?" Donny asked.

"Tell him I'm still thinking about it."

"You're too much. Really, you are!"

"Many would concur. How's Lester? I didn't get a chance to ask you at lunch with all the overriding concern from your lawyer."

Donny huffed. "Lester is fine. He just got an internship with a poverty outreach program."

"Great news. Tell him I'm thrilled for him."

"I will. With all his experience on the streets, he should be good at it. I'm very proud of him. Plus he's got that band on the side. He's passionate about his horn. Maybe not quite Miles Davis, but you never know. Still no talk of moving away from home, but now that the bird has wings it won't be long before he flies off."

Dan recalled Kendra's comment about Ked's unwillingness to abandon him.

"Funny, Ked's the opposite. He's afraid to leave me on my own."

"He knows you too well."

"Yeah, there's that." Dan looked up at the house. "I just got home. Call you later."

"Think about the case!"

Ked stood watching him from the shadows. These days he seemed to hover a lot, Dan thought. Wasn't that what kids were always accusing their parents of doing? Ralph, a geriatric ginger retriever, lay on a pillow in one corner. His eyes flickered occasionally from one to the other of them if he heard a word that sounded like it promised food or a walk.

"How's school?" Dan asked.

"Cool. There's a science fair coming up. I'm thinking of entering an idea I had for making a sling psychrometer."

Dan's expression was blank.

"It's a device for measuring relative humidity."

"Great!"

"It's not as dull as it sounds, Dad."

Dan smiled. "I don't think it sounds dull, just a little outside my field of expertise. Is this the sort of thing you'll be studying in university?"

Ked warmed to the question. "Pretty much. It's in the same field of earth, ocean, and atmosphere studies."

Dan nodded. "You'll be meeting a lot of new people soon and your life's going to change in many ways. Have you thought about where you want to go to study?"

Ked looked out the window. "I want to stay here. There are programs at York and U of T. I'll probably get in one or the other of them."

"Is that where you want to go?"

Ked turned back to his father. "Sure. Why not?"

"Those are both good universities. But are they the best for you? If it's a matter of cost, your mother and I are willing to help you make up whatever you don't have the funds for."

Ked looked indifferent. "I just thought it was better for you if I stayed in Toronto."

"For me? Don't do that."

His son's eyes expressed surprise. Not the pleasant kind.

"But —"

Dan cut him off. "Don't live your life to please me, Ked. Or your mother or anyone else. Live your life in the way you see best fit for your needs. It's your future we're talking about."

"But I thought you would want me here." He sounded disappointed.

"Don't misunderstand me. If it suits your purpose, you're welcome to stay here as long as you're going to school. Or longer, if you like. But don't do it for me. That isn't a sacrifice any son or daughter should ever have to make."

"But I don't want you to be alone."

"That's up to me. Besides, I've got Ralph. We've made peace in our old age."

Dan smiled to himself. *Parenting? What parenting?* If asked about his fathering style, he would profess that he didn't have one. *When it comes to kids*, Dan advised others, *just love them as much as you can, teach them good manners and respect for others, then get out of the way and let them be. If it works, you can be thankful. If it doesn't, it's probably not your fault.*

"Even Ralph won't be here forever," he added. "Everybody leaves home at some point."

"I guess." Ked still looked perplexed.

"Whatever happens, happens," Dan said. "As we go through life, we learn to deal with whatever comes up. It's not always good. People lose arms, breasts, get cancer, divorce. That's life. You can't prevent it."

"I know that."

"But what you may not know is how it feels." He pointed to his head. "I know you understand it here." His hand moved down to his heart. "But this is where it's going to get you, if you're not prepared. And no matter how much you dislike it, you can't stop it from happening."

Ked frowned as though his father had been lecturing him on his behaviour.

"Sorry, I don't mean to sound like an old-fashioned parent. Next I'll be telling you I'm saying all this for your own good." Dan smiled wanly. "Which I am, of course."

He stopped and checked an incoming text. It was from someone named Lionel, claiming to be an accountant and asking to meet as soon as possible. This, he presumed, was the other half of Donny's "perfect couple." There was a pub listed at the bottom of the text. He hadn't even agreed to take the job. It was presumptuous, but that was how the rich operated.

He looked up at his son. "Think about what I'm saying, okay?"

"Okay."

"If you want me to help you rank the different universities, I can do that, though you probably know them well enough by now."

Ked smiled. "I do."

"Good." He paused. "There's a dog over in the corner in need of a walk."

"Yeah, yeah … I know."

Dan glanced back at the text. He didn't want to disappoint Donny, though that was a feeble excuse for accepting a job he didn't want. Still, it wouldn't hurt to be polite.

He typed a reply: *I'm good for 7.* Then for Donny's sake he added: *Looking forward to it.*

Four

Accountable

Dan cast his gaze around the bar's interior. Brass fittings, rough-hewn tables, hockey pennants on the walls. It wasn't the sort of place he would expect an accountant to frequent, particularly a gay accountant, but it suited his purpose, which was simply to hear the man's story, offer sympathy for his plight as he quaffed a single beer, then politely tell him to refer the case to the police. Due diligence done. His favour to Donny signed, sealed, and delivered. He'd offered to listen and listen he would. After that, it was out of his hands.

The man who came through the door was dressed in a bulky sweater over a track suit. Nicely muscled forearms and solid chest. Easy on the eyes. More athlete than accountant, Dan decided. Which went a long way toward explaining the casual sports pub atmosphere. He plunked himself down on the bench like a tennis player who had just played a particularly challenging round, winning both game and tournament.

"Hi, I'm Lionel."

He smelled of cool things, minty and fresh. Dan could imagine running his hands through this man's hair. *Well, you can't blame a guy for trying.*

"Dan."

They shook and a waiter took their orders.

"Good eye," Dan said. "How did you spot me so quickly?"

"Charles described you well. I think he might say you're somewhat of a 'type.'"

"I've heard that before."

Over in a corner, someone scored a goal on a wide-screen TV and the bar was pandemonium for a moment before settling back into its dull routine of drinking and watching.

Lionel's eyes met Dan's again. The gaze held.

"Thanks for meeting me." Lionel blushed. "I wasn't sure at first if it was a good idea. I didn't want to involve you and compromise anything to do with your work principles, but Charles insisted I at least hear what you have to say. He seems to think we're all on common ground. Charles isn't the most trusting person, so when he said you were on the level, I took his word for it."

Dan didn't say that being given the thumbs-up by a lawyer wasn't his measure of a vote of confidence.

"I understand a little about your predicament," Dan said, "but maybe you could fill in a few gaps. Whatever you're comfortable telling me. I know that some of the things you did for Yuri Malevski may have skirted the bounds of regular accounting practices. I won't pry, but at least be assured you can be as frank with me as you choose."

Lionel's face showed relief. "Thanks. It makes it easier for me to talk to you just knowing that."

Dan watched him. In that instant, the breezy athlete was gone and a slightly world-weary accountant with real-life human concerns took his place.

"Since the murder, the police have been snooping around Yuri's accounts, both business and personal. I've been advised by Charles to be truthful in my responses without offering up information that might implicate me in anything questionable."

"That's a smart stance," Dan agreed.

The waiter returned with two pints of beer. Dan took a long, satisfying swallow while the hockey game rumbled on overhead.

"At first it was very routine. They wanted to hear the message Yuri left asking to meet when I returned from Mexico. Luckily I still had it on my phone, so I played it for them. Then the questions started. How often did we meet and what did we discuss and were there any unusual payments made by the bar?" Lionel leaned closer. "I told them I was aware Yuri paid for what we euphemistically called 'security,' but I didn't say that I knew where it went. Technically, I didn't know who or what he paid in that regard. In actuality, we're talking about substantial payoffs to the police to leave the bar alone for various reasons, particularly because of the association it had with drugs."

"Did Yuri ever ask you to make the payments personally?"

Lionel shook his head. "No. I made it clear from the start that I was not going to doing anything illegal, with or without his express consent. I did, however, make financial transactions at Yuri's request, always in cash, from the bar's profits. I handed them over to someone who, I assume, paid the police directly, but never in my presence."

"And who was that?"

Here, Lionel's gaze shifted to the far side of the bar, as though he sensed eavesdroppers. The other patrons were so oblivious to anything but the match being played out on the screen that it was hard to imagine anyone's taking an interest in their low-key conversation.

Lionel locked eyes with Dan again. "At first, Yuri had a couple of drug dealers running the money for him, but then one of them got busted and that ended that. Over the last couple years he'd been dating a young Cuban guy. That was who was making the pay-offs for him."

"This was Santiago Suárez?"

"Yes. My part was simply to take a percentage from Saturday night's payroll and give it to Santiago in cash. What he did with it or who he gave it to, I have no idea. I always insisted I didn't want to know."

"Did you keep records of the payments?"

Lionel nodded. "Yes. Scrupulous records, even detailing the denominations of the bills I used to pay him. The transactions were always listed as 'security.' Yuri might have passed it off as payment to the regular bouncers the club employed."

"Did the police inquire directly into those payments?"

Lionel shook his head. "No, not yet at least. They have the records, but you know how it goes when police investigate their own. My feeling is they know what the payments were for and they're trying to see if I know as well."

"What will you tell them if they ask?"

For the first time, Lionel looked afraid.

"I'm going to tell them I don't know what they were for other than basic payments to ensure the business was run smoothly. Of course, they don't know who took the payments from me."

"I understand Santiago is an illegal?"

"Yes."

"Which will make it difficult for him to come forward with what he knows, if anything."

Lionel nodded.

"Are you worried the police may find something in Yuri's personal financial records that would make things difficult for you?"

Lionel's cheeks expanded and forcefully expelled air.

"A lot of what Yuri did bordered on the illegal. As far as I'm concerned — and Charles has already advised me on this — I was just doing what I was paid to do in a strictly legal capacity. I wasn't there to judge or even snoop around and ask questions. I merely passed money over to one person or another. What those individuals did with the money was between them and Yuri. I made it clear I didn't want to know about drug payments, for instance. Less dangerous for me. It was just easier that way."

Dan nodded. He had probably done more overtly illegal things in pursuit of his own career activities.

"Money's a funny thing," Lionel said. "We all use it in various ways to accomplish many things. Much of what Yuri did with his money helped a great many people in need. It's funny that so much of it was made in questionable ways. He was sort of a Robin Hood, as far as the gay community was concerned. I mean, we all knew about the sex and drugs that went through his club. He was well aware of it; in fact he even benefited, exacting a percentage from everyone who used his premises for such activities, but he seemed to think it was his duty to use those profits for good." Lionel looked meaningfully at him. "Whatever may be said of him, I think Yuri Malevski was a hero, not a villain. Everyone in the community turns a blind eye to the goings-on in bars. Yuri chose to embrace it and use it for a positive end. He knew the AIDS community was under-funded for years, long before anyone in government admitted it. I think he chose to do the things he did in order to settle some old scores and balance a few ledgers that were sorely in need of adjusting. We shouldn't judge him for it."

Dan smiled. "I don't."

Lionel gave him another of those soulful glances. "I hope you can do something about this. If I told the police what I know I'd be putting myself in jeopardy. Not to mention Charles. It's just …"

His words were drowned out by the racket as another goal was scored. The gaps between real life and its electronic simulacra were not so far apart, Dan thought. There were always going to be winners and losers, no matter what you did or what you tried to avoid.

The commotion died down again. Lionel reached across the table and gripped Dan's forearm. "You see ... I feel responsible for what happened to Yuri."

"How could you be responsible for what happened?"

"I advised him to stop the payments to the police. I thought, what was the worst they could do? Fine him? Close his bar for a week or two? I didn't know it would turn out like this."

The final words caught in his throat. Dan saw a man who felt a deep accountability for what had happened to his former boss because of a personal conviction aired at the wrong moment. Many of his own clients professed to feeling the same, their lives torn apart by a lie or a harsh word that resulted in the disappearance of a loved one, compounded by the unending grief and guilt that followed.

Lionel released his arm and sat back. "Charles keeps saying I couldn't have known what would happen. He says I should stop being so hard on myself. But that doesn't bring him back, does it?"

Their waiter passed by balancing a tray on his finger tips, looking for all the world like a trained seal. Dan signalled for two more of the same without disturbing Lionel's tale of recrimination. Guilt was a funny animal, he knew. It deserved to have its own cage in the zoo, labelled "Armed and Extremely Dangerous."

"I went past the bar the other day," Dan said. "It was being renovated. What's going to happen to it?"

"They'll sell it. Some developer will tear it down and build condos. We could be talking several million in development fees. It's a prime downtown location. A small part of it will go into a fund Yuri set up for his employees. I think he also left a good chunk to Santiago."

"So the ex-boyfriend benefits, even though they were estranged?"

"The estrangement would probably have been temporary, knowing Yuri. He always had trouble with one person or another, then a week later they'd be on good terms again. He was temperamental. It was just his way." Lionel smiled wistfully. "The rest goes to charity. He was a very charitable fellow, Yuri. Always looking out for someone else's benefit. There would probably have been a lot more, but a good deal of the profits went to drugs. I used to pad the budget with costs that were in actuality drug payments. He probably spent tens of thousands over the years."

"What of the people who were in his close circle of friends?"

"Well …" Lionel shrugged. "That depends how you define 'friends.' Suffice to say Yuri had a lot of hangers-on. A big party crowd followed in his wake like seagulls following a fishing boat. He was a good catch, as they say. He could be pretty indulgent: all-night parties and the like. Charles and I attended a few of them, but they weren't really our crowd. Too many hustlers and drug users. You'd walk in and there'd be people smoking up or giving someone a blow job over in the corner while someone else videotaped it." He laughed. "It could give you a jolt if you weren't used to it."

Dan listened with curiosity. Lionel's description of his former boss's personal life was taking on all the drama and outsized proportions of the newspaper headlines that had feasted on the goings-on at his home over the past two months. He was disappointed not to hear a fresh perspective.

"So I guess it's true what we're hearing about his lifestyle."

"Pretty much, yes."

"Was there anyone in that circle who seemed a little to the left of shady, in your estimation?"

Lionel gave a big, friendly laugh. "Just about all of them on any given day! Do you want me to make a list?" He grew serious. "I didn't make a point of getting to know any of them. It wouldn't have been worthwhile. I'd never have trusted them enough to want to be friends. Yuri seemed not to worry about such things."

Dan looked up as two fresh pints arrived on the seal's well-balanced tray.

"I've got it," Lionel said, handing over a twenty rather than a credit card designed to inspire awe.

He was, Dan noted, a quietly attractive man, unlike his flashier husband. His ruminations were interrupted as the air suddenly issued with resounding *boo*s. The game had ended, but not to the satisfaction of everyone in the house.

"Were you familiar with any of the police officers who might have come by the bar to pick up their payments?" Dan asked.

Lionel looked up, amazement written all over his face.

"Wow!" he said. "I can't believe I didn't think of this earlier."

"What?"

"One of the regulars at Yuri's late-night parties was a police officer. I only found that out when I saw him in uniform by sheer coincidence. About a year ago, Charles and I were in a small accident and he was the first officer on the scene. I don't know if he knew who I was or not. Charles was driving, so my licence wasn't in question, but I never forgot him after that."

"Do you know his name?"

"Yeah — it was something like Trposki." He spelled it. "It's one of those scrambled Eastern European names. But he was a *gay* cop. I was shocked to find that out."

Dan nodded. "There are a few. For the most part they try to stick together. It's pretty hard being out and gay in the police force. From what I understand, you're better off if you don't make an issue of it."

"I can imagine," Lionel said. "The world isn't that progressive — not yet, anyway. I'll look on the ticket for the spelling to be sure. I keep everything. I'm a dot the *i*'s and cross the *t*'s kind of guy. For sure it'll be in a file somewhere."

They quaffed their beer and looked around at the disgruntled faces. Impossible to say what bets had been won or lost in this crowd, but clearly the tone was downcast overall.

"Tell me a bit more about Santiago," Dan said. "Had he and Yuri been going out for long?"

"About four years," Lionel replied. "Though, as I mentioned, it ended recently."

"Do you know why?"

"Nothing I could put my finger on. All I know is that they quarrelled and Santiago disappeared."

"And no one has seen him since the murder?"

"Well, no one I know." Lionel smiled. "You could ask around."

An idea struck Dan. "Can you get me access to Yuri's house?"

Lionel looked at him curiously. "You think Santiago is hiding out there?"

Dan shook his head. "Not if he's on the run, but it might help if I had a better idea who Yuri was. To do that I'll need to get a look at what's inside the house."

Lionel nodded slowly. "Sure, I can arrange that. Until it changes owners, I still have access to the house." He looked Dan over. "So, are you saying you'll take on the case?"

"I'm saying I'm curious about it. I'll do some preliminary looking around. I'm not promising anything yet."

"Fair enough. When do you want me to get you into Yuri's place?"

"The sooner the better," Dan said. "Assuming the police have concluded their investigation and won't show up while I'm there."

"I can't promise you that," Lionel told him. "But I'll see what I can do about getting you in for a look around. How would tomorrow morning suit you?"

"Perfectly."

Five

Due Diligence

Dan rattled the gate with his bare hands then glanced up at the stone mansion towering over its neighbours. It got top marks for atmosphere. This was a scary witch's sort of house, with granite walls, slate tile roof, and a widow's walk. The veined outline of elm trees flailed their branches around it, as though protecting it in an airy embrace.

He fished through the bars until he felt the heavy lock, retrieved the key Lionel had given him, and unfastened the clasp. The gate swung open of its own accord, as though urging him in before he could change his mind. A wide, unpaved drive led up to the front steps. Spring had released tulips and daffodils from their underground hideaways, bright blotches of colour arcing over the damp earth. Someone had cleaned up last season's dead leaves, either recently or back in the fall. It was still early for the gardens to look overgrown and abandoned, but they were clearly luxuriant. A month or two of neglect would turn them into a jungle of weeds and drooping flowers, as sad as an untended grave.

This was one of the city's grandest houses, though it lay far from the protective enclave of wealthy Forest Hill. A plaque beside the front door proclaimed its historic significance as having been built by "noted entrepreneur J.S. Lockie" for his wife, Edna.

Parkdale had always been a contentious community, Dan knew. A mid-nineteenth-century census showed barely enough inhabitants for it to claim status as an independent village. Afterwards, the cry went round that someone had paid a band of gypsies to sign on as local residents to make up the numbers. The Toronto Home for Incurables on Dunn Avenue added to the area's reputation with its gloomy, eponymous title. Dan pictured parents of the time passing the forbidding structure, pointing stern fingers in warning and spreading fear into the hearts of wayward children who refused to heed admonitions about personal hygiene and the eating of one's vegetables.

The neighbourhood's proximity to Lake Ontario and the Canadian National Exhibition made it a desirable place to live, expanding significantly in the 1920s with infill and sidewalk extensions. It prospered further with the opening of movie theatres, the Sunnyside Amusement Park, and Palais Royale, the latter becoming a favourite venue for big bands in subsequent decades.

All that prosperity came to a crashing halt in 1955 with the building of the Gardiner Expressway, itself a controversy as much for its exorbitant cost as for cutting the neighbourhood off from the beachfront.

Parkdale's popularity plummeted and it faced a decline from which it never recovered. Of its once-glorious mansions, few remained, but Yuri Malevski's was one of the most notable.

Dan took the yard in at a glance as he made his way up the walk. A pair of curious eyes watched his progress toward the house. A pudgy face, unshaven and lined. Funny turned-up nose. It was the sort of mug you distrusted on sight, he thought. What his Aunt Marge would have called "unsavoury."

Dan nodded an acknowledgement. The man had been raking leaves. He stopped now.

"You a prospective buyer?" he asked from across the wood fence.

"No, just a bit of maintenance." Dan paused. "Do you know the owner?"

"Yeah. Dead now. Got what was coming to him, that's for sure."

Dan expressed surprise. "Not a nice guy, I take it?"

The man snorted. "The worst." With that, he turned back to his raking.

Dan punched in the numeric code Lionel had provided. A light turned from red to green. He grasped the handle and entered into a vigilant silence, gazing down a long hallway with a green and ivory harlequin pattern. While re-arming the system, his nose picked up the scent of cleaning substances covering something disquieting that might have been the smell of embalming fluid. A perfectly preserved tin ceiling spread overhead while a staircase cascaded behind Dan's right shoulder. The walls were polished rosewood. High double doors led off from both sides of the hall. The first set opened into a sitting room offering a tableau of stuffed chairs, antique lamps, and a wide brick fireplace. It was like stepping back a hundred years.

At the far end, a white grand piano sat perfectly framed between bevelled lead windows. Dan ran his finger along the polished top, leaving a faint trail in the dust beside a glittering candelabra above a keyboard that seemed to be awaiting the tinkering fingers of a Liberace-come-lately. A portrait of Jesus with what looked like an exploding purple heart stood propped against it for that added touch of kitsch. Had the notorious bar owner and sex-trade proponent been a secret religious acolyte on the side? Dan recalled seeing a documentary on notorious drug dealers, surprised to learn that one of them, a ruthless killer who had her enemies assassinated, was also a doting grandmother captured by the FBI while reading her Bible in a Florida hotel.

The second set of doors led to a dining room with a mahogany table that sat twenty. On the walls, a series of tempestuous seascapes in oil were mounted in hand-carved frames, while a vintage bookstand cradled a scrapbook stuffed with newspaper clippings and old registries. A page from *The Society Blue Book*, subtitled "Toronto's Social Directory for the Ages," listed J.S. Lockie at the present address as though he lived there still. Time never failed to make mock of human pretension.

On the reverse, *Boyd's Business Directory for 1875–6* credited Lockie as manager of the Canadian Bank of Commerce beside an advertisement for "DOCTOR

J BELL'S TONIC PILLS FOR NERVOUS DISORDERS — WE NEVER FAIL
TO CURE." A few of those might put him to rights when
he was having a bad day, Dan mused, wondering just
how much cocaine was in those pick-me-ups back then.
Those were the days.

The Canadian Mining Manual of 1890 followed
one page over, with ads for the Hamilton Powder
Company ("Manufacturers of Gunpowder, Dynamite,
Dualine, and the New Eclipse Mining Powder") and I.
Matheson and Co. of New Glasgow, Nova Scotia ("The
Best Place in Canada for Gold Mining Machinery").
Lockie was listed again, this time as director of the
Haliburton Mining Company, incorporated with "a
capital stock of $100,000 in shares of $1,000" to work
mineral lands in the nearby counties of Haliburton,
Victoria, and Peterborough.

A short article on architecture noted an addition
to the house in 1892. Then, in 1905, another write-up
stated that it "had passed hands to Mr. Frederick S.
MacGregor, bachelor, age 35." *Suspiciously old for a
bachelor back then*, Dan thought. "Mr. MacGregor
receives 1st, 2d, 3d Thursday of every month," the
piece noted, while mentioning the various sports groups
he belonged to, including the Toronto Racquet Club
and Toronto Canoe Club, where he was noted as a
"vigorous and lively member."

A portrait of MacGregor showed an intense, handsome young man with high cheekbones, well-formed
ears, and deep-set eyes. His sporty build and muscular
chest were well-defined by a collegiate sweater. *Well,
Fred, you're a real catch in my books*, Dan thought.

I'd visit you on just about any Thursday, even if you're over a hundred now.

In the kitchen, two-fours of beer had been stacked against the far wall, revealing Malevski's taste for micro-breweries and Belgian lager brewed by Trapist monks. The fridge contained water bottles, yoghurt containers, and a half-empty carton of eggs. A damp mop and plastic bucket sat behind an outside door, the inevitable attendant to late-night party-giving, as though Malevski had intended to be prepared for all eventualities. The bottom of the sink held a residue of dust and sand where someone had emptied a pail of dirty water, probably the last time any cleaning was done.

Dan followed the hallway to the far end. A final door led unexpectedly to a greenhouse. It was like entering a small jungle. Plants sat on the floor, hung from beams, reached to the sky. Cacti proliferated. Those were the lucky ones, Dan noted. Most of the others had been left to die, shrivelling like the skin of a nonagenarian. He recognized a peyote plant, its small, button-like formations sprouting telltale pink flowers. The waxy leaves of orchids, equally neglected, dangled above with their jointed, mostly-flowerless stems spiking the air. As a gardener, Yuri Malevski seemed to have lacked a green thumb.

For the most part, the house was in good order, not in any state of neglect or abandonment. It was clear that someone with taste and money had lived here, at least until recently. Dan wondered which had been the party rooms where Malevski's guests took their drugs and played out their little dramas of the high life.

The second floor consisted of several bedrooms and a sitting room replete with a small library. A quick glance at the spines showed the man had been a fancier of biographies: writers, artists, actors. People of accomplishment. They seemed to accuse him, Dan felt, as if asking whether his life had been of any special significance compared to theirs.

It struck him the house was too big for one person. J.S. Lockie had had a wife and, presumably, a family. MacGregor, a confirmed bachelor, would have lived alone. Or had he? Perhaps he'd taken in a friend to relieve him of boredom and loneliness. Someone to help chase away the gloom. Maybe a squash-playing pal with benefits. It was no wonder Malevski had entertained. The problem was that the sort of company available for late-night get-togethers tended to want more than companionship. Sex, drugs, money. Clearly, Malevski's pool of friends hadn't been culled from the pages of *The Society Blue Book*. His friends came from bars and were probably as transient and temporary as they got. Had he been trying to buy their affection? Put a roomful of drug users and sex addicts in the hands of a rich man and the inevitable problems would arise, expectations rising with them.

Dan snapped pictures with his cellphone as he went. There was nothing unusual, just a house that felt empty and, because it was empty, lifeless, as though its owner were away on a long vacation. As yet, he had nothing to report to Lionel and Charles. Fair enough. He still wasn't sure he wanted to take on the job. Business of late had kept him flush enough that he could afford to be choosy.

Emptiness and silence weighed on him like a dull pressure at some underwater depth. As he opened a final door, ghostly laughter emanated from the walls. Dan started as he caught a dim movement at the far end of the darkened room. His hand flew to the light switch. Quicksilver galvanized the walls as he confronted his mirror image. He waved and saw his relieved-looking twin wave back, glad not to have to explain his presence to anyone more demanding.

"Sorry for disturbing you," he said, the reflection's mouth moving in silent accord.

An echo of the laughter filtered in from the street, some passersby sharing one of life's amusing little moments. He leaned against the wall and felt the urge for a serious drink. A good Islay Scotch with plenty of peat. Something that would burn as it went down. The yearning had come over him more often lately. He resisted, of course. Alcohol was a companion he'd learned to control only after it spent years controlling him. A promise to his son still hung over his head. Social drinking — one or two at most — was permissible. No more. But the urge to sit and drink in an empty room surrounded by silence had a pull that was hard to resist.

A soft padding pricked his ears, like raindrops on pewter. Only it wasn't raining. He stopped to listen. Nothing came to him. What was it about empty houses that set the imagination stirring? He'd just convinced himself it was an illusion when he heard a soft *click* upstairs.

He crept down the hallway to a set of stairs, climbing carefully, lifting each foot and setting it down as quietly as he could. Halfway up, he stopped to listen once more. Again, there was nothing. He began to think his nerves were getting the better of him.

The only door led to the master bedroom. The furniture here was unexceptional, functional in the extreme. An outside wall angled down on a slant, its window well jutting outward. This, he presumed, was where the notorious bar owner had died.

Over the bed, a portrait of a rugged, attractive face in late-middle age arrested Dan's gaze. The perspective was shoddy. The eyes stared straight ahead, bright blue forget-me-nots, with a wooden gaze and flat features common to amateur portraits. It looked recent, so this wasn't J.S. Lockie or his successor, Frederick S. MacGregor. Dan guessed it was Yuri Malevski. Unlike the dining-room seascapes, this work had little artistic merit. Not art then, just someone dabbling with a brush in an attempt to create a likeness of a man who had in all probability paid him. It didn't suit the mental picture Dan had of a fastidious collector with well-defined tastes.

The scrawl at the bottom right caught his eye. A flamboyant pair of *S*'s, with their tails twisting away beneath. *Santiago Suárez*, Dan was willing to bet. You wouldn't put up with mediocrity from Sotheby's, but you might from a sexy, young boyfriend, even if it meant hiding the painting upstairs out of view.

He wandered to the window and looked out over the back garden. A cherry tree was in bloom, smoky tendrils of whitish-pink spreading over the ground. Spring had taken a firm hold. He was about to turn away when a figure slipped into view. Dan felt a jolt run down his spine. He hadn't been alone after all.

Someone in a dark overcoat and cap had just left the house by the rear door. From that distance, it could have been anyone, male or female, young or old. A quick backward glance over the shoulder revealed the face of a young male wearing pale makeup. Dan stepped back from the window. That was all he saw before the boy disappeared through the gate.

Six

Rich Men

He was back in the sports pub with Charles and Lionel. Lionel was pensive, making him seem even more appealing, while Charles simply looked out of place in his grey striped suit and wide pink necktie. (*Though a lawyer would probably call it coral*, Dan noted sourly.)

"He had dark, curly hair. Young. Early twenties, maybe even a teenager. Pale face. He wore a long, grey, trench coat and a newsboy cap."

Lionel was listening carefully. He had been startled when Dan told him about the intruder he'd seen leaving Yuri Malevski's Parkdale mansion.

"Sounds like Ziggy," he said at last. "He was one of Yuri's hangers-on. Just a kid, really, though I think Yuri said he was a drug dealer. Maybe even a heroin addict. Do you remember, Charles?"

Dan glanced at Charles, whose gaze seemed anchored to a potted plant on the windowsill. His face was expressionless.

"Not particularly," he said at last.

"Any idea what he might be doing there?" Dan asked.

Lionel shrugged. "I have no idea. None at all. I don't know why anyone would be there. He was sort of a sad kid, a lost boy. I used to see him at the Saddle, even in the daytime. It was like he had nowhere else to go."

"How would he have gotten inside the house?"

Lionel looked bewildered. "He must have the code. You can't get in without it."

"Wasn't it changed after the murder?" Dan asked.

"No." He looked sheepish. "Once the police finished the investigation, I reset it to the original code. Just an accounting thing." Lionel turned to Charles. "You don't remember Ziggy? Sort of a Goth look?"

Charles shook his head. "Not specifically, no. Yuri's place was a zoo, with all kinds of people hanging around." He turned to Dan. "Is it possible you left the door open and he followed you in?"

Dan shook his head. "I was careful to latch the door behind me when I arrived. I didn't want anyone to know I was on the premises, apart from a nosy neighbour who didn't seem to care for Yuri."

Lionel shrugged. "Then there's no question: he has the code."

"How would he have got it?" Dan asked.

"Yuri must have given it to him. There were always a few people who knew it. If it became a problem, he just reprogrammed it for a while. That happened a couple times a year, but he always set it back to the same code afterwards. His birth date. Easier for him to remember."

"Who else had the code that you know about?"

Lionel considered. "Off the top of my head, I can think of a few people. Santiago always had it. Probably one or two of the kids who hung out here."

"And presumably they could have given it to others?"

Lionel nodded. "I suppose."

Charles snapped his fingers. "What about that trannie?" He looked over at Dan. "There was one in particular I took a strong dislike to. I think he — she — it — whatever the correct term for a transgendered person is —"

"I believe the correct pronoun is 'ze,'" Dan said.

"Okay, then *ze* was probably a transsexual, but I never had my suspicions confirmed."

"Do you recall a name?"

"It was one of those neutral names." Charles looked at Lionel. "Wasn't it Jan?"

Lionel nodded. "Yes, that's it. Jan used to work there from time to time."

"Doing what?" Dan asked.

Lionel looked perplexed. "I couldn't really say. I got the idea Yuri hired Jan as some sort of party warden."

"A drug enforcer," Dan offered.

"Maybe. All the kids were in awe of Jan, though I never understood why. It was as if Jan had some hold over them. Whatever it was, I never learned."

"Can you give me a description?"

"Besides scary?" Charles smirked. "Well, at first glance you'd probably say woman. Spiked hair, shaggy eyebrows, lots of piercings and make-up, but if you looked long enough you'd start to second-guess yourself. Big shoulders, muscular arms. That's what I recall.

There were enough qualities of both sexes to make things confusing. As often as I ran into Jan, I could never say for sure what sex I was looking at."

"How did Jan and Yuri get along? Any bad blood there?"

Lionel thought this over before answering. "Nothing I could put my finger on, but I once overheard an argument they were having. Yuri said, 'If you can't do this for me then you can find another donor to bleed dry.' That was the phrase he used."

"Do you have any idea what wasn't being done to Yuri's satisfaction?"

Lionel shook his head. "None at all, though I remember I was instructed not to pay Jan that month. Jan must have known not to expect anything, because I was never asked for anything."

Dan considered. "It might be interesting to find out what it was."

"I can try, but Jan pretty much stopped coming around after that. As I said, there were a lot of people Yuri might stop speaking to for a period of time, then resume just as suddenly for no apparent reason."

"What about this policeman you mentioned, the one you saw when you and Charles had the accident? Did he have the entry code?"

Lionel frowned in concentration. "Not that I know of, but I couldn't say for sure. And by the way, I looked him up, as I said I would. I was right. His name was Trposki."

"Was he one of the cops taking bribes?"

"I'm sure he was."

"And then Yuri stopped paying him. So, if anyone were to get hot under the collar about it, it might be this Trposki."

Lionel nodded. "It makes sense."

"So there were a number of people, some of them at odds with Yuri, who had access to the house. Besides Ziggy and other occasional partygoers, there was an ex-boyfriend, a transsexual who was hired and then fired, and a corrupt cop taking bribes. It's not a very exclusive list, even if you consider that Yuri changed the code from time to time."

"Sadly, no. He even gave it out to delivery men and such. There was always a shipment of something coming around. Alcohol, food, flowers. Exotic plants were Yuri's passion. He didn't want them left outside, so he gave the florists the code and told them to leave the goods inside the door."

"I saw his greenhouse. It must have been impressive when it was in bloom."

Lionel nodded. "Yuri spent a lot of money on plants. Orchids in particular, especially rare ones. He could talk about them forever, when the mood hit him. I think he preferred plants to humans, to tell the truth."

"The passions of the rich," Dan concluded.

Lionel smiled. "He had a few of those. They weren't all bad."

"Maybe not, but one of them might have got him killed," Dan said. "When you have a moment, I'd like the names of people who definitely had the code. I'd also like to know who was given discreet payments for the running of the club or anything to do with his house."

Lionel gave him a questioning look. "You want a list?"

"It doesn't have to have your name on it. Nothing official, just names and addresses if you have them. If anyone asks, I'll say I got them from the bar's files on my own."

"Okay."

"So then you're taking the case?" Charles asked, just as his cell rang.

Dan smiled. "It would appear so."

Charles nodded and reached for his phone. "Good. Excuse me a moment."

He stepped out of the room.

Dan looked across at Lionel. "I assume you still want me to take the case?"

"Sure, it's just that ... well, we didn't think you would."

"You have to bear in mind that even if I do find this Santiago Suárez, he has no reason to talk to me, especially if he's an illegal on the run from the police. He's going to be very wary of any contact that would get him in trouble or thrown out of the country. I don't know what the official policy is for Cuban illegals, but I'm pretty sure he won't want to be sent back."

Lionel gave a short laugh. "I can confirm that. The last thing Santiago wanted was to get sent back there. He hated his homeland. He said it was as homophobic as it got."

"He probably hasn't been to a Muslim country," Dan said. "Were he and Yuri a real couple?"

"What do you mean?"

"I mean was there anything more between them than sex? I just wonder why Yuri didn't marry him to grant him full citizenship status."

"I know there was talk of it. My guess is they just never got around to it, or else Yuri was making sure the boy was really in love with him and not just after his wealth. Santiago is very attractive, so he might have wandered off once he got citizenship. I think Yuri knew that. Also, there was a huge age gap between them. At least twenty-five years. It doesn't mean they didn't love one another."

"You think he was the killer?"

Lionel shook his head. "No. I don't have any reason to suspect him. More than Jan or the police, I mean." He hesitated. "I guess you can't work on assumptions, but if you do find him, please be careful."

"I will. If only because finding missing people is sometimes like cornering wild animals. You can't predict what they'll do or what they're capable of. If they don't want to be found, anything can happen."

"I can believe it," Lionel said.

"What about this kid, Ziggy?" Dan asked.

"I don't really know much about him, to tell you the truth. I thought Charles did, but apparently not."

Dan thought this over. "Maybe it'll come to him. Do you know if Ziggy and Santiago hung out together? They were close in age, by the sounds of it."

Lionel laughed. "I doubt they had much in common, but you never know."

"If anything comes to you, let me know."

"I will." Lionel gave him an assessing look. "It must be exciting. What you do, I mean."

Dan smiled. "It's mostly dull and repetitious. Anyway, I do it because I'm good at it, not because I'm an excitement junkie."

"Good to know."

Lionel had dressed in track pants and runners again, as though it was his habitual uniform.

"You're a runner?" Dan asked.

"Yes, though I stopped being obsessive about it. I was up to ten k a day for a while. I've tapered back. I was neglecting Charles. Well, according to Charles, at least."

"We should go running together sometime," Dan said, hoping he wasn't sounding flirtatious.

Lionel gave him an encouraging nod, as though to disarm the thought. "I'd like that."

Charles came back into the room and glanced at the two of them.

"All good here?"

"Yes," Lionel told him. "Dan's going to take the case."

Charles looked at Dan. "That's great. Thank you."

"I'll do what I can," Dan said.

They shook hands.

"We have to go," Charles said. "Please keep us updated. You've got our numbers. Anything else you need to know, just ask."

"I will," Dan said. "Oh, one other thing. "I'll need your permission to mention your names if I speak with the police."

Charles looked alert. "What will that entail?"

"Simply that I'm talking to you. I won't divulge anything sensitive." Dan looked at the two faces staring at him. "In strictest confidence, of course, especially given the nature of the situation."

"No, I can't authorize that," Charles said.

Dan waited. "Okay. But seeing how I'll be working for you, I have to make sure I don't step on anybody's toes at headquarters. They don't take kindly to outside investigations, as you can probably imagine."

"I never really thought about it," Lionel told him.

"Occupational hazard," Dan said.

Charles shook his head. "Please keep our names out of it."

"All right." Dan nodded. "You have my promise. I won't say or do anything to jeopardize either of you."

Seven

Slow Train Coming

Dan's day-timer lay open on his desk. The page was blacked out from 2:00 to 4:00 p.m. that afternoon, as it was every Tuesday. It was time for his weekly meet-up as he accompanied one of his oldest friends in the city while she endured her chemotherapy appointment.

He got in his car and headed downtown. No matter what time of day he arrived, shadows covered the outside of the hospital on Elizabeth Street, the least interesting of several medical buildings on hospital row, like a plain elder sister ignored in favour of her younger, prettier siblings.

The elevator was crowded with worried-looking faces. Dan imagined cartoon thought-bubbles over the heads of the various riders, with words like: *Please God, I can't live without him!* Or *This can't be happening to me*, or *I hope she dies soon — I need the money.*

They rose in silence as the elevator made its way to the sixth floor. A bell pinged and the doors opened.

"Chemo ward," someone called out a little too cheerfully.

Several faces looked up, disconcerted by the announcement. They'd all breathe easier once the doors closed on them again, Dan knew. He made his way down the hall to a large room at the very end. Here the faces were grimmest of all. He recognized a few regulars, the stalwarts who came each week.

He saw Domingo's shock of white hair over by the far wall. It hadn't always been that colour, he recalled. It had grown in that way after the first round of chemo six years earlier. *My first reprieve*, she called it. This was her second.

At her side sat the stern, disapproving Adele. If Domingo was a playful balloon, her girlfriend Adi was the lead weight attached to its string. She exuded joylessness and disapproval at every opportunity. At least now, Dan thought, she had a reason for it.

While there were days when Dan didn't think highly of human beings in general, Adi made a habit of disliking men explicitly at all times. Domingo, on the other hand, seemed to like everyone. She made being joyous her primary aim in life.

"I hate men," Adi told Dan when they first met, whether as fair warning or a challenge to make her like him, he couldn't tell.

"Any particular reason?"

"Because men oppress women. Because they're violent. And because they run the world and they do it badly," she answered.

"No argument there, but by that reasoning, we should hate all straights. They oppress us every day of our lives. The world is preset for heterosexuality. But oddly, I don't hate them."

"Maybe you're a coward," she said with a humourless smile.

Further discourse seemed pointless. Dan endeavoured to meet Domingo on her own after that. In fact, he'd spoken to Adele fewer than half a dozen times in all the years they lived in the same neighbourhood. Despite their disparate natures, however, the two women had remained together for more than twenty years. If nothing else, he would respect their love for one another.

Adele looked up at Dan and raised a finger to her lips, as though she would like to shush the entire world. She nodded over to the bed, where Domingo lay sleeping.

Domingo stirred as though she felt his presence. She opened her eyes and smiled. Dan went over and took her hand. Adele watched him like a guard dog watching a stranger approach its master.

"It's okay, Ad. Why don't you go have a coffee?"

Adele stood and looked down at Domingo.

"All right. I'll be back in half an hour."

Dan understood her reluctance. When your beloved is possibly in the last stage of life, you would want to be there every moment. On the other hand, the emotional toll it took was impossible to calculate. A coffee break would have to be a good thing at some point. She left with one last look around the room, as if she might later need to recount these details to a police officer asking for specifics of the last time she saw her partner alive.

Dan looked around. Chemical pouches were strung up on metal racks like plump purses on lean scarecrows. He sat on the edge of the bed and tried not look at the PICC line. On his first visit, Domingo showed him the port valve protruding from her right biceps. He flinched when she told him she had twenty-nine centimetres of plastic tubing embedded in her arm. During the course of treatment, the nurses cheerfully showed her the bags with her name affixed to labels, letting her know the timing for each solution. *This bag will take forty-five minutes, the next one will only take thirty-five.* Dan and Domingo sat together while the solutions drained silently into her body on the off-chance that a small percentage of the chemicals would target cancer cells and stem the tide of illness.

The room was hushed and dim, while the day outside was bright with the promise of spring. The sky seemed to beckon Dan onward, tempting him to run away rather than spend the afternoon in this theatre of sickness and death.

"So what's the good news today?"

Domingo smiled. Her normally bronzed skin was pale and taut. She'd lost weight since their last visit.

"Glad you asked. My white cell count was up this morning."

"Which means they let you do the chemo."

"If you like to put it that way. I prefer to think of it as now I can't get out of doing it."

He nodded.

"Tell me how you're feeling," she said, as though he were the one to be concerned for. "How's Ked? Everything okay at home?"

He knew she just wanted distraction. She didn't care if he said anything relevant or simply rambled; it was all the same to her. She had little energy left over from the combined assault of cancer and the chemicals that made her shiver and feel cold all the time. She was grateful it was coming up to summer. At least it would be warm outside.

"Everything's good. I got a couple of new clients today. Friends of Donny's. He said to say hi."

"Ah! The lovely Donny. Hi back from me."

He filled in the details of the case for her.

"That's good news," she said. "I know your restless mind. You need to keep busy. Speaking of, how are you finding the meditations?"

Dan shrugged, half shy, half embarrassed. "Not that great."

Domingo studied his face. "Tell."

He hesitated. He wasn't about to admit he hadn't done any of the exercises she had prescribed to counter the effects of a recurring post-traumatic stress disorder.

She sighed. "Look, Danny. You know this helps me, too, so don't be stingy with the details."

"Sorry, I forgot."

"What about the dream? The one with the rusty pail with the hole in the bottom?"

It had haunted him, leaving him with a feeling of despair each night as he lifted the child's pail and saw water gushing out.

"No, that one ended when I stopped dreaming about my mother. I can't really remember any others." He smiled hopelessly and shrugged. "Sorry, I'm useless. How about you? Anything good to tell?"

"Depends how you define good."

"Good as in 'positive,' 'encouraging.'"

"No. Not in that way."

"Then what way?"

"These days it's almost always the tunnel, following the train station."

She'd told him when she had the first dream of a train, convinced it meant her cancer would recur. In fact, she was right. A month to the day, her test showed positive. Her prescience always unnerved him, to the point where he'd had to sever the friendship for a while, rekindling it only in the past few years.

"So you were on the train again?"

She nodded.

"Yes. I'm on the train and hesitating at the station, trying to decide whether to get off, but I wait too long and the train starts to move again. At first I feel panic, but then I realize it isn't so bad. The train continues and in the distance I see a beautiful mountain. It looks like the train is going to crash right into the mountainside, but at the last moment a tunnel appears and the train is swallowed up in darkness."

Her gaze was far off, looking at something over his shoulder.

"I can't see a thing inside. All I can hear is the whistle screaming above as we race along in the darkness. Finally, the train throws a stray light ahead of it, illuminating everything in its path. That's usually when I wake up."

She'd had visions since she was a kid, insisting they were psychic insights into the future. She tried to describe them to him once. *It's like a door that opens and things flash past and I glimpse the scene inside before it closes again.* She waved her hands before her eyes, indicating the door as it opened and closed again. Dan tried to joke with her. Was it big and wide or more like a narrow screen affair? Did it have a window at the top and a doorbell to one side? If there was a party going on when it opened, would you ask to be let inside? What about a sex scene, possibly accompanied by gasps and a rude slamming in her face?

She refused to let him put her off. *It's just what I see*, she told him. More often than not, he had to admit there'd been validity to what she told him, even if it became apparent only with hindsight.

He was watching the change in her eyes, the leaden greyness coming in to chase out the light, the zombie reflexes that passively accepted the poison drop by drop. Absorbing, conquering her. Taking over her will until there was nothing left to fight with.

She smiled and reached for his hand.

"Old friend," she said. "Thanks for being here."

"I'm always here for you."

"I know. I'm well taken care of. It's Adele I worry about. If I go first, I don't know what she'll do. She acts tough, but she's a softie inside."

"Let's worry about that when the time comes. For now, make sure you tell me if there's anything I can do for you."

"There's only one thing. You already know what it is."

She didn't have to tell him: a decade earlier, her teenage son had gone missing. The boy, Lonnie, had shown signs of personality disorder at the time, though

Domingo hadn't fully understood the extent of the problem. He'd been experimenting with drugs and she put his strangeness down to that. Then he disappeared. Despite everything, he'd always been a loyal, loving son. There was no reason for him to vanish outright.

Dan pursued the case whole-heartedly at the time, but nothing came of it. Then he and Domingo had a falling out and he'd let it linger at the back of his filing cabinet. Now she lay in a hospital ward undergoing chemotherapy in a fight to save her life. It was time to reopen the investigation.

In the ensuing years, Domingo had convinced herself that her son was dead. No news was often not good news in Dan's business, but it was a reason to stray on the side of hope rather than despair. Sometimes people went on hoping for years — the eternally optimistic — despite having nothing to go on. Maybe it was a talent for faith or just a better choice than premature grief. Domingo wasn't one of those. She expected the worst, but mostly she wanted to know the truth before her health failed completely, another thing she was not optimistic about.

Right before he vanished, Domingo and Adele took Lonnie for counselling, but he refused to continue after a second visit. He claimed the doctors were purposely messing with his head and he wanted none of it. At her wit's end, Domingo asked Dan to help. He tried talking to the boy. They'd always had a good rapport. Lonnie had looked after Ked on more than one occasion when Dan was strapped for a sitter. But by then Lonnie had gone from a friendly, outgoing boy to a sullen, suspicious young man. Dan said his bit then gave up. He could tell he wasn't getting through to him. He concluded by reminding Lonnie he could always talk to Dan in confidence any time. A week later the boy left, taking with him a knapsack and a change of clothes. Not much to live on. They all thought he'd be back, but it was the last time anyone heard from him for months.

Then, nearly a year after vanishing, he called his mother out of the blue at Christmas from an area code just outside Quebec City. She told Dan he sounded disoriented, but managed to say he was living with a group of young people. He declined to say where he was exactly, but said he was happy. Two minutes later he was crying and telling her he missed her. Domingo begged him to come home, riveted by the fear that something terrible would happen if he didn't. He refused. By the following year she was convinced he was dead. He'd come to her in a dream, she said. He was trying to fly, while all around him people were yelling, "Jump! Jump!" She watched him fall.

Since then the trail had dwindled to nothing. Lonnie had successfully disappeared, taking with him his burgeoning soccer skills, a drug habit, and whatever chemical imbalance was affecting his thinking. In the meantime, Dan sent out queries and requests for a follow-up. A few police contacts sent possible leads. All of them came to nothing. Dan tried another round of inquiries, but they too led nowhere. The trail had gone cold. Since then, nothing. Now, he was determined to try once again for his friend who lay dying in a hospital bed.

Dan looked up. The bags were empty.

The door opened. Adele was back with a rush of air, giving him the sour look she always had reserved for him. It was time to go.

Eight

Demimonde

On Tuesdays, Ked played basketball after school before going for pizza with his friends. Dan had no desire to eat alone, so he made his way to the gaybourhood upon leaving the hospital. His feelings were conflicted regarding the four square blocks that constituted his community. Some days he found them too shabby, too confining. Nothing that was easily defined, just that they were lacking in pizzazz. They needed more "Ooh-la-la!," as Donny put it.

Dan's former therapist suggested the nagging voice in his head was a reflection of his low self-esteem, making him hold the Church-Wellesley neighbourhood in parallel low regard. Self-hatred, self-inflicted homophobia. It was the psychology of being seen as a minority. Maybe, but Dan didn't mind being a minority. He would happily declare that every-one is a minority of one sort or another. *Just look hard enough and you'll find the divide between you*

and every other human being who walks the earth,
was his thinking. In any case, there wasn't another
community he could opt into if he opted out of this
one. If wishes were horses, beggars would ride. Like it
or not, this was his second home and he knew enough
to be grateful for it, however begrudgingly.

Wandering north along Church Street, he could
see the neighbourhood was changing again. He still
recalled the days when the ghetto sprawled in from
Yonge Street, stretching as far north as Isabella where
two of the more popular bars, Chaps and Komrads,
ruled. Back then there'd been little of note on Church,
but rent was substantially cheaper than the gouging
that went on elsewhere. In the space of a year, two
new bars opened and the tide came east, helping create a unified neighbourhood with its first openly gay
city councillor and a bi-weekly press. With unification
came money, however, changing the tone and forcing
out the smaller establishments, like the bookshops and
clothing boutiques that couldn't compete with bars
and strip clubs. Wherever you went, there were always
going to be winners and losers. The losers were the
ones Dan missed most.

A decade earlier, he could have told you his favourite bar in the neighbourhood. No longer. His old haunts
were gone. In a pinch, the Black Eagle served a purpose,
and that purpose was to socialize lightly and sometimes
meet a hook-up — seldom more — when the keening
edge of loneliness came over him. If nothing else, on
those long, lonely nights he could hang out unnoticed
in its darker corners where his scruffy sex appeal hid

its allure for the wrong sort. No matter how old he got, Dan discovered, there was always someone he wasn't interested in trying to hit on him, even when he gave off all signals to the contrary.

Like it or not, he'd become a known commodity at the Eagle. If he stuck his face into the light long enough to be recognized, that is. The bartenders greeted him affably, joking about after-hours dates, which he always politely declined. Not a snob, he simply chose not to hang out with bar workers. He vividly recalled the days when one drink inevitably led to five or six or sometimes more, inebriation following in its wake. He hoped they were gone forever. He didn't need to remind himself that risky sex had on occasion been a part of that dark picture. Somehow, little thanks to himself, he'd survived his youthful folly and looked forty in the eye without blinking. It seemed the edge of oblivion for most gay men, but he was grateful to have reached it.

A handful of patrons sat around the downstairs bar. Dan knew the type: pleasant, non-aggressive fixtures on the scene, always on the lookout for company or comfort. A good man or a full glass, it didn't matter much, one served as well as the other on any given day. Half a dozen heads turned to clock Dan's entry. From a few came a friendly nod. He returned the acknowledgement. That was all for the present. Come closing time, he'd no doubt be on several mental checklists with unspoken captions like, "Where did that sexy, dark-haired dude go?" Later on they might be glad to see him still standing in some corner or else perplexed that he'd got away without being noticed.

The place had recently been refurbished, transforming the Eagle's interior from a derelict grunge bar to a sleek hangout, Manhattan-style. This was largely an older bunch, unlike the twinks at Woody's or the flashier dance crowd at Crews & Tangos. When the Saddle closed, its patrons had washed up here, though the move wasn't entirely willing. A simpler type of bargoer, for whom a costume served as a personal greeting, they found the Eagle intimidating, too chi-chi despite its hardcore S&M roots. It was a matter of knowing your style. A latex bodysuit was not a substitute for denim and a riding crop. Still, the management didn't turn patrons away for breaking any sort of unspoken dress code. It was a friendly bar, all things considered.

Dan sidled up to the counter, ordered a pint of Keith's, then proceeded to tour the place. The second floor yielded a total of a dozen men, most of them planted on the outdoor patio to smoke. Inside, others listlessly watched porn in the wan afternoon light on oversized screens secured above the bar. The effect was unsettling. You might come in thinking of your grocery list or the chores you needed to accomplish that weekend, but you always left in a zombie-fied stupor, usually alone, thinking of sex. It was that simple. Addictions made easy.

Dan watched the screens for a while, then turned away. No matter the performer, the accoutrements or the setting, the story arc was always the same. There were just so many variations on desire before the theme got monotonous. He'd just finished his beer when an ethereal blonde caught his eye. Dan watched him approach, dreamy and distant. He waited to see if the man would lose his nerve and falter before veering off to the bathroom. Whatever he was on seemed to keep his will focused, even while his steps were unsteady. He walked up to Dan and put a hand out.

"Gerry."

"Hi, Gerry. I'm Dan."

Dan waited for him to make a quick excuse and bolt once he got a closer look at the unshaven face, the scar angling from his right eyebrow, but instead he stayed and his smile grew. Gerry seemed to have a taste for the darker things in life.

"Dan the Mysterious Cowboy."

"I've been called worse," Dan admitted.

"I hope you deserved it, whatever it was."

Gerry reached out and groped him. Encountering no resistance, he went in for more, massaging Dan into a semi hard-on. Dan wondered why he even let this begin, since he was only going to break it off in a moment with no intention of carrying things on later.

Gerry increased the offensive. Dan felt a tightening in his groin, the one that said he might soon change his mind. Another thirty seconds and it would be a round of fellatio in the back room. He thought he'd put those days behind him.

He pulled away. Gerry's expression was pure bliss, though Dan suspected it was at least partly chemically induced.

"Wow," Gerry said. "I could do with a night of that. Hell, I could do with a lifetime supply."

"You're cute as hell," Dan said. "We should set up a date some time when we both have a lot longer to hang around."

"Ah." Gerry looked disappointed. "I was hoping you were here to stay."

Dan shook his head. "Nope. Just buzzing through. Looking to score, though."

Gerry's interested piqued again. "E? K? H?"

"All of the above. You know a guy name of Ziggy who might be able to fill my order?"

A smile flitted over Gerry's face. He was obviously a devotee of the drug seller.

"That little cutie!" A frown followed. "I used to see him at the Saddle all the time. I don't know where he hangs out now."

Dan finished his beer and set it aside. "What about a Cuban named Santiago?"

"Nah. Haven't seen him for a while, either. A piece of work, that one." He shrugged. "Doesn't matter. I can hook you up. Whatever you need."

Chemical delights twitched and writhed at the edge of his mind like three lemons hanging over the visual field of a chronic gambler. Once you saw them, you could never erase the image.

"Got a number?" Gerry asked, running a tongue over his teeth.

Dan shook his head. He didn't want Gerry calling to offer him anything in the dead of the night, as tempting as a cute, willing young man could be in times of need. But no. Not a good idea.

"Sorry. Just switching providers. How about you give me yours and I'll call you in a couple days when I'm hooked up?"

Even stoned, Gerry could see through that one.

"Forget it. If you're not interested now, you won't be later."

Dan watched him stagger back across the room. On reaching the doorway, Gerry turned and waved sadly, heartbroken, before heading down to the main floor.

Dan was conscious of being watched from another corner of the room. A face came into focus.

"What was wrong with him?" the bartender called out, wiping a glass on a towel.

Dan smiled. "Nothing. I'm not on the market today."

"I've been trying to get a date with you for years. If he's below your standards then I haven't got a chance. The usual soda water for you?"

"Yes. Try not to blink." Dan paused. "On the other hand, no. I'll have a second Keith's. Believe it not."

"Testing your limits?"

"What have I got to lose?"

"Not your virginity, I'll bet."

Dan gave him a wry smile. "You know what they say: it comes back after seven years. I'm due for a return."

The bartender pulled a pint of gold-and-cream froth, set it on the counter and shook his head when Dan offered to pay.

"Tuesdays virgins drink for free."

Dan smiled and thanked him, then wandered off to the patio where several men eyed him warily, though none approached. That was fine, as far as he was concerned. There was no sign of Ziggy or anyone else selling drugs.

He finished his drink and wandered back inside, shaking his head when the bartender nodded to his glass for another.

"Back to the soda water."

"So how are you these days, sexy?" the bartender asked, setting a glass in front of him, again declining his cash.

"Good enough," Dan said, toying with the drink. "Do you know what I do for a living?"

The bartender looked him over and shrugged. "I heard you're some kind of private eye."

"That's pretty much it. I find missing people."

"I go missing once in a while. I'd love you to come and find me."

Dan stopped to take stock of the situation. Here he was, being flirted with by a highly attractive man who seemed to have his head screwed on straight. Muscular chest, longish hair, goatee: he was just the right degree of scruffy.

He held out his hand. "Dan."

"Hank."

They shook.

"Been in the business long?"

"Ten years."

"Did you know Yuri Malevski?"

"Sure. We all knew Yuri."

"What did you think of him?"

He shrugged. "Nice enough, though he had a temper, I hear. Always ready with a handout for a worthy cause."

"Any ideas what might have got him killed?"

Hank lowered his voice. "Word on the street is that his boyfriend was leaving him for a woman."

"The Cuban?"

"That's what I heard. He was bucking to get married for citizenship. I guess he got tired of waiting for Yuri to pop the question. What have you heard?"

"I heard he was being pressed for kickbacks. Do you ever get approached for payments so your bar isn't inspected on certain nights? Anything like that?"

Hank gave him an assessing gaze. He ran a hand through his hair. It had just the right bounce.

"You're talking about the police, I assume?"

Dan nodded.

Hank looked away again. "Not something I feel comfortable talking about in the bar ..."

Dan nodded. "It's okay. I get it —"

Hank cut him off. "I need a smoke. Meet me on the patio in two minutes."

Dan smiled. "Sounds good."

A few minutes later, Hank handed him a cup of coffee as he came through the door. They sat on stainless steel chairs at the far end, away from the other patrons.

"I remember you from way back," Hank was saying. "I used to see you around a lot more back in the day."

"That was a long time ago. No real desire to come downtown these days."

"Married?"

"No, though I've been in and out of relationships. Just bored, mostly. You reach an age. You know. And I've got a teenage son."

Hank gave him an assessing look. "Cool."

Dan fingered his coffee cup. "Why do you remember me?"

"Besides your sex appeal? Your edge."

"My edge?"

"Back in the day, everyone had attitude. You know — we were all too good for this, too good for that. Always wanting more. Learning a little about life along the way didn't help either. It only made us want what we didn't have. I know people who are still bitter, thinking that life overlooked them. But that wasn't you. You never had that kind of vibe. You never got bitter. To me, you just seemed in a permanent state of anger. Even when you stood off by yourself in a corner, it shone like an angry halo."

Dan laughed. "An angry halo. That sounds like me. I'm sure my son would agree. Maybe I shouldn't find it so funny."

"It was sexy. It said, 'I'm dangerous — don't get too close to me.' So, of course we all wanted to."

Dan nodded. "I haven't been very good at letting people in. Not for a long time. Maybe not ever."

Hank winked. "It's not too late."

"Maybe I'm just a work in progress."

Now Hank laughed out loud. "Aren't we all!"

"Speaking of danger," Dan ventured. "Care to share what you know about protection money?"

Hank looked around, noting that all the others were absorbed in conversation. "I assume you're asking for professional reasons and not just to make small talk?"

Dan nodded.

"All right. Then I can share a bit, though I keep my head down and my nose clean for the most part. If there's something a little too spicy going on in the bar,

I just duck behind the counter till it blows over. But yeah — shit gets said, and I overhear it now and then."

He paused. Dan felt himself leaning forward, a boy anticipating a secret revelation.

"There are guys — I'm pretty sure they're cops — who come in every once in a while. Never in uniform, of course. When they show up, the owners give me a look that says I need to disappear. I usually go down to the basement and count cases of beer. When I come back up, the till is a little emptier and the owners are a little more sombre, like they've just had a scare and aren't ready to talk about it."

"Do they ever ask you to give anything out if they're not around? Maybe an envelope?"

Hank made a face. "No. And I hope they don't ask."

"Why do you think the guys who come in are cops?"

Hank gave a rueful shrug. "Because every time they come in, the owners get slack about the head count for the next few weekends. Like they've been told they don't have to bother with all the bodies in the place. Meaning they can let a lot more people in. Sometimes we go over the legal limit, which in turn means more beer sold, which also means they can start to make up for whatever payments they just handed out."

Dan nodded. "A nice, clean system. So in the end, nobody really loses out."

"You might say it's a win-win situation."

"Until there's a fire. But so far as you know, the payments have always been made?"

Hank's brow wrinkled. "Couple of years ago, when things were slow, I know we weren't doing so well. I think the payments were smaller. The bar was fined a few times. Once it was a long weekend. We had a full house. Wall to wall people. We got closed for a week for overcrowding, but I got the feeling they were just testing us. Just showing us what it would be like if we didn't go along with their scheme."

"It sounds like what was going on at the Saddle. What about the other bars? Are they getting tapped, too?"

Hank's smile was grim. "I think we all are. But the Saddle, especially. They were always over the limit and everyone knew it. It wasn't just luck that they got away with it again and again."

"You think they pick on gay bars in particular?"

Hank gave him a funny look. "You mean, because we're minorities the cops think we must be knock-overs? That sort of thing?"

Dan waited.

"I guess it might be true, but then again we're known as a successful bar. If they were after minorities, they'd be hitting up some of those small Jamaican bars on Vaughan Road. But they don't, unless they're making money. Why squeeze someone who isn't worth tapping into, right?"

Another of the bartenders came out to the patio, knocking butts into a pail. He glanced at Hank, nodded, and left.

"One of your big fans from downstairs," Hank said with a laugh. "You should start a club. Or maybe I'll start one for you."

Dan grinned. "Did you ever recognize any of the cops who came in to the bar?"

Hank looked away for a long while then turned to face Dan.

"There's one who comes in sometimes. Not often. I haven't seen him in months, but I wouldn't forget him. Thin, muscular. Wiry build. Intense black eyes. He made a scene one night. I remember he was very drunk. That's when I learned he was a cop. He looked as though he could get out of hand if you pushed him. One of those mean drunks you hear about."

"Was his name Trposki?"

Hank thought it over. "Yeah, that sounds right. Take my advice — stay as far away from him as you can." He stubbed out his cigarette and stood. "Gotta get back, sorry."

"Thanks for your time."

Hank nodded. "I could probably find out more, if you're interested. Of course, you'd have to come over to my place for supper to continue the conversation."

Dan smiled and looked at Hank's muscular forearms, his facial hair. "I wouldn't say no to a dinner date."

Nine

The Approach

Dan left the bar thinking about everything he'd just learned. A lot of fingers seemed to be pointing to an Officer Trposki of the Toronto Police. A gay cop hitting up a gay bar for protection. He took out his wallet and fiddled with the blue-and-white-striped card he kept hidden in its soft folds. So far he hadn't used it, but once the chief of police had asked for his help. With reluctance, Dan had given it. Maybe it was time to ask for a favour in return.

He pulled out his cellphone.

Not exactly friends, still they were allies in an undefined way. The conversation was brief. Dan had no hesitation saying precisely what was on his mind: police officers were taking kickbacks from bars in the gay ghetto.

The chief didn't insult him by denying it. In fact, he surprised Dan by being forthright.

"Does this have anything to do with the Yuri Malevski case?"

"That's it," Dan told him.

"*Quid pro quo.* What do you know about it?"

"Not much, but I've been told the official investigation may run into some roadblocks because of the bribery allegations. Cops don't rat on cops."

"You know I don't like hearing that kind of talk."

"I wouldn't say it if it weren't true."

The chief mulled this one over.

"I'd like you to talk to someone," he said at last. "Have you got a pen?"

"Shoot."

Dan wrote down the name and number.

"One of my best. She's in charge of an internal investigation into police corruption. You can talk straight with her. She'll treat you the same."

Dan hung up and left a message with Inspector Lydia Johnston. She phoned back within five minutes, asking to meet. Half an hour later he was sitting across from an attractive, forty-something woman with shoulder-length brown hair, sporty build. She beamed confidence. They were at Fran's Restaurant on College, one of Toronto's culinary institutions whether you were a connoisseur of diners or not. Johnston glanced around at the other customers. "I like to chat here," she said. "It's always so loud and busy that no one can overhear you."

Dan smiled. He'd wondered about the wisdom of talking in public, but she was right. The buzz was deafening. The only drawback, as far as he knew, was that the coffee was nearly undrinkable. "Burned" and "scorched" seemed to be the only noticeable flavours it possessed.

Inspector Johnston put him at ease at once. She didn't carry that tough outer persona most cops projected on the job, and which more often than not seeped through to their private lives until friends and family found it difficult to distinguish one from the other. But he'd been given access to her through the chief of police, so perhaps she felt it was in her best interests to impress him.

Dan told her the little he knew: word on the street was the police had been taking bribes from the Saddle and Bridle, milking Yuri Malevski through various employees designated to put money in other hands for a dubious form of protection.

"And you know this how?" she asked.

"Through one of his employees."

"Name?"

Dan hesitated.

"If I'm going to trust you, then I'd like you to trust me."

She wasn't hard-balling him, just stating her position. There was no aggression or intimidation in her voice.

"I'm sorry. I promised my source anonymity."

She nodded. "Okay. Fair enough, but the more you tell me, the more I can help you. Let me be frank: I can't prove that whatever you tell me is safe, but I want you to know my aim is to rid the police force of corruption inasmuch as that is possible in a force this large. I have no hidden agenda. The bars are part of it. There are drug deals, as well. Lots of messes to clean up. But I don't screw around with confidential information or the lives and reputations of police officers. I've merely been assigned a task and I'm trying to carry it out as well as I can. We will all benefit from a cleaner police force. Do you have any questions?"

Dan liked her so far. "Where do you get your zeal? What makes you suitable for this job?"

Her gaze was unblinking. "My father. He was a good cop. One of the best. He taught me to be honourable in all things. He taught me that although there are unjust laws, there are a lot of good and meaningful laws on the books. You don't break laws simply for your own convenience and especially not for personal gain. My father didn't like graft and corruption. I don't either."

Dan started to speak, but she cut him off.

"And in case you think that's a pretty speech, I'll tell you that my father died in the line of duty. I don't take his memory lightly."

"Okay, I believe you," Dan said. "Forgive me if I don't name names. I gave my word, and that means something to me. In fact, it means everything to me. I will ask for permission to spell things out to you personally, but give me credit that for now I simply cannot."

"Cool. Let me know when you can."

"For the moment, however, I can give you the name of one of your own: Trposki." He caught a flicker of interest behind the self-assured gaze. How deep the interest went, or why, was impossible to guess with certainty.

"What about him?"

"I'm told he was one of the officers who might have received bribes from the Saddle and Bridle."

"And this comes from your source?"

"Yes."

Her mood had darkened, but only slightly. He saw the outward signs, and was glad he hadn't revealed everything. Obviously the name meant something to her. Dan recognized the look. He'd seen it in his clients, the ones with things to hide. They didn't necessarily turn away when you asked the hard questions about why someone might have vanished: *Did you ever hit her? Were you having an affair?* These were the sort of questions that made most people blink, though a few had played poker long enough to know that an averted gaze was as good as an admission of guilt. But there were others, like Superintendent Johnston, whose aversion tactic was barely discernible. Dan thought of it as lips being out of synch with the words in a film. Something was mismatched. If asked to describe it, he would have said she seemed to be thinking one thing while saying another, the words going in one direction while the flickering traces of thought on her face went elsewhere. It was his own internal polygraph, but he'd never known it to be wrong. A lie was a lie, no matter the reason for telling it.

"I'm curious," she said at last. "What's your interest in this case?"

"My source is also my client. I think I can safely tell you that much. I'm looking for Malevski's ex-boyfriend, Santiago Suárez."

She sat back. "Interesting."

"As far as I know, Santiago was responsible for passing the payback money along to the police officers who were taking bribes."

"I'm sure you won't be surprised to hear we already know this?"

"Is he a suspect? In the murder, I mean."

"As much as anyone who knew Yuri Malevksi is considered a suspect at present."

"What about the killing itself. How was it done?"

"Nasty and swift. A long-handled knife was used. From what we can tell, he was attacked in his kitchen before being carried upstairs afterwards. There were a few residual bloodstains on the stairs. Everything else had been cleaned up. The front door was double-locked from inside and the back door alarmed. He was all dressed up when they found him. Almost as if he was going somewhere. In any case, he probably died in his bed."

"Sounds like someone went to a lot of trouble to hide the body."

"Seems like it. He was discovered pretty quickly, however, when he failed to show up at work and missed an accounting meeting he had planned."

Dan nodded. "Word is the ex-boyfriend left Yuri for a girlfriend. Do you know anything about that?"

Johnston's smile lit up her face. "That's what we heard, too. I thought at first it might just be an alibi thing, but we found the girl and she confirms his story. A quick conversation with some of the neighbours told us he'd been coming and going for some time. So it seems as though it might have been real. At least back then. We put a watch on the apartment, but he never returned. Probably never will, is my guess. If it helps, I can give you her name and address."

"I'd appreciate that."

Inspector Johnston took out a notebook. "She's in the Jane-Finch Corridor. If he's hiding out, it would prove easier for an illegal alien to hide out there, far from the downtown core, rather than in other culturally diverse areas like St. James Town."

"True enough," Dan concurred as he wrote down the particulars.

"What else do you know about Officer Trposki?" she asked.

The turnaround surprised him, but it shouldn't have. She came across as pleasant, but she was still canny.

"He's gay."

She finished her coffee.

"Okay, leave this with me. Do I have permission to call you at home?"

Dan nodded. "Any time you like."

"Good. And I'd like you to feel free to contact me any time as well." She stood and offered her hand. "Lydia, please."

"Dan."

Dan had a couple of hours to kill and an appetite to appease now that he'd overdosed on bad coffee. He headed back to the ghetto. The Village Rainbow Restaurant seemed the quickest option on the strip. He wasn't above cheap food when his appetite was on autopilot. He went in and took a seat.

The waiter's immaculately cut hair was the only clue he cared about his appearance. The trousers pushed down around his hips seemed to say, *I can't be bothered to worry what you might think about my butt.* He was arrogant with the scarcely considered beauty of youth — untouched, untutored, and altogether radiant.

The burger was barely noteworthy, but Dan wolfed it down anyway. Fries were always in season. When the bill arrived, Dan pulled out his wallet. The blue-and-white-striped card fell onto the table. He picked it up and thumbed the edge before tucking it back inside.

"Yeah, thanks," the boy said coolly, when Dan tipped him for his meagre efforts.

His look was sullen, as though he hated to be beholden for something as inconsequential as money.

Afterwards, Dan stood on the sidewalk outside. Apart from meeting Hank, there'd been little memorable about his afternoon in the ghetto. It simply reinforced his belief that he didn't belong there. He was a misfit among misfits. But the neighbourhood wasn't the problem, he realized. Now he saw it simply for what it was: an underprivileged bit of turf that attracted a particular type of person. Why did the LGBT community need to stand out? Wasn't that what his therapist had accused him of: trying too hard to show the world that he belonged? Maybe the boy who served him his burger felt the same: *Take me or leave me*, he seemed to say. *I can't be bothered to waste my time trying to impress you.*

Dan remembered walking down these same streets for the first time as an eighteen-year-old. The city had seemed immense to him, having just come from small-town northern Ontario after leaving behind a brutal upbringing where love was expressed with fists and curses by his alcoholic father. Back then he'd felt it was all he could do to survive, but somehow his future had been forming quietly in the background, taking shape while he walked the streets and grew more and more comfortable with the cityscape.

Images passed through his mind, a parade without end. Now, more than twenty years on, the buildings no longer seemed so high, the city less crowded than in his memory. He'd scaled its heights, bringing it down to human proportions. Of course, raising a son had contributed to that. There was nothing like being responsible for another human being to make reality assert itself.

He saw them up ahead, a trio of twisted sisters. They were a splash of local colour, a stage designer's *trompe l'oeil*, like exhibitions in the Church and Wellesley display for curious tourists. "If you look to your right, ladies and gentlemen, you'll see some of the favoured clichés of the LGBT community …"

The first was male, at least in appearance: red hair, freckled shoulders, and muscular physique, though the walk and talk said otherwise. Why go to the trouble of pumping yourself up if the voice and personality didn't match? Security, of course. You could beat up a wimp, but you'd think twice before tackling someone with a construction worker's build. The second was also male, nothing much to write home about, though the third had Dan perplexed. Shoulder-length hair and wide hips, but with a broad back and a boy's voice that cackled and whinnied and carried on. The message was as loud as it was clear: *You may think we're freaks, but don't*

mess with us. We won't be silent. The latter leaned over
to the first and kissed him on the mouth.

"Longer and wetter, sweetheart!" came the cackling
command.

Even when Dan passed them by, casting a sidelong
glance to see if there were breasts — hardly any to
speak of — he still couldn't be sure. Then it dawned on
him: the spiky hair and bushy eyebrows. This was Jan
the transsexual. Normally, he looked for signs of aber-
ration: an unusual scar or an overly obvious tattoo —
something to tell him the thrust behind the personality,
where a person came from and how they'd been formed.
Clues that gave hints about the likeliest approach to
finding someone should they disappear. But this was an
overload of signs and signals in every sense of the word.

Before Dan could make a move, Jan held up an
arm and let out a whistle, stopping a passing cab. The
unlikely trio climbed in, the cab whisking off even
before the doors were shut properly.

Dan watched it pass down the street and out of view.

Ten

Outskirts

There was nothing particularly frightening about the Jane-Finch Corridor when seen from the perspective of someone driving past at fifty kilometres per hour with little or no intention of stopping. It was the stopping that got you in trouble. Conceived of as an "instant suburb" in the 1960s, Jane-Finch was the product of an altruistic We're-All-Equal mentality bent on creating a socially diversified community, while giving little credence to the infrastructure necessary to making such a vision work. The concept of "equal but different" did not apply solely to unjust marriage laws, Dan knew, and it might cynically be said to have found a better fit here, fostering a population with one of the most culturally diverse criminal gangs and low-income, single-parent families, as well as the highest hospitalization rates for trauma in the entire city. Not your average success story. But still, it was home to some.

That Santiago Suárez had considered marrying someone from the corridor said a lot about his desperation to acquire citizenship. Ostensibly, he was a man trapped between three hostile worlds: first, that of the Canadian legal system, where he would be viewed as a murder suspect as well as an unwelcome refugee claimant; second, of his past, where he was an escapee from a dictatorial country whose citizens were not allowed to travel; and third, as a homosexual in a macho Latino culture that derided the *mariposa*.

Dan knew Canada's record for deporting refugees back to regimes where their safety and their lives were at risk. Currently, Haiti, North Korea, Iraq, Afghanistan, and the Congo were on that list of no-go zones, though every year dozens were returned to those very countries. While Eastern Europeans might claim financial deprivation as a legitimate reason for not wanting to be sent home, others like Santiago faced imprisonment, physical danger, and possibly death if they were extradited. Dan knew to tread lightly as he approached Santiago's girlfriend's door.

Judging by the building's exterior, she wasn't living a life of luxury. If Santiago had been well kept by Yuri, he hadn't upgraded by turning to Jane-Finch. Dan glanced up at the brown high-rise with its paint-flecked balconies. Bullet holes pocked a NO PARKING sign to his left. While it might have been the dream of many immigrants to live in a building towering high above the world, some of them had probably hoped to share it with better neighbours.

The door opened on a very plain young woman who stared at him through stringy bangs with sullen regard.

"Are you Rita St. Angelo?"

"Why?"

"I'm looking for Santiago Suárez."

"He's not here."

She started to shut the door, but Dan held his hand against it. She didn't put up much resistance. "Bored" was how he read it. His appearance on her doorstep might at least offer a distraction.

"I'm not with the police," he hastened to add. "I'm a private investigator. Do you mind if I just ask a few questions about him?"

"You can't come in," she said, though Dan wondered how much resistance she would give on that, too, if he pressed her.

"I promise I won't take up much of your time."

"I have to go to work."

Her hair was a snarly mess and she was dressed in a housecoat and slippers. A TV blared in the background. Dan doubted work was her priority. She had "fag hag" written all over her, but in a language he couldn't read. Her skin was oily and she could have done with a manicure. He doubted she would be much of a sexual draw for someone like Santiago, even if he were straight. She practically had "free citizenship" stamped on her forehead.

"Do you love him?" he asked.

Her eyes flickered. He'd caught her attention.

"Yes. And he loves me."

"Then maybe I can help you."

Her hand stopped pressuring the door. She waited for him to continue.

"I know you told the police he vanished. Do you know where he's gone?"

She shook her head, eyes misting over. Dan believed her.

"If he loves you, he should be here. Why isn't he here with you?"

"He's afraid they'll take him away. He didn't do anything wrong, but they'll try to blame him. The police, I mean."

And the immigration authorities, Dan thought, mentally adding to the count.

"For the murder?"

"Someone killed his boss. But it wasn't him." She seemed resigned to talking to him now. "He was here the entire week that guy was killed. He never went out. I told the police that, too."

Standing by her man, Dan thought. "Even while you were at work?"

"I wasn't working that week."

"So he never left the building?"

"Just to get milk and cigarettes at the corner store."

"Did Santiago tell you that he and his boss lived together?"

She flicked a fluff ball from her arm.

"He said he was just a friend who needed help to pay the rent, so Santiago moved in with him for a while. But that man was crazy and jealous as they come. He was delusional!"

Watches too many talk shows, Dan concluded, thinking of all the misguided people conned into putting their personal problems on daytime television, believing it would help.

"What happened? Can you tell me?" he prompted, feeling like a talk-show host coaxing his guests into revealing the details of their lurid lives.

"He threatened Santiago. Said he would make sure he couldn't come back here. He even phoned me on my own phone!" Her expression said she was impressed by this revelation and expected Dan to be too. Her eyes narrowed. "He said if I knew what was good for me, I'd leave him alone."

"How do you know it was his boss?"

"I know the type," she said, her eyes flashing with a woman-in-love defiance. "But Santiago said never mind, when we got married we would move to a nice house somewhere."

Paid for with what? Dan wondered.

"Where did you meet him?"

Her smile flickered back to life. "In a Cuban bar. The Little Havana. Afterwards, we went salsa dancing at El Convento Rico. He was the handsomest man there. He always is."

Dan knew El Convento Rico, a Latin bar where straight closet cases could grind up against the gay men and drag queens on the edge of the dance floor without causing a riot.

"How long have you known him?"

"Four months."

Dan calculated back: that was around the time Santiago and Yuri were supposed to have had their big break-up.

"Isn't that a little quick for a marriage?"

"Not when two people are in love like we are."

"Did you ever think that maybe he wanted to marry you for citizenship?"

Her face turned pouty. "He wouldn't do that."

"You'd be surprised what people do," Dan said.

She was undeterred. "I approached him, if you want to know. I offered to marry him to help him stay here. He never asked me for anything."

A nice-looking Latino illegal flirts up a storm in a bar and gets offered marriage and citizenship. Not bad for an evening out, Dan thought.

"Is that what you told the police?"

"It's the truth."

Dan pulled a card from his wallet and handed it to her with a fifty-dollar bill.

"Give this card to Santiago when you see him." He thought of editing *when* to *if*, but stopped himself. "The fifty is for you. I'm not with Immigration. I just want to ask him about payments he made so the police would leave his boss's bar alone. If he can help me pin that on anyone in particular, it might help with his case."

The door stayed open after he turned away. He could practically feel her eyes on him as he headed down the stairs. Someone had threatened her to keep away from Santiago. Dan doubted that was Yuri Malevski's style. In any case, Santiago would not likely be coming around here for a while, unless he ran out of money and got desperate. Dan hoped he'd put enough doubts into Rita that she would call if the Cuban returned.

Eleven

My Life So Far

Heading south from the corridor, Dan made his way down to Parkdale and pulled up outside the Lockie residence. The place looked as unwelcoming as it had on first sight. He traced the roof with his eyes, reconstructing the sloping wall in Malevski's bedroom and following it along the eaves. Several antennae and a satellite dish sat cockeyed above. Power lines joined in like snaking trellises, the gridlocked residue of the previous century's technological onslaught. One of those wires connected with the security system. How had it failed so spectacularly, letting a killer trespass with the intention of silencing its sole inhabitant? Yuri had changed the code a week before his death. Had he felt threatened? Was it to keep Santiago out or someone else? In any case, it hadn't worked. Someone who knew the code had got inside, unless there was another way in that bypassed the alarm system altogether. If so, it wouldn't be known by just anyone, only an intimate who was aware of hidden entrances.

Dan let himself into the yard and approached the house with a view to breaking in. There were three ground-floor entrances. The master bedroom had a small balcony, but surely that too would have been wired by the alarm system. If not, it was still a long way up and an unlikely bet for anyone trying to get inside unnoticed. Dan scoured the ground beneath. The garden looked undisturbed, the shrubs showing no sign of broken branches or damaged stems, so unlikely in that regard as well.

He followed the perimeter, making a thorough circuit of the whole house. Each of the doors — front, back, and side — was clearly linked to the security system. Any attempt to breach the locks or bypass the code would set off an alarm, bringing whatever response was set up to stop an intruder. He kept his eyes peeled for an alternate route: a basement window or coal-delivery chute from days past. There was nothing.

His attention kept coming back to the greenhouse. Once inside, you could get to any or all of the floors, the only problem being that you would still have to break a window, which again would be connected to the security system. Regardless, there were no broken panes. Could someone have removed the glass and entered the house, then replaced the window once he or she were back outside? It seemed a trifle elaborate, but no doubt it could be done with a little effort, in which case there would be signs it had been replaced. Dan ran his finger along the paint-sealed frames. Everything was intact and the silicone caulking undisturbed. Where did that leave things?

He glanced back up. Something about the roof-line seemed out of place. A small porthole showed near Yuri's bedroom, a little lower down. Dan tried to reconstruct the hallway in his mind, but couldn't recall seeing it from inside.

Dan stepped back and turned around, nearly walking right into the figure standing behind him.

"Whoa!" he cried, jumping aside. "What the —?"

For a second, it didn't register. Then he recognized the snub-nosed neighbour he'd seen watching him over the fence on his first visit. The man stood there, unmoving, dressed in a plaid jacket and dark jeans. He was creepy and ominous.

"You're back," the man said.

"Yes, I'm back. Why are you sneaking up on me?" Dan demanded.

"I thought you could be someone trying to break in," the man said. "Who are you again?"

"Property maintenance," Dan told him. "I've been hired by the estate."

"You looked like you were trying to break in."

Not an inaccurate description of what he'd been doing, Dan thought, except he wouldn't have been so obvious about it if he were.

"Well, I'm not trying to break in. I'm trying to see if anyone has tampered with the security system."

The man nodded. "Uh-huh. So you got the code and everything?"

"Yes, I have the code." Dan looked him up and down. He was just as grubby and rumpled-looking as the first time he'd seen him. If he met this man on the street, he might have thought him homeless. "So you keep your eye on the place. Ever see anyone coming and going?"

The man grinned. "Not since the murder. Until then, all the time. Oh, yeah."

"Well, Mr. —?"

"They call me the P-Man. Short for Pig, if you wanna know."

He gave a hyena-like snort.

"Well, P-Man. I'm glad to know someone is keeping an eye out." Dan pulled out a notepad and wrote his name and number on it. "If you see anybody hanging around trying to get in, please give me a call."

The P-Man looked over the note. "All right, Dan."

Dan left him standing there and went to the front door. He tapped in the code, watched the light turn green, and then went up to the third floor. It struck him instantly that Yuri's bedroom door was closed, though Dan had left it open. Had someone been inside since his last visit? It was an old house, so it could have been a tilt that slowly closed it on its own. Dan had lived in enough wonky places to know that was a possibility. He opened it and flicked on the light. Nothing seemed to have changed. He took a photo to check against his previous shots.

A bevelled lead window threw coloured light rays at the end of the hallway, but that wasn't what Dan had noticed from outside. Red roses dominated the pattern, intertwined here and there by green stems replete with thorns. Even in artistic expression, the impulse to preserve life's menacing aspects remained. If it had been a landscape with a cloudy horizon, no doubt one of them would be a thunderhead, grey and heavy with the threat of rain. Was it human nature to imagine perfection and leave the worm in the bud?

The walls were finished with raised wainscoting, all very old and pricey to reproduce. The lacquer had cracked and wrinkled, yellowing with age. Anyone wanting to gut this house would walk away with a fortune in reusable material in top shape. The salvage business would always be booming so long as the past was in vogue.

Dan's eyes followed the panelling along the corridor and stopped where he presumed the missing window would be. Right there. It was easy to spot once you knew what you were looking for. A single panel of wood that appeared less worn than its fellows. His knock resounded on the framework. He pressed and felt a slight give right before it sprang open.

Inside, the space was small and cozy. Light filtered through the window and splashed over an unfinished floor. It was little more than a cubbyhole, but one that had been afforded the luxury of a small porthole. The attic beams were drywalled over. It would probably retain heat in winter, at least enough for sleeping. The ceiling wasn't quite high enough for standing, but sitting wasn't a problem.

A narrow futon lay across the floor with a single pillow, a sheet, and hand-knitted throw draped over it. A small lamp sat on the floor beside a baggie of cannabis — what was referred to as a private stash. Hardly a drug dealer's den. Dan recalled the mysterious odour he'd smelled on his first visit. Someone stayed here, no doubt about it.

A child's school report, pale blue, lay under the window. What he'd called a "scribbler" in grade school. Dan flipped it open to the title page: *My Life So Far* by Ziggy. Lionel had been right. Dan wondered if the police had discovered the room, but he doubted it. Otherwise, the notebook would have been seized along with Ziggy and his magic bag of tricks.

Dan quickly scanned the pages. It was filled with daily happenings, ranging from April of the previous year right up until a few days ago. It began with an account of how Ziggy came to take up lodgings in the Lockie House, describing his introduction to Yuri at the Saddle and Bridle, and how thrilled he was when Yuri offered him a place to stay. There was no mention of sexual favours or payment in return.

Further along, he wrote about going to clubs and trying to fit in, or how he wanted to be a journalist. Subsequent entries dealt with day-to-day minutiae of the house: *Yuri received another shipment of orchids today. They're worth $10,000 each! Santiago fusses over them like he owns them.*

Then Dan turned a page and saw a name he recognized: *Small party here tonight. I made it in the bathroom with a lawyer named Charles while his husband was downstairs. He said I looked like Santiago's younger brother. Amazing how everyone's in love with Santiago!*

So much for the perfect couple routine, Dan thought. He wondered if Lionel was fooled or simply turned a blind eye to his husband's doings.

Another entry stated: *Day 30 of being clean! I am finally through with drugs. I told Yuri and he congratulated me. That was the condition he let me stay here: that I keep off the hard stuff.*

Clean. Dan could relate. At twelve, it hadn't been hard to get alcohol. There'd been plenty around the house and his father never missed it when Dan helped himself. He'd liked the light-headedness that came with a few gulps, the buzz that followed after a few more. He'd gone to school drunk a half-dozen times before he passed out in the locker room and his secret was discovered. Counselling followed, but he insisted it was just a lark, something he did for kicks.

By the time he reached his thirties, it was a habit that followed him and dogged his footsteps like a shadow. His willpower was strong enough that he could control his drinking and function reasonably well at the best of times, but there were other times that weren't so good. His son had seen it. So had Donny. Together, they helped him walk away from it, like stepping backwards from a car crash one footprint at a time.

Ziggy probably didn't have a family to shame him into sobriety, but it sounded like he'd had a friend in Yuri Malevski. He found other entries detailing parties, conversations with Yuri, and even small, essay-like pieces on Ziggy's hopes for the future. Then: *I fucked up! I used and Yuri found out. Not sure what he's going to do. He said I had to leave until I get clean again.*

The pages that followed were blank. Dan skipped ahead, around the time Yuri was killed: *Finally back in! Stayed with friends while I got clean. I'm through with that shit. Fucking H! It makes me a crazy person. It's like I don't even know who I am or what I'm doing when I'm on it. Yuri doesn't know I'm back yet. Don't know what he's going to do when he finds out.*

Four days passed before he wrote again. *Yuri's dead. Fuck! I had to wait till the cops stopped coming around. That was a crazy few days. Not sure where I'll go next. I don't think they found my room.*

He wrote a short passage about death and what it meant. Then a single line at the bottom of the page: *If there is no morality, is killing wrong?*

Dan took shots of the recent entries and replaced the book exactly as he'd found it. He had Ziggy's diary, but where was Ziggy? And what happened during those blank four days? He withdrew from the space, closing the panel behind him.

Twelve

The Keening Edge

Dan looked around from the embrace of a rocking chair, taking stock of the home he and Ked occupied. It wasn't big, but it was cozy and comfortable. Even the back-yard, glimpsed through the kitchen window, was an extension of their living space, at least in the temperate months. Compared to others, their lives were the envy of much of the world. They could eat and drink without fear of contagion, travel where they wanted, love and marry whom they chose, educate themselves, take up professions, aspire to public life without fear of assassination, spend or save as much as they could manage, and fall asleep without fear. What must their existence seem like to those outside the tiny bubble in which they lived? An impossible dream? It was difficult even to comprehend such good fortune while standing at the centre of the charmed circle.

Ralph nuzzled his fingers, hinting that a treat would be appreciated, or even a walk should he feel so inclined.

Dan and Ralph had long since made peace from their days of mutual antagonism. Dan suspected a good deal of Ralph's newfound submissiveness had come with age rather than any testosterone reduction resulting from his neutering, which seemed to have little if anything to do with his outward behaviour and passive-aggression toward Dan in particular. Now when there was an accident in the house, Dan knew it was a senior moment on Ralph's part rather than any youthful rebellion.

Dan had several hours to kill before nightfall. They took a long, leisurely walk, with Ralph stopping to sniff at every opportunity and Dan taking time to reflect on the tranquility of his neighbourhood, still amazed by its growth spurt over the past decade. When he first moved there, Leslieville was in a deplorable state of physical and aesthetic decline. He'd been the first on his block to landscape. The following year, a few tepid attempts by the neighbours showed initiative to at least try to match his. Rotting roofs were replaced, paint splashed on walls. The skinheads at the end of the block moved out and a lesbian couple moved in. But it was a beginning. Now there were trendy cafés, film studios, and even — sign of the times — gelato shops.

After unleashing Ralph, Dan went up to his office and dug out the file on Domingo's son. His last correspondence on the subject had been more than four years earlier, when he sent out circulars with Lonnie's photograph. All his queries were returned with nil responses.

Dan reread the file, but nothing came to him. Without a fresh lead, there was simply nothing new to try. He'd have to ask the old questions again, hoping things might have changed on the other end. The Quebec area code was still the best bet.

He sent of a couple of emails and set the pages aside. His mind turned to Santiago Suárez and his recent interview with his girlfriend, if indeed she was his girlfriend.

He called Lionel, giving a rundown of his conversation with Rita St. Angelo.

"So she did exist," he said.

"Didn't you believe in her?"

Lionel laughed. "I thought it was just one of those rumours. I'm pretty sure he's gay. I guess you can fake anything if you try hard enough."

"She claimed he was with her the entire week Yuri Malevski was murdered. I don't know if I believe her, but at least he has an alibi."

Dan described his discovery of Ziggy's hideaway behind the panelling, but made no mention of the diary or the entry detailing Ziggy's tryst with Charles.

Lionel was silent for a moment, and then said, "I guess it's all right to let him stay for now, seeing how he's been there all along. I'm legally in charge of the house until it's sold, but I doubt there's any point in making him leave."

"I don't have any advice to give you on that count," Dan said.

He hesitated on the next point, Lydia Johnston's request to be told the names of Dan's clients. Lionel surprised him by being forthright on that one.

"I spoke with Charles about it and we both agree it's all right for you to use my name in your conversations with the police investigation, so long as they can guarantee confidentiality. We don't want them to feel we're being uncooperative or subversive in any way."

"Good, that'll be helpful," Dan said. "Are you okay with being contacted by them directly, if they request it?"

"As long as you're confident it's the right thing, then I have no problems with it."

"Thanks, Lionel. I appreciate your trust."

The conversation concluded. Dan was left sitting in the vacuum of his home, contemplating a similar feeling he'd had in Yuri Malevski's empty mansion.

Afterwards, he called Lydia Johnston and told her his client had reconsidered his request for anonymity.

"The chief was right," she told him. "He said your client would turn out to be the accountant. My money was on the bar manager."

"I won't take any bookie tips from you then," Dan said.

"Gambling's not my thing. I only go for sure bets anyway."

He updated her on Santiago's girlfriend.

"So you think it likely there wasn't much in the nature of true romance there?" she asked.

"I'd call that a sure bet," Dan said.

Downstairs again, Dan heard Ked breeze in and out, stopping long enough to turn down Dan's offer to make supper. He was on his way to meet his girlfriend, Elizabeth, who had more or less become a permanent fixture in his life. Dan was glad he approved of her; he'd hate for a woman to come between him and his only offspring. He'd heard enough of the sort of tales that divided families to ever let that happen to his.

Ked stood at the door looking guilty. "I'm sorry I won't be here for supper."

Dan almost laughed. "Go. Enjoy yourself. My greetings to Elizabeth."

Ked lit up with a smile. "Okay. I won't be late."

Alone again, Dan turned to the kitchen. Cooking for one was high on his list of dreary tasks to avoid. Just one notch above that was eating alone in restaurants. While he wasn't a fan of cooking for its own sake, he had over the years become a decent hash-slinger with some culinary coaching from the ever-capable Donny. If need be, he could spend a half hour in the kitchen and retreat with a fairly respectable meal for his efforts.

He opened the cupboard, picked out an unopened jar of pesto and a bag of pasta. A plateful of greens scooped from a plastic container did not dampen his enthusiasm for salads, fortunately, as this was the easiest way to balance his diet without a great deal of washing and chopping. In his estimation, food should be fun and not a chore.

While waiting for the water to boil, Dan went to the living room and drew out the final volume of Proust's *In Search of Lost Time*, which he was diligently making his way through for the second time. Proust's love life hadn't been all that successful, Dan knew. Mostly, it had been obsessive and unrequited. As a consolation, he reinvented and endlessly replayed it out in the pages of his massive epic. If he'd lived in the age of television, he probably wouldn't have written nearly as much.

Dan drained the pasta and poured pesto over it. He ate quickly and without relish, then washed the dishes and put them away. Duty done.

He stopped for a moment and glanced at the cupboard over the fridge. Once it had contained his stash of liquor bottles. Now it held cleaning products. After he resolved to stop drinking, he hadn't tormented himself by keeping alcohol within reach. While he considered it a battle largely won, he thought it wise not to stock up on temptation.

Whenever he felt the twinges of loneliness, as he did on days like this, it would have been simple to console himself with a drink that could easily turn into a second and a third. Back then, it seldom stopped with one. That was the problem. Not the passing through, as with Jane and Finch, but the stopping and staying.

He picked up his book and read till the light dimmed outside the window. Just as the words on the pages were becoming incomprehensible, he reached overhead and clicked on the reading lamp. Despite his obsessions, Proust was a good companion, equally lost as Dan when it came to love. Dan was pretty sure he'd known the same loneliness, the melancholy of azure skies at twilight. But Proust was dead; Dan was still alive and living his solitariness every day. Maybe Ked was afraid of more than abandoning his father. When it came to alcohol, leaving Dan on his own was not a good option.

Ralph had retired to his bed in the kitchen. He lifted his head and sniffed when Dan came in again, resting his chin on the side of his basket. Dan poured himself a glass of cranberry juice, plunked in several ice cubes till it threatened to overflow, then lifted the drink to Ralph. It looked like a cocktail, but it would taste very different.

"Here's to independence, Ralphie."

Ralph sniffed at the air, decided it was nothing he was interested in then let his chin sink back onto the pillow. Dogs were fine companions, Dan thought. And usually they were easier to get along with than humans; they just didn't have a lot to say. Still, there was his date with Hank to look forward to Friday night.

He eyed his glass of cranberry juice. At least he knew he wouldn't be waking up sprawled on the sofa, an empty bottle of rye on the floor beside him in the morning. Sometimes not giving in was as good as it got.

Thirteen

Let's Dance

It was a nice evening, the spring air slightly cool on his skin as Dan arrived at Hank's condo. He felt a slight trepidation when he realized he couldn't recall his last date, but the feeling vanished as Hank greeted him with a chaste kiss, dressed in nothing but a towel. Before anything could start, Hank whisked himself off to the bedroom, returning coiffed and neatly dressed in chinos and a crisp navy T-shirt. This time he gave Dan a longer, more intimate kiss.

Dan breathed in Hank's subtle scent, relishing the minty taste of mouthwash on his lips. Hank pulled back and abruptly left the room again.

"I can't forget I'm your host as well as your chef," he called over his shoulder. "Besides — we need to get through the main course before we try the dessert."

Enticing aromas wafted in from the kitchen. Dan followed and leaned up against the counter. Hank uncorked a bottle of wine, splashed the contents into two glasses, then handed one to Dan.

"To passion," he said with a wink.

Dan smiled. "To passion and its possibilities."

"I'm making Peruvian chicken with fennel ragout." Hank grimaced. "I didn't ask. Do you object to eating animals?"

"Only if they're still alive when I eat them."

"Not a vegetarian then. Good! I hate pandering to other people's weirdnesses. I'm a complete carnivore myself, but I like to experiment. And not just with food, by the way." He leaned in and kissed Dan again, pulling back with an intoxicated expression. "I'm tempted to forgo dinner and drag you off to the bedroom right now, but I put a lot of effort into this meal."

"Then let's not waste it," Dan said. "Besides, I came hungry."

"I promise you will go away fulfilled." Hank downed his glass and poured a refill. "I did a little asking around about your problem. Although my bosses were not entirely forthcoming, they told me a few things. They tried to laugh it off and make it sound negligible, but I gather they get squeezed regularly. Nothing too outrageous. After all, you don't want to squeeze the bar owners out of business. You just want to get them into the habit of coughing up when they can."

"Do you know if anybody ever gets threatened if they don't make the payments?"

"I think it's been suggested that it wouldn't be wise to turn down a request. On the other hand, I don't think anybody was worried about being killed. Just being shut down for a few days."

"That was my first thought," Dan said. "As you noted the other day, it's a win-win situation if everybody plays nice. So why upset the apple cart?"

Hank shook his head. "Ego, maybe. Nobody wants to be told what to do. From what I heard, Yuri could be headstrong. If he decided he didn't want to play the game then maybe he just opted out and thought to hell with it. He was probably prepared to have his place raided and would have had a good doorman for the weekend crowds — there's always a million guys waiting to get in and have fun on a weekend. But I doubt he would have expected to be murdered because of it."

"I agree," Dan said. "It doesn't make sense for them to kill him. Why risk a murder investigation?"

Hank shrugged and drained his glass again. He held up the bottle. Dan shook his head. Alcohol, he knew, was like sex. The first kiss was magic, the second sloppy, and then it was all pretty much down to business after that.

Hank smiled indulgently. "Chef's prerogative. I cook better when I'm drunk. We need to speed you up a bit. Otherwise I'm going to be too far ahead of you."

"It's not a race," Dan said. "You take things at your pace and I'll go at mine."

"Ah, you really aren't a drinker! I was right. We need to loosen you up."

Dan had no intention of telling this attractive man that he was a former drinker who had faced the abyss only recently. First impressions were better edited with time. In the past two years, it had become a badge of honour to imbibe without overdoing it. He could have a single drink and stop. In good company he allowed himself two, with a long wait between the first and second. Seldom had he advanced to a third. A fourth was out of the question.

Dinner went well. The ragout was followed by a salad of butter lettuce topped with roasted walnuts, shaved parmesan, and a citrus dressing. Dan was on his second glass of wine, sipping slowly, when dessert arrived straight from the oven: a flourless chocolate-bourbon cake. Hank had gone all out to impress him.

"Ready for the next course?" Hank asked when they finished the meal.

"Your move," Dan said, setting his glass down.

In the bedroom, they shed their clothes without awkwardness. Hank's touch was surprisingly gentle and expertly tuned to his pleasure. As his toast had promised, he wasn't a man who kept his passions on a leash. Lips met lips as erections probed each other's thighs. As it turned out, Hank was well-endowed.

They were just beginning to get into it when Dan's phone rang. He grabbed it and saw Lydia Johnston's number.

"Sorry, I should answer this."

He heard Lydia's soothing voice asking for him. When he identified himself, she said, "Thought you'd like to know we've had a Santiago Suárez sighting."

Just then, Hank's lips met the head of Dan's penis.

"Oh!"

"Yes, I knew you'd be excited," Lydia went on as Dan tried to control himself.

"That's, um … great news. Was he in touch with the girlfriend?"

A pair of hands cupped his balls and gave them a good yank. Dan let out a little sigh.

"What?" Lydia asked.

"Sorry, just catching my breath. I've been jogging."

"Hey, good to hear. I'm a jogger, too."

He hoped she wasn't about to launch into a casual conversation about their mutual fitness interests. Dan looked down to see Hank grinning up at him, working his shaft with one hand. Dan shook his head, but didn't push Hank away.

"So. The sighting?" he managed.

"It was pure coincidence. One of my officers went by Rita's place to do a follow-up and saw Santiago coming down the stairs as he arrived. Although the man denied being Santiago, my officer swears it was him."

Hank's actions were having a telling effect. Dan could barely keep his mind on the conversation. He tried to control his breathing.

"So he's sure it was him?"

"As sure as he could be from having seen him only in a photograph."

Dan bit his lip to keep from gasping.

"So he didn't actually get much chance to talk to him?"

"No, unfortunately."

"Mm," Dan murmured as Hank's tongue hit a hot spot.

"I know, it's a drag," Lydia said. "By the time he got back to his car the guy was gone."

Dan exhaled. "Did he talk to the girlfriend?"

"Yes, she answered when he knocked. He said she still had a fresh smile on her face. She was wearing a very flimsy nightgown. She probably thought it was the boyfriend coming back."

"So they … they were enjoying a moment of pleasure together?"

"No doubt Santiago wanted to make sure he still had a place to stay if he needed it."

"You think?"

Dan felt the pleasure building. He tried hard not to groan. Hank was expert at what he was doing.

"It seems likely. We know he isn't staying there full time or we would have caught him by now. I wonder if your little visit the other day triggered something. All that poking around you've been doing. Anyway, that's my theory."

"Right!" Dan exclaimed, a little too loudly.

"Are you okay?" Lydia asked.

"Very," Dan said. "And I agree totally."

"Good."

Hank stepped up the pressure with both tongue and hand. Dan felt himself getting close. "I …"

"Sorry? What?"

"I better let … let you go."

"Okay," she said. "I'll keep you informed."

"Yes," Dan said. "Thanks very much. Thanks …"

"Talk to you when you're a little less busy."

The cell clicked off.

"Oh, gawd!" Dan's body bucked as he dropped the phone on the bed and lay very still. Hank's face hovered above him. "You are very, very wicked," he managed.

"Said the bishop to the altar boy," Hank chimed in. "Ba-*dump*!"

They showered together. Hank stood back, apprising Dan's body as they towelled off. "Very, very nice!"

"Thanks," Dan said. "You, too."

"It's been a fun evening. Would you like to continue at the bar? I could do with a little dancing!"

"I'm not much of a dancer," Dan said apologetically.

"I can teach you. You know what they say: dancing is an art."

"I don't mind coming with you, but can't I just appreciate it from a distance?"

Hank grinned. "I want to see you live a little. You need to learn to relax, Danny boy."

Dan considered. "All right. But not too late."

"Of course not. We need to get you back home before the Great Pumpkin comes calling for you."

Zipperz specialized in music from his youth, as Dan discovered. He hadn't been on a dance floor in years, but slowly he let go and began to enjoy himself. Hank bought him a beer. It was his third drink of the evening and Dan was dead set on making it his last. It was all a matter of self-control.

Not only had Dan not danced in public for a decade, it was probably the first time he'd danced with an alcoholic beverage in hand since his twenties, around the time he met Donny. He stopped to consider: it actually felt good. Hank was right — he needed to unwind and relax. Otherwise he would petrify, becoming a fossil before his time.

The lights rippled as the music enveloped him, reminding him of how much fun he used to have before the responsibilities and worries and everything else that dragged you down with time. For just tonight, he wasn't that person anymore. He was free to be who he wanted.

Hank walked off the floor and returned with two more bottles. Dan shook his head, but Hank pouted. How many years since he'd had such meaningless fun? Dan wondered. He was flying now, his feet lifting with the beat pulsing around him. Everywhere he looked, people were having fun. Healthy, normal people were enjoying a night out with a little beer and companionship to tide them over. He could manage it, he thought. It wasn't asking too much. And it was better than staying alone at home. He nodded and grabbed the beer.

Hank gave him a contented smile. The student was coming along nicely.

"But this is absolutely the last drink tonight," Dan shouted in his ear.

"Absolutely! You're fantastic, buddy!"

Hank gave him a thumbs-up and Dan drifted off to the centre of the dance floor. He could have done a back-flip out of sheer physical enjoyment. The man next to him glowed. Dan looked around in amazement at all those smiling, happy people pressed into one small space. He felt euphoric and wanted to hug them all. He turned to look for Hank and saw him shimmying with another man across the room. Others were coming on to the floor now. How could he have forgotten there was so much joy in dancing?

It was during the next song that he felt his pulse racing. It accelerated so quickly he wondered if he was having a heart attack, but then it slowed again. He stepped off the floor, feeling flushed. He waved to Hank to say he was going to take a break. Hank smiled at him and kept dancing.

Dan staggered to the bathroom, reaching out to the walls to steady himself. At the urinal, he released a dark stream of piss and watched in fascination as it discoloured the ice before flushing away. He felt better, but only momentarily. The heat and the pressure in his head were building again. He lurched into a cubicle and bent low over the toilet, forcing himself to his knees as he gripped the rim. The sudden stream of alcohol mixed with the remains of Peruvian fennel ragout were disgusting, though he felt immediately better.

Once he could stand again, he carefully exited the stall. Hank stood just inside the entrance, watching him with concern. Dan propped himself against the wall, taking deep breaths to quell the fire inside. A security guard looked him over: if this guy was going to give him trouble, he'd be one hell of a dude to mess with.

Hank put an arm around Dan's shoulder.

"I think we'd better take you home, cowboy," he said softly in Dan's ear.

Music pounded in the background. For a second, Dan thought he was going to be sick again. *Wimp!* he thought. Not drinking for a couple years had rendered him a complete washout. The irony!

He let Hank lead him from the club then stumbled into a cab when Hank opened the door, all the while apologizing for the scene he was making. He tried to talk, but he wasn't making sense. If he didn't lie down, he felt he would collapse. Finally, he gave in and sprawled across Hank's lap.

"Sorry, sorry …"

"No worries, big guy," Hank said soothingly.

The cab took them to Hank's condo. The driver scowled even as he took the twenty Hank proffered through the window. Whether he disliked drunks or faggots, they were both and his distaste was clear. The cab swerved off again.

Dan was a contestant on a game show. Someone asked him to guess the identity of the people who loved him, but one after another the doors slid open on empty space. He felt a sense of despair as he approached the final door. At last, it opened with a flourish. There was his son, with Donny and Kendra. Relief flooded over him. Better late than never.

Pain split his head like an axe stroke. He sat up and looked around, but he wasn't in his room. The events of the evening started to come back, shadowy and vague. He was back at Hank's condo after being out at a dance club. A used condom lay on the floor beside his castoff underwear. That meant they'd had sex upon returning, though Dan couldn't recall taking part in the event. This was like so many wasted nights of his youth.

Hank was asleep on the far side of the bed. Dan dressed hurriedly and let himself out of the condo, embarrassed as hell by his conduct the previous night.

So much for self-control.

The house was dark when Dan arrived home. Ralph gave him a questioning glance, but let him pass. No use rubbing it in, his look seemed to say, though it stopped short of outright commiseration. Dan went directly to bed and slept until afternoon.

When he got up, his urine was nearly black. Something clicked as he stood over the toilet, propping himself with one hand against the wall. He wasn't drunk. His first thought was food-poisoning. Then the other shoe dropped.

He stumbled to the kitchen. There were three messages from Hank asking how he was and did he need any help. Each one sounded a little more panicked. Dan picked up his cell. Hank answered on the first ring.

"How are you, buddy?" Hank asked on hearing Dan's voice. "I was very worried about —"

"I'm all right now," Dan said, cutting him off. "I wasn't last night. Care to tell me what happened in the hours between leaving your place and returning home again?"

There was a pause. The line hummed between them. Dan waited.

"I didn't know you'd be so susceptible," Hank said with a nervous laugh.

"To what?"

"MDMA."

"You gave me MDMA?"

"Just one," Hank said. "I slipped it into your beer at Zipperz. I'm sorry."

Dan was momentarily stunned. He'd heard of the dangers of mixing alcohol and Ecstasy. It was little short of date rape.

"What the fuck? What were you thinking?"

"I'm sorry, Dan. I just thought it would be fun, a little something to help you relax."

"That is the stupidest fucking thing anyone has ever done to me."

"I'm sorry. I won't do it again."

"No, you won't, you fucking idiot," Dan raged. "Because you won't see me again."

"Wait, I'm sorry —"

Dan slammed down the phone, then stumbled back to the bathroom for a painkiller.

Fourteen

Run Wild, Run Free

His resurrection was a little slow in arriving. Dan looked like hell in the mirror, but his body was beginning to feel normal again. Whatever normal was. He ate a bowl of yoghurt, drank some coffee, and felt considerably relieved. He was just thinking over what his day might hold, in a productive sense, when the phone rang.

The voice on the other end sounded panicked, something about an unexpected phone call. It took Dan a moment to recognize it as Lionel's. He pictured the accountant's attractive features and tried to match them with this frenzied-sounding person.

"Slow down, slow down," Dan told him. "Who called you?"

"I ... I think it might have been that cop we talked about. The one who showed up at Yuri's place a couple of times."

Lionel's breath was coming in short, excited bursts.

"Trposki?"

"Yes. I think so. Maybe. I only vaguely remember how he sounded."

"Did the caller identify himself as a cop?"

There was a short pause. "No. He didn't. I just jumped to the conclusion because of what he said about how I should butt out of the investigation. I assumed he was a cop."

"It's a logical assumption," Dan assured him. "Tell me what he said."

"He said I should forget anything I knew about the payments for bar protection."

"Did he threaten you in any way?"

"No, not exactly, but that deep voice breathing into the phone telling me to forget this and forget that was threatening enough. He didn't have to spell it out." Lionel paused. "He said someone had been snooping around in the investigation and I had better not get involved."

Dan felt the sting of realization. It sounded as though someone knew he'd been talking to Inspector Johnston. He recalled the look in Lydia's eyes when he mentioned Trposki's name.

"I'm sorry this happened," Dan said. "I'll look into it."

They spoke for several more minutes until Dan suggested it might be better not to continue on the phone.

"It's possible your phone is bugged. We need to keep you out of this to make sure you stay safe."

"Yes, but this means we're on to something. It won't go away by having me hide my head in the sand."

Despite the gravity of the situation, Dan almost laughed at Lionel's gung-ho attitude. He recalled his comment that Dan's work sounded exciting. To a mild-mannered accountant, it probably would. "Well, there's brave and there's reckless. We don't want anything happening to you."

"I appreciate that, Dan, but please don't give up now. I want to know that whoever killed Yuri is caught."

"Look, I'd like to come and talk to you in person. Is there a discreet place for us to do that?" An idea clicked. "How about a run? We'd be free to talk then."

Lionel sounded relieved. "Perfect."

They settled on a time and starting point then Dan rang off.

His next call was to Inspector Johnston. While it was possible the threat to Lionel had nothing to do with their recent discussions, Dan couldn't get Trposki out of his mind. How likely was it that the investigation into police corruption had been compromised from within? Dan had no doubts about the chief of police. It wouldn't be possible for him to sabotage his own investigation. It wasn't even imaginable, from Dan's knowledge of the man. He was as tried and true as they came. But Lydia Johnston was a dark horse in his estimation, even if the chief had personally selected her to head up the inquiry.

She answered on the first ring.

"It's Dan Sharp, Lydia. Have you got a moment?"

"Yes, Dan. What is it?"

"I just heard from my client. He received an anonymous call warning him not to talk about the Malevski murder, especially as it related to bar payments."

She drew a sharp breath. "What did the caller say?"

"Just that my client was to keep out of it. The implications were clear."

"And what did you tell your client?"

"I told him I would talk to you."

"Does he have any idea who called him?"

"He mentioned the name Trposki again."

The pause was barely perceptible.

"In what context?"

"Just that he thought it could have been him."

"Why?"

"Just a hunch, though I understand my client saw him more than once at Yuri Malevski's home. When I asked you earlier about Trposki, you didn't say anything about him."

Again he felt the tightening, the withholding. She definitely knew something she wasn't going to share, at least not with him.

"We are aware of Trposki. I can't tell you anything else at the moment."

The chief had told him she would be open with him. This did not sound open, but he let it pass for the time being. There were other issues at hand.

"Was my client mentioned by name at any point by you?"

She hesitated. "Of course I had to name your client when I discussed him with the chief."

"Anyone else?"

"Not ... really."

It was the gap between those two words that struck him forcibly.

"So, yes, then."

"Dan — I can't tell you these things."

He exploded. "Damn it! I gave you a man's name and now he's being threatened. Tell me what's going on."

"All I can tell you is that everything has been discussed in the strictest confidence. Yes, I spoke about him to the chief, but I certainly put nothing down in an email or anything to that effect. I doubt this call has anything to do with us or anything coming from headquarters."

Dan's head was spinning. His previous doubts about Inspector Johnston had increased exponentially. "Who else would know about it?"

"Someone might have guessed! He was Malevski's accountant. It only makes sense we're going to query him at some point about the money and ask him for details."

He heard the exasperation in her voice.

"Look — I want you to continue to co-operate with us, but all I can tell you is that everything I do is monitored with the utmost caution. This is a very high priority for the chief and neither he nor I take any of this lightly. Not for a second. So whatever was said to your client, I guarantee there were no slip-ups coming from us. I can't say it any clearer than that."

The line went silent for a moment.

"Are you there?" she asked sharply.

"Yes."

"Look — I'm sorry, but you have to trust me. It didn't come from us." She waited for this to sink in. "Do you want us to put some protection on your client?"

"I don't know," Dan said. "I'll have to ask him. He's still willing to co-operate with the investigation. He wants Malevski's killer caught. That's his bottom line. My bottom line is that nobody gets hurt on my turf."

"Understood, Dan. I want you to know we are in complete agreement on that. So, will you let me know when you hear whether or not he wants protection?"

"I will," Dan said. "I'm meeting him this afternoon."

"Then I will wait to hear back on that."

Despite her assurances, Dan hung up feeling angry and dazed.

The rise above the track at Riverdale Park was one of Dan's favourite views. It kept the high towers of the city's economic engine at a distance, making them look decorative and less self-important. Far below, tiny stick figures jogged, threw balls, walked dogs. Somewhere down in those trees lining the river, Dan knew, a small community of the homeless lived in tents from summer through winter. There were still outcasts in the land of plenty.

Dan felt the wind on his cheeks, watched clouds scudding along the horizon. Instinctively, he longed to be in motion, knowing how his blood would quicken with each stride of his legs. He turned to his left, where Lionel was straightening from a round of stretching, his face flushed with anticipation.

"I thought this was a good idea," Dan said. "I mean, since you're a long-distance runner."

Lionel gave him a shy grin. "Somewhat of an exaggeration, I'm afraid, unless you put it in the past tense. I'm just getting back into it after a couple of years. I had to stop because of an extended bout of tendonitis."

"How far do you like to go?"

"I was up to twenty kilometres at one point. Lately, I find ten to twelve is comfortable, though it's not difficult to stretch it out a bit more."

"It's about fourteen klicks from here to Edwards Gardens. The elevation gain is around sixty meters overall. We can stop at any point you choose. Don't be afraid to tell me if you're in pain."

"Right-o, chief!"

They set off at an easy pace, across the track and over the bridge spanning the Don, passing dog walkers and couples pushing strollers. Rain had swollen the river, leaving the water unusually high and threatening the banks with erosion.

"Sorry for getting flustered on the phone earlier," Lionel told him. "I can't tell you how shocked I was. It really caught me by surprise."

"I don't blame you," Dan said. "I made a phone call to the police after we spoke. My contact, who happens to be investigating police corruption, swears your name wasn't mentioned to anyone except the chief of police himself."

"Is that a good thing?"

"It is if it's true."

"Are you saying you don't believe it?"

Dan considered. "I don't have an answer for that. At present I have no reason to contradict it, but I still question it. It doesn't make me happy to know you were threatened."

"Nor me."

They were running effortlessly now. A GO train scuttled by on a rise above them.

"Anyway, we're safe talking here," Dan said, as the greenery buzzed past.

"I trust you, Dan."

"Thanks."

"I've been looking through some of the bar records over the past few days and I may have come up with something. It's a file with a record of payments and a series of numbers. No names, just initials. The letter *T* was prominent."

Dan glanced over. "You think it's Trposki? Could these be the police payments?"

"I don't really know. It's a bit confusing, because I can't tell what the numbers refer to. They may be codes or possibly dates. I think the payments correspond to the weekend income counts and some of the amounts I handed over to the guys who paid the police for protection, but there's something else I can't figure out."

Dan gave him a quick look as they bounded over a tree branch lying in their path.

"Anything I should know about?"

"Just some irregularity. I'll let you know if I figure it out."

"Okay, you're the accountant. I'm curious — what does Trposki look like?"

"Last time I saw him? Short hair buzzed close to the skull. Dark eyes with very thick lashes. Almost as though he wears mascara, though I doubt he does. Thick shadows on the face and jaw, too. If you like hairy men, he'd definitely fit the bill. A wiry build, but very muscular from what I recall."

Dan was thinking it sounded like the cop Hank had described.

"Was the file on a computer?"

"No. It's handwritten. I found it in Yuri's office. It's his writing, for sure. It screamed out at me. It's sloppy and imprecise. Definitely not my style of accounting. I'm a dot the *i*'s and cross the *t*'s kind of guy. Perfectionist tendencies. If it's not right, I toss it out and start again. Unhealthy obsessions."

"I hope you were being careful wherever you were looking. Is it possible your search prompted the warning call?"

Lionel's eyes darted.

"Wow! I never thought of that. You're right. It could have, though I can't think just how at the moment. Maybe someone noticed the file had been moved. I don't know how many people would have known what it was, but it's possible someone did."

"Do me a favour," Dan said. "Don't do any more investigating on your own. If there's a file you want to look into, bring it to me."

"All right." Lionel paused. "I was a little surprised to find these records. It means Yuri was keeping a separate set for his own purposes. He must not have wanted me to see them, though of course I'm probably the only one who might guess what they are."

"I'd like to see them for myself."

"All right. I can do that."

Dan looked over. "If there's anything unusual, I'll probably have to take them to the officer in charge. You know that, don't you?

Lionel nodded. "I know."

"Which means I'm going to have to tell her it came from you."

"Her?"

Lionel looked surprised by this news.

"Inspector Lydia Johnston. She's the chief liaison in this investigation."

Their legs were pumping harder now, flying beneath the Bloor Viaduct and the subway trestle where it spanned the river.

Lionel grinned. "I don't know why it struck me as odd that it should be a woman."

"Best choice for breaking the old boys' network, if that's what it is. By the way, she told me to ask if you wanted protection."

"That occurred to me, but I can't decide."

"I would strongly advise you to accept, if only for your peace of mind."

They passed a couple of slower runners and pounded along in silence for a while.

"I'm really enjoying this. We should try trail-running some time," Lionel said. "Maybe somewhere on the Niagara escarpment."

"I'd be up for it," Dan said. "If Charles won't accuse you of abandoning him."

Lionel came to an abrupt stop. Dan shot past him then jogged back.

"Did I say something wrong?"

Lionel was bent over, hands on his knees, breathing hard. He looked up, a dark expression haunting his face.

"It's just that Charles keeps getting angry with me. He says I should stay out of it and let things settle themselves. To be honest, I'm a little afraid of him these days."

Donny's description of the pair as the "perfect couple" came back to Dan. Inside every dream home, he knew, there was always a shiver of discontent, a stifled scream. In fact, his work often depended on the dissatisfaction that split homes apart, but he didn't want to make Lionel more anxious than he already was.

"He's probably worried for you. He's seen these things from the other side, from the viewpoint of the courts and the police."

Lionel nodded. "That's what he keeps saying. He wants me to let the police pin everything on Santiago, but I'm not convinced Santiago is to blame. Until I know for sure, my conscience won't let me do that."

"Why does he want Santiago blamed?"

"An easy scapegoat, maybe. I'd hate to see him framed just to put this all in the past."

"Do you think that would be blaming the wrong person?"

Lionel hesitated. "Let's just say I'm not convinced he's behind it."

"Would Charles have any special reason for believing Santiago is the guilty party? Is it possible he knows something he's not sharing with you?"

Lionel stared at him. "That never occurred to me. But I think Charles is just unusually suspicious by nature."

"He's a lawyer, so he would be, but surely he wouldn't risk framing someone."

Lionel sighed. "Some days I don't know what Charles might do."

Dan heard the concern. "Even lawyers can get a little panicky when their partners are threatened."

"I didn't tell him about the phone call today. I don't want him to know. Please keep it to yourself for now."

"All right, if you think that's wise. But if there's any reason to be worried, then it might be best to let him know."

"I've thought of that. I … I won't let him be put in jeopardy. I just need to find the right time to tell him what's going on. He keeps asking me things. About what you and I talk about, for instance, or what the police have been asking me. If anything, he's the one who's stirring things up. He's worried about this corruption probe, but I'm not sure why."

Dan put a hand on Lionel's shoulder. "He's probably concerned most about how it will affect the two of you. You're a couple, so what hurts one will hurt both. As far as I can tell, we can trust the officers looking into the corruption issues. Try to reassure him about that, at any rate."

Lionel gave Dan a rueful smile. "I don't have much choice, do I?"

They took off again at a brisk pace. Ahead, a riding academy crowned the hills over a track where students practised mounting and dismounting in crisp white jodhpurs, black jackets, and riding caps. An instructor demonstrated posting techniques to a group of young riders in the distance.

Lionel pointed to the stables.

"We keep a couple of horses there. Charles spends most afternoons here when he isn't working. In fact, he's probably there now." He turned to Dan. "Does your partner worry about you?"

Dan's mind did a little flip. Was Lionel asking about his availability? He pushed the thought from his mind.

"I don't have a partner. But when I did, my work drove him crazy. It was the major factor in our split."

"I'm sorry to hear it."

"He wasn't able to ignore the risk he felt my job put me in. He had a nervous temperament to begin with, and the thought of the danger I faced was too much for him. We had to end things for his sake."

"What happened? Where is he now?"

"He's happy on a little island in B.C."

The wind whipped past as the stables disappeared behind them.

"What will you do now?" Lionel asked. "To find Santiago, I mean."

"I want to go back to Yuri's house and have another look. In the meantime, I'll keep asking around until I find him."

"I certainly appreciate all the work you're doing for us. Don't get me wrong about Charles — he appreciates it, too. We'll have you over for drinks some time. We've got a great view from our balcony."

"Something to look forward to," Dan said, wondering how wise it would be to get close to the pair as long as they were his clients.

The trail veered around a corner. They raced along like a pair of adventurers flying off into the unknown.

Fifteen

Menthol or Unleaded

Dan had barely spoken to Donny since the initial meeting with Charles. Once his most reliable go-to source for consolation and commiseration over life's inanities, Donny's current relationship with an attractive man named Prabin meant that he and Dan now spent far less time together than at any point in their friendship. The absence was significant.

If truth be told, Dan missed the sound of cigarette smoke being inhaled on the other end of the phone. It had come to seem as comforting as the click of knitting needles to children under Grandma's care, knowing all the vigilance and devotion it signified.

Donny had been there for Dan from the time Ked was a small boy. He was one of the few people with whom Dan had shared his history, who knew of his mother's tragic early death, and of his father's brutality. He was always first to caution Dan away from the edge of the abyss. "What's done is done," he would say. "Mourn the loss and move on."

Donny the Practical. Donny the Wise. Dan felt in need of a little good common sense right now. It was confession time.

They stared at one another across coffee cups filled to the brim. Donny had discovered yet another dark and dingy café to satisfy his low-life urges. Dan never failed to find them dreary, though the advantage of speaking without fear of being overheard, or even understood, in a roomful of immigrants was not to be underestimated.

Dan looked disconsolately at the saucer where he'd slopped a small tide of brown liquid. The napkin sopped it up like a chemical spill on the banks of some Eastern European river. If he looked, he might find wildlife flapping out the last of its life under the silverware.

"Do you even think there's caffeine in here?"

Donny picked up a menu and pointed to the word "coffee" then to its equivalent in Korean characters.

"You see that lettering here? I happen to be an expert in Korean. I should have translated it for you before you ordered. The exact translation for coffee is not, as one might imagine, 'coffee,' but rather 'brown drink.' So no, I suspect it does not in fact have caffeine of any sort. And if you look over here under flavours, it says 'menthol' and 'unleaded.'"

"That's not reassuring."

"Probably not. Anyway, it's the atmosphere I come for."

Dan glanced around at the handwritten pages of menu items Scotch-taped to the wood panelling. "Yes, some serious decorating for sure."

"Never mind all that. Sorry to hear Hank was a bust. What a jerk. I didn't think people did such childish things outside of high school, where it's practically *de rigueur* that you do terrible things to the other kids as a rite of passage."

"Did you do terrible things to the other kids?"

"No. I was the kid they were doing terrible things to. Children are horrid. They can tell when you're different. Someone once hung a sanitary napkin dipped in ketchup on the outside of my locker. They were calling me a 'bloodcloth.' That's not an expletive to be taken lightly in Jamaica. I got the distinct impression they didn't like me."

"Nasty. Though I think anything would be preferable to what Hank did to me."

Donny gave him a knowing look. "Well, look at it this way: at least you found out early on that he's a waste of time. He didn't make you wait till after the wedding."

Dan rolled his eyes. "All the same, I'm beginning to think marriage isn't in the cards for me in this town. Not now, not ever. People are here for their careers, not to find a partner."

"You know what the French say about marriage. It's like a besieged fortress. The people on the outside want in, and the people on the inside want out."

"There's consolation for you."

"You know me — I'm just trying to make you feel better."

"Keep trying. How is Prabin, by the way?"

"Divine, as always. He sends his love. The stock market keeps him busy. When it doesn't, we do silly things like go to Ripley's Aquarium and find that we're vastly entertained by the wildlife. All those jellyfish going up and down in slow motion in glowing colours. It's exciting. We spent three hours there last weekend, in fact."

"Sounds reassuringly mundane."

"It is, but don't worry — I'm not going to try to sell you on the benefits of Grindr. That little app has probably put an end to long-term relationships forever. But there must be something you could do to improve your love life." Donny smiled. "You know, I just read an interesting article. They've discovered that house mice court their mates with ultrasonic sounds."

"Very creative. Is that a dating suggestion?"

"In your case, it couldn't hurt." Donny's eyes flickered around the room. "Funny how you're the one who wants a relationship, but I'm the one who's in one."

"Is that supposed to make me feel better, too?"

"No, but I would like to go on the record and really put my neck out by saying that dating a bartender is not a good idea for someone with a disreputable past when it comes to alcohol issues."

"I'd already considered that."

"Then consider it a lesson well learned." He paused. "What's going on with Charles and Lionel? Have you solved their problems yet?"

"Not yet, but I visited Yuri Malevski's house. It's quite a museum piece. Huge, filled with tasteful antiques rather than the junky kind. You'd be impressed."

"I've heard the lore. It's a legend on the party circuit."

"Ever been there?"

"No. I never really made it with the country-and-western set. Not to say I'm a snob, but horses just aren't my thing. I knew Yuri, of course — who didn't? — but I never made a closer acquaintance with him. Too many drugs in that crowd to interest me."

A rough-looking character came in the door, big, cumbersome and on the "tetchy" side, as Dan's Aunt Marge might have said. Dan caught sight of the man's dark glances and scowling face, thinking it fortunate they were in a public place. If this bruiser was a gay basher looking for trouble, he could certainly give a few people a run for their money. The miscreant looked over, caught their table on the fly and headed directly down the aisle toward them. As he passed, he tapped Donny on the shoulder. Dan's muscles were tensed and at the ready, set to lurch to his friend's defence. The colossus leaned down and whispered in Donny's ear. "Hi, sweetheart," came the gravelly voice. "Haven't seen you around for a while."

Dan caught the residue of lacquer on his nails. He took a second look at that bulbous, ravaged face and thought he discerned another one underneath, dolled up by layers of cover-stick and mascara for her moment in the spotlight. A transvestite by daylight. Carol Channing leered down at them, incognito, having put aside her diamonds and ermine for an afternoon's outing.

Donny smiled. "Hey, Cherry, baby. Been off the market. Finally caught a good one."

"How darling for you! Come and see me sometime."

With that, Carol passed on to her own private booth around the corner.

"You lead such a colourful life," Dan commented.

"Yes, I'm blessed." Donny took a sip of coffee and gave an uncharacteristic look of disapproval, leading Dan to wonder if that was the first time he'd actually bothered to consider the taste. He set the cup back down. "As I was saying, I don't really partake of the drug scene. Never have. My brain has its own permanent happy zone."

"Tell me about Charles and Lionel."

Donny's face lit up with a smile. "Has Charles made a pass at you?"

"Not yet. Should I anticipate it?"

"Don't discount it. It could happen. Though he'll behave himself if you rap his knuckles. They're the perfect couple, don't you know."

"So you keep saying."

"They're a powerhouse. They give great parties. Everyone wants to be on the guest list. They have a penthouse in Radio City. Best view of the city. It looks south over all the towers and high-rises. You can see the lake from all around. CN Tower, whatever. It's all there."

"What's he like?"

"Charles? Mostly a pussycat, but he's got a bit of a temper. That I'll-get-even kind of lawyer's temper. Slow burn. No hysterics, just a telling bop on the head at the right moment."

"Anything violent?"

"Not that I'm aware of. What have you heard?"

"Nothing. I was just wondering."

Donny gave him a curious look. "I never felt unsafe with him when we dated, if that's what you mean. Not like I had to lock up the razors or anything, but I wasn't dazzled by the warmth of his personality. You might say he's controlling. He expects obedience from his partners and can be quite assertive. But then some people like that sort of thing."

"What about a kid named Ziggy? I'm told he used to hang out at the Saddle and Bridle. Ever hear of him?"

"Sure, everyone's heard of Ziggy. Cute kid, but something not quite right with him."

"Like what?"

Donny considered then shrugged. "Apart from the Goth thing, which is worrisome enough, there's something off about him. I can't put my finger on it. A little spooky. He was brought up in care." He gave Dan a knowing look. "You know what they say. When a kid goes into care they see it all: drugs, violence, prostitution. It can take decades to get over it. Sometimes the street's preferable. I've seen him go off into long, staring-into-space episodes for considerable periods of time. You never know what's going on inside his head."

"You know him from the bars?"

Donny gave him a strange smile. "No, through Lester, actually. Ziggy's a ghost from his street days. I don't encourage Lester's association with him, for obvious reasons, but he slept on our couch once or twice when he didn't have a place to stay."

Dan started. "When was this?"

"He stayed with us a few times last year. Lately, not so much, though he was there for nearly a week a couple months ago."

"Mid-February? Right around the time Yuri Malevski was killed?"

Donny went silent for a while.

"Could be," he said at last. "I gather he had a more permanent place to stay, but couldn't get in for a while."

"Yes. Yuri Malevski's."

Donny gave Dan an assessing glance. "Really?"

"In fact, I think he still lives there. In a cubbyhole in Yuri's upstairs. I found his diary."

"Well, I hope he gave me a good write-up. I served him a veritable feast of back bacon with blueberry-glazed crepes one morning."

"Not to worry. He gave your cooking five stars."

"Glad to hear it." Donny sat quietly for a moment. "I have to ask. Is he a suspect in the murder? He really was a bit weird. Troubled, you might say."

"Not as far as I know, but I don't know much about the investigation yet."

"Yet? Meaning you might know more later?"

"Remains to be seen. For now, I'm concentrating on finding the missing Cuban boyfriend."

"Ah, yes. The one with the shady past and the slipperier present. Yuri always had a taste for wild boys."

Dan shot him a look. "As in?"

"The scruffy, dangerous ones. I gather Santiago was a handful when Yuri took him in, but he tamed him quickly enough."

"What did you think of him?"

"Of Santiago? Not much. I met him a few times at the club. I wasn't all that impressed, to be honest. I gather Yuri was grooming him to take over as manager. If you didn't know better, you would have thought Santiago was the owner, the way he lorded it over the clientele. He certainly had the gold-digging gene and pretensions of grandeur to go with it."

"Do you know anything about their history?"

Donny wiped his mouth with a napkin and set his cup down. "I'm a bit iffy on the details. I think he and Yuri met when Santiago was still a teenager. Maybe four or five years ago? Probably at the club. I don't know if it's true or not, but I heard he left Cuba by hiding out in the cargo of an Air Canada jetliner and nearly froze to death on the way here. He's a survivor, though, and by the time he met Yuri he was looking for a sugar daddy. A real beauty, that's for sure. He charmed the pants off half the gay men in Toronto, not to mention a few women who were susceptible to his charms. He isn't that discriminating. And when I say he charmed the pants off them, I mean that quite literally."

"How did he and Yuri get along?"

Donny's eyes had drifted outside the window where two smokers were lined up to have their nicotine levels boosted. Dan clanked a spoon against his saucer.

Donny's eyes bounced back. "What?"

"He and Yuri. How did they get along?"

"Oh, like cats and dogs. I gather it was a rough-and-tumble relationship from beginning to end. Lots of scrapping. I can't say over what, but probably the usual — older man meets younger boy. One wants commitment, the other wants credit cards charged to the max. A young man's financial needs are not easy to fulfil. Nor are an older man's demands for sexual exclusivity."

"Nevertheless, they managed to live together for the last four years?"

"From what I heard, yes."

"Do you think he killed Yuri?"

Donny stood up. "I would hate to incriminate anybody with a careless word spoken in haste. I'll go get another cup of coffee and think about that before I answer."

Dan shook his head. "You're being far more evasive than normal."

"It comes with domestication. You learn to keep secrets."

Sixteen

Under the Eaves

Dan left the coffee shop thinking about Yuri Malevski's "wild boys." He knew some gay men liked to get close to younger guys who appeared threatening on the surface — tattoos, muscles, rough talk. It was one way of making peace with the demons who'd terrorized them in high school, but few of them expected to be murdered in the process. Malevski, it seemed, had wanted a wild boy to domesticate. Apparently he thought he'd found that in Santiago Suárez, the missing Cuban. Ziggy, on the other hand, seemed to be more of a dark horse. He was a moving target waiting for an expert marksman to hunt him down. Whatever there was to be learned about him was still inside Lockie House.

Dan parked across the street. From the front stoop, everything looked the same. He punched in the numbers. Red turned to green. Definitely something to be said for all that accounting consistency.

It was still daylight, making the false twilight inside seem eerie. Dan's MagLite swept a beam along the floor. No need to announce his presence to the world outside. Had Fred MacGregor still lived here — Dan dispensed with formalities, feeling he knew the man well enough by now — had *Freddie* still lived here, this might be one of his at-home days when he received callers, but Dan wasn't in a receiving mood.

He made his way to the third floor and looked around. All was calm. He pressed the panel and watched it swing open, just the way things did in the movies. And why not? Movies had to take their inspiration from somewhere.

Ziggy's diary lay beneath the window where he'd left it, the baggie of dope still in place. He skimmed the pages, moving backward in time to when Ziggy first came to stay with Yuri. *My family*, he'd called Yuri's collection of friends and misfits. Still, he had his perspective right: *All families are weird*, he wrote, *so this one isn't that different from any other. At least I feel at home somewhere.*

Dan could relate.

Yuri didn't seem to have asked for anything from Ziggy for his room and board. In fact, if the diary was to be believed, Yuri's interest lay more in rehabilitating the boy: *Need to get clean. Yuri told me that a month ago. I have to stop doing drugs and get my life in order. A little grass now and again is cool, he said, but he won't tolerate hard drugs in the house. He said my days of drug use are over if I want to live with him.*

That, Dan thought, was a different Yuri from the one everyone else seemed to think they knew. Ziggy expressed admiration for Yuri several times in the passages he read. The only note of dissent lay with his feelings about Santiago, who appeared as the villain in the pages. *Santiago has another lover! I saw them together and now he hates me. He cheats on Yuri with everyone. Should I tell Yuri before he tries to get rid of me?* Two days later, Ziggy confided to the diary's pages that he'd told Yuri about Santiago's lover: *Yuri was furious. He said he didn't believe me, but they had a fight and now Santiago is gone.*

Rather than exult in his triumph, Ziggy felt remorse for having hurt Yuri: *Why do I always hurt the ones I love?* he lamented. *Way of the world*, Dan wanted to tell him. Oscar Wilde wasn't the first to note the sentiment. He read further till he caught the name *Charles* again. There was no mention of sex this time, just anger that Charles had told him he couldn't repeat the episode, being a "happily married man." *Happily married!* Ziggy wrote. *Ha! That asshole. Then what was he doing with me?*

An apt question, Dan noted, though there seemed little concern from either party on Lionel's behalf. He felt a surge of anger for the absent accountant. Why was it always the nice guys who got used?

He felt his emotions tug as he discovered that Ziggy had contemplated killing himself, his anger at being rejected by Charles compounded by guilt over having hurt Yuri. *Dear Darkness, I want to die*, he'd written. *I shouldn't care what Charles thinks, but Yuri is my friend. I need to make him see I'm the only one who treats him well, even though he doesn't care. Instead, he treats me with disdain. Maybe I should just end this here and now.* Anger, confusion, manipulation, sadness. It was a regular soap opera in those pages. But, as Donny said, that wasn't unusual for someone brought up in care.

Dan heard a throat cleared behind him. He turned and saw large dark eyes set in a pale face. It could have been a vampire, if such things existed. Instead it was Ziggy, dressed in full Goth regalia, standing in the doorway watching him. Black velvet jacket over a black T, ruffled lace at the cuffs and collar; "Back in Black" emblazoned on his chest in case the visual hints weren't enough. He looked like a mourner dressed for a very theatrical Victorian funeral.

"Find anything interesting?" he asked softly.

"The mysterious tenant," Dan said.

"Yes, I stay here when I want. Yuri gave me permission."

He crept in and sat on the futon, legs crossed in front of him.

"That permission might have expired now that Yuri's dead."

Ziggy cocked his head and regarded Dan curiously. "According to whom?"

Dan left the question unanswered. "My name's Dan."

"I'm Ziggy, as you probably know from reading my diary."

"Is that German?"

Ziggy gave a funny, lop-sided smile. "No, just a nickname from when I was a kid. I used to run funny, sort of zig-zagging. They called me Ziggy for short."

"So, Ziggy. Aren't you worried about staying here since the murder?"

"I'm not afraid."

Outside, a pigeon landed on the windowsill and began cooing to some invisible mate. Dan thought of the superstition about birds in the house.

"You're not afraid of being killed?"

Ziggy shook his head. "What would I lose? Yuri was my only friend." He gave Dan a close look. "If you think I'm being dramatic, I'm not. It's the truth."

"Who do you think killed Yuri?"

Ziggy reached for the bag of weed and produced a slender joint.

"Maybe some hustler."

He lit it and took a toke, then held it out. Dan shook his head.

"Why do you think that?"

Ziggy stared at him for a moment, and then shrugged. "Yuri was in love with this Cuban guy named Santiago. Santiago wasn't very nice to him, so Yuri told him to leave. After Santiago left, Yuri went a little bit crazy. He wanted them to stay together. Like, probably forever. There were a couple of guys who stayed the night with him after that. Rent boys. Maybe he hired some hustler to come in and things got out of hand."

"Had that sort of thing happened before?'

Ziggy took another toke and thought this over.

"Once or twice Yuri threw a couple of hustlers out of the house for behaving badly, but no one ever tried to hurt him before."

"Did Yuri seem afraid before he died? Was there anyone in particular he worried about?"

Ziggy shrugged. "Not that I know of. But maybe he just didn't tell me there was."

"Are you planning on staying here in the house?"

He shrugged again. "Till they kick me out, I guess. It's not like I have anywhere else to go."

"I read in your diary that Yuri locked you out for a while."

Ziggy glanced down at the pages. "He didn't like it when I did dope. Heroin, I mean. He said it was messing up my future. So he kicked me out and told me to come back when I got clean. I wanted to apologize, but I never saw him again."

"It's ironic, but you stayed with some friends of mine. Donny and Lester."

"Really?" Ziggy looked more amused than surprised. "You know Donny and Lester?"

Dan nodded.

"Cool," he said, stabbing the joint out on a beam above his head. It dissolved in a flare of falling sparks. "Anyway, for now I'll stay here. At least until someone changes the code. Then I'll be screwed again."

"How did you get back in last time?"

"Pure dumb luck. Yuri wasn't answering my messages. I thought he was mad at me for using, so I came over to apologize just as Irma was coming by. I sneaked in when she got here. I found the code on his phone that he texted to her."

Dan looked at him. "Who's Irma?"

"Cleaning lady. She's a trip. Eastern European something or other. Wicked accent, like Bela Lugosi." He grinned. "Irma thought Yuri was evil. She used to leave religious pamphlets around for him. He laughed whenever he found them."

Dan recalled the picture of Jesus with the exploding heart. "What did Yuri think of Irma?"

Ziggy struggled out of his jacket, revealing a thin chest and arms. But no track marks, Dan noted. He was still clean.

"You mean, like, was he afraid of her?"

"Sure."

"Nah. Yuri thought she was a joke. He loved teasing her, but he wouldn't fire her. I think he felt sorry for her. Santiago liked her. They were both illegals. I guess he could relate."

"Why didn't Yuri marry Santiago and help him get his citizenship?"

"They talked about it. I think Yuri was testing him to see if he'd remain faithful. Santiago couldn't be faithful to save his life. Yuri wanted to rescue everybody. He should have been rescuing himself."

Not bad advice, Dan thought, *though a trifle late on the delivery.*

He felt Ziggy's hand on his forearm. The other snaked down to Dan's crotch. Dan pushed the hand away.

"Please!" Ziggy said. "Am I a freak? Do I look repulsive?"

"You're not repulsive," Dan said.

"The last guy I had sex with said I was attractive."

"Was that Charles?"

Ziggy's eyes flashed. "Did you read the entire thing?"

"No," Dan said. "But I know Charles."

"He used me."

"He's in a relationship."

Ziggy rolled his eyes. "I know. He's married to the accountant."

"Married men don't stick around."

"Tell me about it." He gave Dan a sidelong glance. "What about you? Are you married?"

"No."

"Then why aren't you interested in me?"

Dan looked the boy up and down. *Rule number one of the gay dress code*, he thought. *Don't wear make-up and skin-tight jeans unless you want to look girly.* But how to tell him he was attractive, even under that garish get-up?

"Can't you find me attractive?" he pleaded.

"You are attractive."

He ran a hand over Dan's chest. "Then touch me."

"How old are you?"

"Twenty. Just touch me."

Half my age, Dan thought. He tried to recall the distinction between pedophiles and pederasts. Pedophiles had unsolicited sex with minors, while pederasts shared the bodies of willing, or in this case aggressive, younger men. As a teenager, he'd often been on the other end of the equation, but now he was the older one. A thousand thoughts went through his head: his discovery of sex with grown men, his fears at not being attractive enough, his worries at being discovered to be queer. Hell, most of his sex education had occurred beneath a train trestle in the clear light of afternoon once he realized the twelve-year-old girls who pursued him at school could do nothing to satisfy his sexual urges. It was their older brothers he'd wanted.

"Be a man. Touch me!" Ziggy commanded.

Dan sensed his own adolescent bewilderment and anger in Ziggy. Like this boy, he too had known what he wanted from men as far back as he could remember.

"Not while you're stoned," Dan told him. *And not ever*, he thought to himself.

Ziggy must have sensed his reasoning. "It's because I'm too young. Don't worry, I'll say I was the aggressor. I went after you. I don't know why people always think it's the older person."

"It's just the way people think."

"Why aren't you married? Or are you? It's okay, you can tell me."

"I'm not married. I told you the truth. Did you tell the truth about your age?"

"No. I'm only nineteen. So what's wrong with you then? Why aren't you married?"

"I'm not the marrying kind." Better to discourage any further hopes on Ziggy's part, Dan thought. "Some days I'd rather have a good conversation than sex."

Ziggy smiled. "What are you anyway? A psychologist?"

"No."

"A cop?"

"I'm not a cop either, no." He paused. "Have you had sex with cops?"

Ziggy nodded. "One."

Dan decided against asking if it were Trposki. "I'm just trying to help out on the murder."

"I thought you were a cop because you were reading my diary. I thought maybe you were looking for something to say I was a psycho and that I killed Yuri."

"Did you?"

The face that stared at him was all seriousness. "Yuri was my friend."

"Friends kill friends. It happens all the time. Sometimes it's just an accident."

"I didn't kill Yuri." Ziggy's eyes narrowed. "I'd be more likely to kill myself. If I did, I'd just lock the doors and unplug myself. No one could get in until it was too late."

Dan thought of the diary entry he'd read. "I hope you won't. It's seldom that easy. Besides, you know what they say: it gets better. I can vouch for that. I come from a shit background, too, but life turned around for me."

"Yeah, whatever. You probably didn't grow up in care. I grew up in care. It doesn't get better for someone like me."

He looked away, as though they'd touched on something too raw to discuss.

"I'm sorry for intruding on your private space." Dan turned to leave. "If you ever just want to talk or anything …"

Ziggy's eyes met his. "You want to get together again? Not as a date or anything. Maybe just to meet up for a coffee? Don't worry, I won't stalk you."

Dan smiled. "Sure. I'd be happy to."

He held out a business card. Ziggy turned it over and tapped it with his index finger. "Missing persons? I could design a nice little skull for you on the back, if you want."

"Not exactly the sort of message I'd like to deliver to clients."

Ziggy laughed. "Yeah, right."

Dan pushed the door open and stood in the hallway. Ziggy watched him closely.

"Will I see you again?"

"You've got my number," Dan said. "Contact me and I'll get back to you."

"You promise?"

"You have my word."

Seventeen

Desecration

The house was dark again when he got home. Ked was out. Ralph came to greet him briefly then returned to his bed. Dan knew he'd better get used to it.

There were no messages on his answering machine. But what he found on his laptop turned out to be far more interesting. His e-mail in-box held a response from the *Sûreté du Québec*. He had an inkling even before he opened it. Inside lay the answer he'd been seeking. Or, rather, the answer he'd been hoping not to have to face. Nothing one-hundred-percent conclusive, but certainly leaning in that direction. He responded as quickly as his French would allow and sent it off. If the reply came soon, it meant putting off the search for Santiago Suárez a few days. It looked as if he'd be going to Quebec.

He slept uneasily, unsettled by dreams of young men with pale faces. A little before five he woke and couldn't get back to sleep. He gave up trying and got out of bed, feeling disoriented. Middle age was turning out to be a bitch. He thought of the e-mail he'd received and went to his office, but there was no reply. The Quebec police had probably wisely stayed in bed.

Dan hadn't seen Domingo since the previous week. She was due for another round of chemo that afternoon. There was no need to get her hopes up when he saw her, but he felt he should at least broach the subject of finding Lonnie and the probability that her son was no longer alive.

He arrived early at the hospital. The waiting room was crowded, as usual. He made off down the corridor to her room, but stopped when he heard voices coming from inside. Women's voices. They weren't raised, but he felt the tension. After a moment, footsteps approached and a woman emerged. She checked her watch, an unsettled look on her face, then headed to the elevator. Dan thought she looked familiar, though he couldn't have said why. Then it clicked: she was an older, harried version of Domingo.

He heard Adele say, "Can you believe that? The fucking church! How dare she come in here and upset you on your chemo day?"

Domingo mumbled a reply Dan couldn't make out.

"How dare they desecrate our relationship like that? A relationship of twenty-two years built on love and truth. That woman is immoral! If they want you to go to church, tell them you'll go to the gay church, where you're welcome. If she believes in God, then she'll know that God doesn't care what denomination you pray in."

Again, Domingo spoke too softly for Dan to overhear.

"I'm sorry," Adele said, her tone changing. "I'm sorry for getting angry."

Dan heard the sound of a scraping chair. He stepped into a doorway, out of sight.

"I'll be back to pick you up at four."

He waited till Adele's footsteps died out then went in. Domingo was sitting up in bed. She smiled wearily when she saw him.

"Hi there!" Dan tried to be as cheery and nonchalant as he could. "Are you ready for today's adventure ride?"

She looked away.

"Everything okay?" Dan asked.

"Not really."

"Test results not good?"

"Apparently I was fine yesterday. Blood was good. Sleep was good. Mood was great. Then this morning I got a visit from two of the Furies."

"Oh-oh," Dan said. "I thought I saw Adele leaving a minute ago."

"She's half the problem. The other half was my sister."

Dan nodded sympathetically.

Domingo shrugged. "It's the church. All that family and religion stuff. We West Indians are full of it. They want to drag me off to repent, while Adi's having a fit about it." She sighed. "My sister and I haven't spoken six words in all the years Adi and I have been together. When I got sick, I called her. I probably shouldn't have. They're all praying for me — the whole nine yards."

"So let them pray. It can't hurt."

She pushed aside a half-finished breakfast tray in front of her.

"It's just having my sister coming in here ranting about giving up my sinful life and coming back to Jesus. I said, 'Ranee, I have no problem with Jesus, but giving up the woman I love is not an option.' Then she sits there and stares at me while Adele throws daggers at her with her eyes. Both of them staking out their territory and that territory is me. I know they mean well, but I really wish they wouldn't fight over me like that."

Dan took her hand and felt its lightness. Definitely not a day to tackle the subject he'd considered taking up with her.

"Is there anything I can do? Do you want me to talk to Adele?"

"No, that wouldn't have any effect. Anyway, she's right. I should forbid my sister from coming in here and talking like that, but it upsets me to have to do that. And now I've got three hours of sitting here while the doctors pour poison into my system. I'm fighting inside and out."

"You can put it off for another day, if you want to."

Domingo shook her head. "What's the point? I still have to go through it. And psyching myself for a day beforehand is half the battle. That's hard. I know it's supposed to be good for me, but it seems like all I have to look forward to is thinning hair, shaky hands, and feeling chilled even in summer." She squeezed his hand. "I'll be fine now that you're here."

Dan settled beside her in the visitor's chair, feeling as resigned as she sounded. After the first bag of chemicals emptied, a nurse arrived wearing a full-body gown, then proceeded to put on gloves before hanging up the second bag. Dan averted his eyes while she changed Domingo's dressing and reinserted the PICC line. Done, she put everything in a hazardous waste container and left.

Dan struggled again with telling Domingo what he'd heard from the Quebec police, that finding her son alive was as unlikely as winning the lottery at this point, but today it wouldn't help her. He suspected it was just one of many things she'd reconciled herself to already.

Eighteen

Where the River Narrows

The reply from the Quebec police was there when he woke. Dan thought it over and decided a quick resolution was best. He called Ked and Kendra to say he'd be gone for a couple of days. Afterwards, he contacted Donny and Lionel. That covered his Need to Know list. For good measure, he left a message for Inspector Johnston. She called back to ask a few details about the trip, wishing him luck in finding Lonnie. Then he left the city and headed east.

His car burned up the Highway of Heroes, that stretch of the Macdonald-Cartier Freeway where the bodies of fallen soldiers made their final journey between the armed forces base at Trenton and the forensics centre in Toronto. It had earned its nickname from the crowds gathering on overpasses to salute the convoys moving beneath, during what Dan thought of as a misguided war on Iraq as American indignation mollified its wounded pride over being attacked on its own soil. *Not our war*, he thought. Easy to say, of course, but Dan wasn't sentimental about such things: when you go to war, you put your life on the line. It was a given. There were plenty of ways to die, few of them pretty. Dying wasn't always the worst option, what with the burgeoning cases of post-traumatic stress disorder making the lives of returned soldiers even more of a nightmare than what they'd endured in the desert. Dan knew about living with nightmares. Now *that* was brave, he'd have said, if anyone asked.

His favourite time on the road was early morning, before the other drivers came out to ruin things for him. He liked the feel of being the only person alive for miles around. No one to talk to, no one to bother him. An eight-hour solo drive to Quebec City was just the thing to quell his burgeoning misanthropy.

Quebec had long held a fascination for Ontarians — Torontonians in particular. It was the "forbidden" land. Montreal had a rep for being Canada's party destination, compared to staid Toronto the Good. When Dan thought of Quebec, however, it wasn't Montreal that came to mind first. But then he'd never really been a party boy. A friend once said of him, *Dan's a nice guy, but he doesn't know how to party*. Dan's response had been pointed: *"Party" isn't a verb*. Not entirely accurate, given the evolution of language, but his friend had been too intimidated to argue. Which seemed to settle the matter.

For Dan, *Vieux-Québec* was the province's real destination, taking its name from the Algonquin *Kébec*, meaning "where the river narrows." He loved

to approach by car and sit gazing up at the promon-
tory. *Cap-Diamant.* Cape Diamond. There, above
the narrowing banks of the St. Lawrence, stood one
of North America's oldest and most elegant cities.
Explorer Jacques Cartier built a fort there in 1535, but
decided it was less impressive than the site that would
later become Montreal, and so sailed on. It remained
French territory until being ceded to England at the end
of the Seven Years' War, igniting a cultural feud that
continues to this day.

Dan understood the resentment Quebeckers felt
toward the rest of Canada. They had every right to
feel slighted by how their causes and beliefs were overlooked and trampled on by the largely unfeeling English
majority. In fact, he had every sympathy for the Quebec
cause. Except one: the French weren't there first. To
his mind, the issue of Aboriginal sovereignty had never
been properly accredited. After five hundred years of
neglect, the land's original owners deserved better.

He pulled into town and quickly found his hotel.
The room was comfortable and, to his regret, thor-
oughly modern. There was nothing of old Quebec here,
nothing linking it with its history and heritage. Still,
it would afford a peaceful sleep when the time came.
He unpacked, hung up his clothes, then went out and
found a *crêperie* with a low ceiling and stone walls.
A fireplace crackled quietly in the corner. Real wood.
Quebeckers went in for veracity. No fake fireplaces or
gas lines for them.

He indulged with a single glass of cider, remember-
ing his promise to his son. You were honest only if you

kept the faith when no one was watching. His crêpes arrived on a long plate that neatly accommodated the crisp rolls bursting with melted cheese and ham slices wrapped around asparagus spears. *Screw the partying*, Dan thought. *This is really living.*

Twilight came on as he finished his coffee. Out on the street again, he glanced up at the Château Frontenac, that stone emissary from another century, massive and upright. Light illuminated its spires like a great cathedral left over from the French Revolution. *None of that chrome-and-green-glass condo crap going up everywhere like a creeping mould that's only going to get worse over time*, Dan thought. Maybe he'd been born a few centuries too late. Perhaps all his malaise and discontent in life amounted to that.

The cobblestones felt at once familiar and strange as he made his way up and down hills, marvelling at the buildings set aglow in the fading light, their colourful interiors at odds with the stern grey exteriors.

In the Faubourg Saint-Jean, he found the sign: Club Le Drague, its exterior adorned with a Quebec flag. He bypassed the outdoor *terrasse* and stepped inside. He could have been standing in any bar in Toronto, with a basement disco and a glittery stage *pour le travesti*. No matter the language, gay bars were the same the world over.

Dan ordered a soda water with his minimal French — just enough for obtaining food, drink, lodgings, and getting the boys to show an interest. Even the smallest effort helped keep things on the friendly side here. Where Montreal was largely a French-English compote,

Quebec City was the bastion of separatist thinking. No surprise in a province where English was not even acknowledged as an official language. Better to supplicate than butt heads unnecessarily.

The bar smelled of beer and cigarettes. Donny would be proud to know there was one last bastion of the Empire that hadn't succumbed to a cowardly intolerance for the weed. Dan took his drink to one corner and sat watching the crowds come and go.

The men were particularly striking, he noted. Many had beautiful eyes. A few of the twinks looked him over. Then, deciding he was either too dangerous or too *anglo*, they passed him by. A leather man glanced his way as well, but there was no mutual spark compelling either party to cross the national divide. Such were the mysterious ways of cruise bar protocol.

He trailed downstairs to *le disco*. It was too early for dancing, apart from a few introverts who preferred their own company, twirling in self-absorbed ecstasy. The DJ warmed up his skills as the lights spun, but the room was largely empty. Neverland had never looked so lonely.

Dan felt a buzzing in his pocket. He pulled out his cell and saw Ziggy's name: *I know I promised not to stalk you, but I just wanted to say you're a nice guy and I'm thinking of you. Maybe we can meet up later this week? Now that the Saddle's closed, I hang at the Beaver Club. It would be a nice surprise if you showed up.*

Dan texted back: *I'm out of town right now. When I get back, I'll look you up at that club!* He thought it best to leave things vague. He knew the obsessive tendencies of teenage boys to form crushes on anyone who paid them attention. Even with a promise not to stalk him, Ziggy could turn out to be a problem.

He was making his way back to the bar when a good-looking guy caught his attention: dark and steamy. Just his type. Dan watched for a moment, trying to read his body language, till the man turned away. No use chasing him. He was just another pretty face in the second of Canada's two solitudes.

He was getting ready to call it a night when a burly bear in leather chaps and harness passed, a pitcher of beer in either hand. In his haste, he bumped Dan with his elbow, spilling his drinks. Dan reached out to steady him.

"Sorry," he said.

"Calice! Maudit anglais," the man growled.

Dan caught the expletive, but he wasn't taking the bait. *"Pardonnez-moi,"* he said to mollify the man, though he wanted to say it wasn't his drunken clumsiness that had caused the accident.

The man stopped. "Why do you fucking English have to come here? Don't you have enough places to go? This is not your province."

Dan stared him down. "Plains of Abraham. We won, you lost. As for land claims, the Natives were here long before the French or the English."

Dan thought for a moment the man was going to throw the beer in his face, but instead he broke into a big, toothy grin.

"Ah! Fuck you, *Anglais,*" he said, moving his bulk smoothly along to his group of friends, who looked back and hooted with laughter as he related what Dan had said.

Dan turned and got another glimpse of the face he'd seen earlier. Was he being cruised? The man was on the small side, but definitely Dan's type: dark and masculine. He caught Dan's eye then turned away. Apparently the attraction wasn't mutual. When Dan looked again, he'd vanished.

He finished his soda and left, wandering along the streets. He put his mind to the task ahead. In the morning, he'd visit the *Sûreté* and follow up his inquiry into Lonnie. One way or the other, it would bring things to an end. If it was an unproductive search, there were no other avenues for him to take. In the meantime, he was in one of his favourite cities, enjoying its sights and sounds.

There were two of them waiting outside his hotel. Something about their size and how they carried their bodies, as if they wore armour, told him these were no ordinary tourists. They reminded him of men surreptitiously photographed around the grave of some recently buried Mafia don. Paying their respects. Dan knew respect had nothing to do with why they were there.

He turned and started walking away, but they'd seen him. Fighting an impulse to run, he slipped across the street. Clip-clopping hooves rang out on the cobblestones as he ducked behind a *calèche* carrying a middle-aged couple whooping it up like newly-weds. By the time the carriage passed, his followers had separated. One of them, Dan presumed, had gone down a darkened side street. The other was heading directly toward him.

He thought of dashing back to the hotel, but they could still catch him in the lobby. There might even be someone waiting for him in his room. Instead, he headed back toward Le Drague. Nothing like a few outraged drag queens to protect a fellow gay, but that would put others in danger and Dan wouldn't consider going inside. He turned a corner and dashed up a hill. A few seconds later, his follower emerged right behind him. The lamps threw shadows all around. People were milling everywhere. Dan sprinted away from the crowds.

On the next block, he stopped and leaned into the shadow of a doorway, hands pressed against stone. When his pursuer passed, Dan lunged for him, grabbing his neck with one hand and his crotch with the other. Fists came up, but Dan was in snug. The man struggled for all he was worth. For a second, Dan thought he was prepared to risk the crown jewels. Then again, they were in the rebel province of Quebec and sovereignty didn't have much sway here.

A fist landed against his throat, winding him. Dan's grip loosened and the man wrenched himself free. A knife flashed, shiny and seductive, released from the folds of a suit. Dan leapt aside.

Before he could strike again, a door opened on the man's right, releasing a noisy gang from the bright interior of a pub. One unguarded glance over his shoulder was all Dan needed. He kicked out and landed a solid blow against his ribs. The knife clattered away as the man doubled over.

Dan watched him lurch down the alley and disappear around the corner. There was no use pursuing him. His partner was still out there somewhere. It would just be asking for trouble.

"Stop following me," he spat out uselessly.

A crowd had formed across the street. Someone was punching numbers into a cell phone. Dan heard the word *police*, which sounded pretty much the same in either language. His pursuers were gone. Dan doubted that would be the end of them, but it would buy him time.

He turned and headed back to the hotel, making his way through the crowds. As he reached the corner, he found himself facing the dark man he'd seen in the bar. It hadn't been a mutual appreciation society after all, but Dan was determined he wasn't going to stop him from entering his hotel.

"Your buddies just left," he said, grappling with the newcomer.

With his head butted against the man's shoulder, and legs entwined, Dan tried without success to force him down. His opponent was small, but wiry and supple. The coupling felt like a form of intimacy, their tangled limbs somehow making them complete. The other fought back expertly. This was a man who knew how to defend himself, Dan thought. Military possibly. Maybe police. It was the latter that worried him most.

Dan squeezed him tightly, pulling them together lest this man produce a knife, too. His opponent drew his arms in close then thrust his shoulders forward explosively, literally knocking Dan aside and forcing the breath out of him. He hit the ground in a low roll, instinctively protecting his vitals from potentially damaging kicks, then lay dazed, waiting for the other's next move.

"Asshole," the man spat out as he walked away.

Not French, at any rate.

Nineteen

The Grain Silo

Dan strode through the lobby and headed up the stairs. Throwing his belongings together, he took time to check his face in the mirror, daub the gash on his cheek with toilet paper, then quit the room. Out in the street, he tossed the key into a mailbox and made his way to an ATM.

Cash in hand, he headed down the road to a small hotel he'd spotted on his arrival. A light gleamed in the front window, the vacancy sign still lit up. A lucky thing, Dan knew. At that time of year, most hotels were booked well in advance in the tourist quarter.

The old man who greeted him didn't hesitate to take his cash. He wrote out a receipt and showed him to a room. *Now this is more like it*, Dan thought, gazing around with admiration at the stone walls and wood beams. Pure *Vieux-Québec*. Probably owned by a descendant of one of the original *habitants*. It would suit his needs, but he couldn't stop and admire it for long. He'd finish his business and head home. Whatever his pursuers wanted from him, they would have it one way or another. But they'd have to find him first.

He kicked off his shoes and put his feet up on the bed, casting around for something on television he could understand. It turned out not to be a problem. With cable, there were far more English stations than French. *One more reason for them to hate us*, Dan thought. *But god forbid they separate and get swallowed up by the U.S. Then they'll really have something to scream about.*

He settled in with good, sensible Jamie Oliver, righting the nutritional wrongs of the world one social class at a time. There was no sense going back out and showing his face on the street again tonight.

Sleep did not come easily. Wary of every sound outside his door, he finally nodded off before dawn. When he woke an hour later, his back felt as if it had been split open, with a rib or two puncturing his lungs for dramatic effect. That he'd hate to die in a Quebec hotel room was all he could think.

He called the *Sûreté* to confirm his meeting then packed and left. The chief of police was as old and wrinkled as a desert tortoise. He looked Dan over with jaundiced eyes as he opened a musty-looking file. Judging by its condition, it may well have predated computers. Dan watched as he turned the pages till he came to the one he was searching for, stabbing it with his forefinger.

"*Ici.*"

Dan saw a handwritten coroner's report in a script

that might have been made with a quill pen. He followed what he could make out with his limited French.

He looked back up at the man. "*Mort?*"

"*Oui, il est mort, bien sûr.*"

"*Quand?*"

The man frowned and looked down at the report. Surely this idiot Englishman could figure that out.

"*Le quinzième mai, deux mille trois.*"

He looked back up with bleary eyes. Dan could practically smell the alcohol on his breath. The man should have been packed away in mothballs and put in a closet, not left sitting at a desk in some backwater provincial police station.

Fifteenth May, two thousand and three.

Dan thought back and felt a chill. That was pretty much when Domingo had started saying she knew Lonnie was dead. He'd been sitting here on some police shelf all that time, waiting for someone to find him. Dan fought a sense of rage over the carelessness of such things. Probably no one had entered it into the police files.

He looked at the report and saw a first name only: *Lonnie*. Someone had added a blurry Polaroid of a boy turned away from the camera, looking back over his shoulder with a wide grin. Elfin. That was exactly how Dan remembered Lonnie. He'd found what he was after.

He wanted to ask what happened, but his French wasn't honed enough to extract such answers with precision. Instead, he tried to convey what he could with facial expressions. He shook his head and tried hard to look chagrined. *Chagrin*. It was a French word. Surely this old codger would understand that.

"*C'est quoi?*"

The old man looked at Dan as though he were the daft one.

"*Qu'est-ce qui s'est passé?*" Dan managed.

"Ah!" Enlightenment shone in his eyes. "*Il est tombé.*"

"*Tombé.* He fell?"

"*Oui.*" The man used his hands to indicate someone climbing then falling in space. He pointed to a grain silo in the background of the photograph. "*Suicide,*" he pronounced slowly, the word taking on a cultivated gravity in French.

Dan picked up the image and examined it in his hands.

He turned to the officer again. "*L'addresse?*"

"*Oui, oui.*" The man made a snuffling sound, swiped at his nose, and then handed Dan a form with the address of the mortuary.

"No, the other."

The man glared as though he were speaking a Martian dialect.

"*L'autre addresse,*" Dan said. He pointed to the silo. "*Je veux aller ici.*"

"Ah!"

Again, the look of recognition passed over the man's face. He bent and wrote something on the form and handed it back. Dan took it and thanked him.

"*Bien sûr,*" he said with a shrug, as though he expected no less.

At the mortuary, Dan was thankful to be greeted by a bilingual attendant who seemed to bear no grudge against him for asking his complicated questions in English. He'd anticipated more trouble on this end. Getting information was one thing, but asking for a cremation was quite a different set of affairs. He handed over his investigator's licence for identification. The attendant looked it over, glanced at Dan again, and then handed it back with scarcely a flicker of interest.

Dan signed a form and answered a few questions. Yes, a plain metal box was adequate. No, he would not mind coming to pick up the remains himself. Tomorrow morning was fine. Business concluded, Dan thanked the man and left.

On the way back to his car, he passed a florist and ducked inside. It was threatening rain as he drove past the Plains of Abraham, those tumultuous fields where the destiny of the country had turned decisively two hundred and fifty years earlier. On the outskirts of town, he parked and approached the silo. It looked tranquil, not the sort of place you might expect to find death. Then again, it was exactly the sort of place you might decide to kill yourself if you were determined to do so. From pain to peace in one short step, but with a world of difference between. Dan well knew the seductive urge. He'd never do that to Ked, but he often thought of the peace that would follow, a respite from the relentlessness of his dreams, should he ever get so desperate. People did all the time.

He stood looking up a sheer wall of cement. The handle on the door was rusted shut. That wouldn't stop him. He'd come this far. He put the flowers down and looked around for something to pry it open. Around back he found another door, this one red and covered in dents. It opened to his touch.

The carpet of dirt was soft and hushed beneath his tread. Inside, the air was stale but comforting, like the scent of an old sweater. The space felt welcoming, as though it had been waiting for a human presence. The shaft disappeared in darkness overhead. An arrow of light pierced the gloom, revealing wooden beams criss-crossing the interior far above. A set of rickety stairs tempted the curious to climb up into the shadows.

Dan looked around. *There should be something more here*, he thought. *The memory of a fall, the trajectory of a body arcing through the air. Something marking the spot where he fell.* As a boy, Lonnie was constantly on the move — bicycles, Rollerblades, running sports. There had to be something more. Not just this emptiness.

He held the photograph up.

"You were a good kid," he said.

He caught the flicker off to one side. Then he turned and saw her. A barnyard Madonna, hair hanging down, classical features etched in the air. Not quite an apparition. She was watching him. No fear on her face, just curiosity.

"*Bonjour,*" Dan ventured, wondering if he was about to be arrested for trespassing. Given the way things had been going, it wouldn't have surprised him. Either that or he was looking at a ghost.

"*Bonjour,*" she answered brightly.

"Do you speak English?"

She smiled. "I am English."

He held out the flowers. "I came here to leave these. A boy died here."

The look on her face said she knew.

"Lonnie," she said.

"You knew him?"

She walked to the centre of the space then looked up into the rafters and down again at the sawdust-covered earth.

"It was here," she said, indicating the spot with her hands. "There were a bunch of us. We all lived here together for a few months one summer. Lonnie, me, and the others." She looked back at Dan. "Lonnie said we'd found the end of the world here. I think he thought we could stay forever. We knew there was something wrong with him, but you sometimes went days without noticing it and you thought maybe he was all right."

She looked him in the eye to see if he understood then went on.

"I think we wanted him to be all right. Then it would show up again. Just odd things, you know. Like one day he found a toad and went around with it all afternoon, cupping it in his hands like it was some kind of offering. I asked what he was doing. He said he was getting the toad acclimatized to being carried. When it was ready, he said, he was going to carry it through town as a symbol for animal-rights abuse. He wanted to walk across the country to make people aware that animals were being poisoned by pollution. That was how he was going to do it."

She cocked her head and looked at him. "You knew him?"

"Yes," Dan said. "I'm a friend of his mother. Can you tell me how he died?"

She looked back up at the gloom. "We were dancing one night. We'd lit a bonfire. Some of us were drunk. Lonnie climbed to the top of the silo. He said he was going to see the world from the roof. Some of the boys were yelling to him to jump and see if he could fly."

Dan watched her as she told him all this with the bright, serene light in her eyes.

"They were laughing. We didn't think he would do it. Next thing I knew, something hit the ground. I turned around and there he was." She looked at him. "It wasn't their fault. They didn't know he was going to do it."

"What happened?"

"One of the boys phoned the police. We all left after that. Before they could come and question us. We didn't know what else to do. We were trespassing. We didn't even know his full name. I still don't know it."

"Rhodes," Dan said. "Lonnie Rhodes."

He offered her the flowers. She took them and laid them on the soft earth.

"I come back here sometimes. I live in town now, but I like to come back. I think about him. He was so sweet."

The wind blew through a crack high above, making a mournful sound.

"Will you tell her I'm sorry? His mother?"

Dan nodded. "I will."

The next day he made his way through Quebec, that rebel holdout from the seventeenth century, back down the Highway of Heroes, carrying the ashes of an unsung hero who would not long be remembered by many.

He had hoped to tell Domingo that she still had a child alive somewhere. That it was all a mistake. Her son had never died. But instead, this box. Ashes. Nothing to warm the heart of a dying woman or bring joy to a face already dazzled with pain and impending loss. Instead, what he was bringing home was grief and a crowd crying, *Jump!* It seemed unfair. Worse than no news at all.

Twenty

I'd Rather Be High

Dan felt his heartbeat quicken as he turned off the 401 and headed south along the Don Valley Parkway. As the towers swung into view, Toronto had never looked so welcoming. Ked had stayed with Kendra while Dan was away. Dan mulled over the question of what to do with him on his return. Now he was home.

Lights blinked on the answering machine in his front hallway. The first call was from Lydia Johnston, asking him to get in touch as soon as possible. No doubt she wanted to update him on the case. She would be surprised by what he had to tell her. He pencilled her number on a pad and pressed *Next*. Lionel's voice came through, low and quiet. It wasn't the panicked Lionel of a few days earlier after being warned by a mysterious voice to keep things to himself. This was a sombre, spooked Lionel.

"… they said it was suicide. I don't believe them."

For a moment, Dan thought he was referring to

Lonnie. He'd mentioned his reason for going to Quebec, but why should that concern Lionel?

He strained to hear the words.

"I don't know how much more I can take, Dan. I'm terrified. Of course, I had to tell Charles this time. I couldn't keep it to myself."

This wasn't about Lonnie. Dan turned off the machine. The eight-hour drive from Quebec had worn him out, but now he felt adrenaline coursing through his veins again.

He picked up the phone. Lionel answered on the first ring.

"Thank god, you got my message."

"I just got back in town, but I'm free now. Could I come over? I'd like to discuss this with you and Charles. I'd rather not do it over the phone."

"Yes, of course. Radio City, south building. We're in the penthouse. Ask for us at reception."

Dan reached the stately towers in fifteen minutes. The powerful-looking man behind the desk appeared friendly and relaxed, though Dan was pretty sure he was armed with more than just a smile and some pricey muscles. If the bruise on his face registered, the concierge didn't show it.

"Yes, sir. I was told to expect you." He nodded to the set of elevators. "Go on up."

The lobby was as grand and silent as the tomb of any self-respecting pharaoh waiting patiently through the centuries. Dan walked quickly through and pressed PH over the illuminated buttons. He stared at the silvery walls during his ascent, trying to imagine all the floors in between, all the whispers of lives unseen and unheard except for a brief murmuring of gears. He pictured Lionel's worried face waiting for him to arrive. Dan had experienced threats of violence to the point where he was able to turn off the fear and simply deal with whatever needed to be dealt with, but, according to Danny, the perfect couple Lionel and Charles lived a tranquil life whose routine was seldom disrupted by such concerns. It wasn't easy to get used to intimidation.

The elevator opened on to high ceilings and a wide, open hallway. Silver and blue dominated the wallpaper's soft, shell-like patterns. More tranquillity. Understatement was the theme here, but Dan knew this was extreme luxury and comfort as far as downtown living went.

Like almost everything else about the building, the penthouse door was oversized, as though built for armies to come and go. In fact, it looked as though it could hold off an armed revolt if things ever came to that. It never hurt to be prepared for the revolution when it came to town.

"They killed Santiago," Lionel announced before Dan had set foot in the room. "They said it was suicide, but I don't believe it for a second. It had to be Trposki or someone like that."

He sounded calmer now, but still frightened. Charles seemed more self-contained. They were bookends of composure and discomposure, the tall, stocky lawyer and the lean, athletic accountant.

Charles registered the bruise and cuts on Dan's face with a curious expression as he ushered him inside. "Come in please, Dan."

The central room was brightly lit, yet sparsely furnished. A wall of windows loomed behind, framing the night sky like a painting that overwhelms the space it hangs in. Outside, the darkness was edged by lights, sketching the horizon in a constantly changing chimera of colours and shapes that mere mortals on the ground could never conceive. Here was Valhalla presented for the entry of the gods.

It was the perfect showroom. It was also, Dan noted, the perfect opportunity for someone in the twin tower opposite to take a couple of clean shots, killing anyone inside with minimal effort and expert efficiency. An assassin's wet dream.

They sat astride cream-coloured couches centred on a geometrically patterned carpet, like figures on a Paul Klee canvas.

"When did the police call you?" Dan asked.

"Yesterday morning. He had my business card in his wallet when they found him. I have no idea why. I told them that. They said he didn't have any family in Canada, so I had to identify him." Lionel ran a hand through his hair. "He looked awful. He was all swollen ... his face ..."

He grew more agitated as he described Santiago's appearance.

"I'm sorry you had to go through that," Dan said. "And I'm sorry I didn't find him first while he was still alive."

"It's silly. I shouldn't get so rattled by it. It's not like I haven't seen death before." Lionel picked up a glass of water. His hand shook as he brought it to his mouth. "When I was five, I lost my older brother. It was a car accident. We were nearly home when we got hit by a truck. I remember the doctors telling my parents he had a fifty-fifty chance of surviving. I prayed all night. He died the next day. I kept wondering what happened to the other fifty percent. I realized then that life is just a numbers game. There's no morality, no god who makes things better or worse for you if you do or don't do what he wants. There's nothing more than the odds for or against something. Some people live, some die. How can you stop it from happening?"

"I have no answer for that," Dan said.

Lionel finally registered the changes to Dan's appearance.

"What ...?" He shook his head. "What happened to you?"

"Small accident. Nothing to worry about," he said, brushing aside the question. "Where did they find Santiago's body?"

"Beneath the Overlea Bridge, not far from where we went running the other day. Close to the stables ..." Lionel glanced at Charles. "That's why they thought it might be suicide. It used to be the Bloor Viaduct where these things happened. That was the most popular spot. But once they enclosed it with wire, people started looking for alternate locations. Overlea is closest."

The city had covered the sides of the Viaduct, hoping to stop the spate of suicides, Dan recalled, but people simply found other places to jump. The numbers hadn't changed. He did some quick mental calculations. Overlea was at least seventy-five metres high. A falling body would hit the ground at more than a hundred kilometres an hour. At that rate, you'd be pretty much assured of an instant death. For jumpers, that was often a factor. No one wanted to injure themselves and just make things worse as a result of not having tried hard enough.

He glanced at the windows. A wide terrace ran alongside, the one-time scene of Lionel and Charles's wedding, as Donny related. At thirty floors up, it too would be a suicide's dream.

"There's more," Lionel said, sounding strained. "While you were away, I kept looking into that file I told you about. I think it's for off-shore investments. Money was being siphoned off from the Saddle and Bridle. Lots of it. I don't know how Yuri managed to hide it from me."

"Have you told the police?"

"No."

"You will probably have to."

Lionel nodded distractedly. "It always struck me as funny that Yuri never wanted me to do a full audit of the books. I never really questioned it."

"Do you think Yuri was into more than just a regular bar and nightclub business? We know about the drugs. Could he also have been dealing in arms, for instance? Something that would bring in a lot of money that he needed to hide?"

"If he was, it was completely without my knowledge. I never saw anything like that going on behind the scenes." Lionel nodded to a sheaf of papers on a sideboard. "See for yourself."

Dan leafed quickly through the documents, noting figures and cryptic letters that could have been account particulars.

"Can any of it be traced?"

Lionel shook his head. "I doubt it. This stuff goes into one account and then disappears into another. After that, no one knows where it ends up. I doubt you'd even find a name attached to it once it left Yuri's hands." He looked at his husband. "Charles has had experiences with this sort of thing. He could tell you about it."

From the look on Charles's face, Dan sensed he had no intention of talking about it.

"Nothing that would be of any help here," Charles said. "But if the police get wind of this, they may target Lionel for running illegal financial operations for Yuri. So far, they haven't said anything, but that could change. We have to be careful to protect his reputation."

And his life, Dan thought. He held up the file. "I think it might be wisest to let them know first. Can I take this with me for now?"

Lionel shrugged. "Sure."

"We need to make sure you both are protected for the next while. The police have offered to help with that."

"We've already discussed it. I'm not sure what they can do," Charles said, sceptically. "Nor do I particularly trust the police. Not now, not ever."

"Then I strongly advise you to hire somebody privately. Get yourselves a bodyguard."

"We're well protected here," Charles said. "You might not be able to tell from the lobby, but you'd need a SWAT team to get in. Why would we need anything more than what we have now?"

Dan nodded over to the windows. "It's pretty open up here. You never know what someone is capable of doing. Don't underestimate the enemy, whoever it may be."

Charles scowled. "Can you recommend someone?"

"I can ask around and come up with a name or two by tomorrow."

"All right. Send them to me and I'll check into it," Charles said. He looked at Lionel and shrugged. "It's what lawyers do, after all."

Dan glanced back and forth between the two. Charles seemed a bit cavalier, though perhaps he simply didn't want to appear to be rattled by the situation.

Lionel's elbow slipped on the arm of the couch. He steadied himself.

"Your sleeping pills are kicking in," Charles said. He turned to Dan. "He's been a wreck the last few days. I think it's starting to take a toll on him."

Lionel nodded to Dan. "I needed to calm myself down. I took them right after you called."

Charles stood and turned to Dan. "Can I get you something to drink? A beer?"

"No, thanks."

"Tea? Coffee?"

"A coffee would be good," Dan said.

Charles went to the kitchen.

Lionel leaned back into the couch. "Sorry if I seem a little out of it. Charles thought it would be a good idea if I really knocked myself out and got a good night's sleep."

"Just don't overdo it," Dan said. "I've had some pretty bad insomnia the last few years, but I still have to be careful how many pills I take."

"I was really worried before, but now it all seems a bit silly. I think maybe I'm feeling a little high."

Dan noticed the edges of a bruise peeking out from under his sleeve. "You hurt yourself," he said.

Lionel looked down and pulled his sleeve over it. "I banged into some workout equipment yesterday. Clumsy."

"Looks like a bad bruise," Dan said.

"Don't worry, I'm okay." He smiled. "Thanks for coming by this evening. We both appreciate it. I'm starting to feel better."

He struggled to keep his eyes open a moment longer, then gave up. His breathing was softly rhythmic by the time Charles returned with the coffee.

Dan took a cup. "Looks like Lionel has had enough for this evening. I'll just finish this and leave."

Charles glanced over at his husband's sleeping figure.

"I hate to see him going through this. He's very sensitive. More than me, at any rate." He studied the cuts on Dan's face. "What really happened to you?"

"I was attacked while I was away."

"In Quebec?"

"Yes."

His brow furrowed. "And you think it has something to do with what happened to Yuri?"

"I suspect it does."

Charles nodded. "Get me those names. I'll look into getting some kind of security for the time being."

"I guarantee you'll be happier knowing you're both safe rather than worrying about it." He nodded to Lionel. "I can help you carry him to bed before I go."

"Don't worry about Lionel. I can handle him. But I'd like to talk to you for a few minutes."

"No problem," Dan told him.

"I don't trust the police," Charles continued. "I've said that already. Still, I'm just not convinced that Santiago was murdered. That seems a bit far-fetched. What do you think?"

Dan considered the question. Despite his experience in Quebec, he was undecided. "I'd like to hear from the police whether or not they believe the death to be suicide. They may not want to reveal too much about the investigation just yet. It could be they think it's in their best interest at present to go along with the suicide theory. At any rate, they can't all be corrupt —"

Charles cut him off. "What do you know of this Trposki character Lionel keeps mentioning? He seems to be at the heart of things."

"I agree, but I don't have an answer for that. I've asked about him at police headquarters, but I don't get much back by way of an answer."

"You have an inside source there?"

"I'm friendly with the chief," Dan said.

Charles's face registered surprise. "I didn't know."

"In any case, when it comes to Trposki, if you see him I think you should avoid him if possible."

"I doubt I'd recognize him if I saw him again." He put a hand on Dan's forearm. "How's your coffee?"

Dan felt the heat in his touch and recalled Donny's warning. Charles leaned forward, his handsome features caught in the light, a stage designer's *trompe l'oeil* that had seduction written on it. Intention lay all over this man, from the cut of his silk shirt outlining hard pectorals to the crease of his pant leg that said he could be conservative and coy if you liked, but better lay in wait if you didn't.

"I'm good, thanks," Dan said.

Charles lifted the hand. Lionel snored lightly in his corner.

"I better go," Dan said, bundling the file Lionel had given him.

If Charles was disappointed, he didn't show it. He stood and walked Dan to the door. A picture on the mantel caught the reflection of a pinspot: Charles astride a well-groomed horse. *Rich men and their hobbies*, Dan thought, determined not to let himself be added to Charles's list of amusements.

"That's Rocket," Charles said, catching his glance.

"Nice-looking horse. Is that the stable in the valley?" Dan asked.

"Yes. Very near to where ..." He shrugged.

"Right." Dan paused. "With Santiago dead, I'm assuming you won't need my services any longer."

"Let's take a few days and think it over. Lionel likes you. It might be in his best interests to keep you engaged for the time being."

"To do what?"

Charles gave him an assured smile. "Maybe you can find out what really happened to Santiago. We can afford to keep you on."

Dan held up the file. "I think my job here is done once I bring this to the police."

"I understand." Charles held out his hand. "Thanks for not worrying Lionel about your attack.

And I won't underestimate the enemy, as you put it. Not for a second."

They shook. The gap in the door narrowed until Charles disappeared behind it.

At home, Dan went up to his office. He pored over the documents Lionel had given him. Substantial amounts of money seemed to have been forwarded to various accounts on a regular basis. Judging by the codes, it would be impossible for anyone but an expert to determine where. As well, there were lists showing smaller amounts indicating what appeared to be a series of regular expenditures. One weekly entry had a cellphone number at the bottom. He dialled it, but the line was no longer in service.

He checked his watch. It was already past eleven. Inspector Johnston had said to call any time, but he wasn't surprised when the call went directly to her answering service, her voice softly compelling him to leave his name and number.

"This is Dan Sharp, Lydia. I got your message. Please call when you get a chance."

She called back within two minutes. He could tell from her voice that she'd been sleeping. He imaged her lying there listening to him, trying to shake off the vestiges of sleep before she dialled his number. Nevertheless, she had called.

He gave her an update on his trip. She calmly offered a security contingent. He accepted it with a sense of relief. After his experience in Quebec, he wasn't going to take any chances.

"Are you home now?"

"Yes."

"Would you prefer to stay there tonight or go to a hotel?"

"My son will be coming home soon."

"I can have someone there after midnight," she said.

That was unusually fast, Dan thought, but then he'd been directed to her by the chief of police. Obviously she commanded a measure of authority and knew when to use it.

"I've also advised my clients, Charles and Lionel, to hire private protection, since they don't seem to want any of yours." He paused. "Ex-clients, I should say. I bowed out of the job this evening."

She seemed to take the news with barely a moment's consideration. "Do you think they'll take your advice about hiring protection?"

Dan hesitated, recalling Charles's apparent disregard at his mention of the likelihood of danger. "I hope so. I can't say for sure."

He told her about the file Lionel had given him. They made plans to meet the following morning, and then Dan wished her good night.

He had just got off the phone when he heard the front door open. Ked was home. It was time to face the music.

Twenty-One

Alarmed Forces

His son stood at the foot of the stairs nodding in time to his iPod, earphones plugged into his head like the tendrils of zombie plants creeping in while he was unaware. It was a whole universe inside those ear buds, Dan knew. Considering the state of the world at large, it wasn't a wonder kids dissociated from it whenever they could. Dan's generation had protested — economies, racism, wars, unjust laws — because they'd been told they could change things. The new generation just wrapped themselves in cocoons and waited things out, like a nuclear winter, hoping it wouldn't get any worse. Their animated heroes fought greater and greater battles on computer screens, while the kids themselves seemed prematurely dogged, knowing they could never have even that much effect on the world.

Ralph brushed past Dan down the stairs to greet Ked, who looked up and saw his father standing there. His smile faded as he caught sight of the bruise on Dan's cheek.

"Dad —!"

"I'm okay."

"What happened?"

Dan saw the panic rising in his son's face. He would have to head this off quickly and deal with it as best he could.

"C'mon — let's sit in the living room. I need to talk to you."

Ked followed as Dan led the way. He sat on the couch across from his father. Ralph flopped himself at Ked's feet. At least someone was taking this casually.

Dan clasped his hands. The gesture made him feel old rather than calm and secure. "I went to Quebec City, as I told you the other day."

His son was holding on to his temper, but only just. "Dad! Just tell me what happened."

"I got beat up."

"Why?"

That, of course, was the million-dollar question. Dan didn't know why, precisely, and what he conjectured about the reasons for the attack could not fail to arouse fear in his son's mind. One of the classic triggers of PTSD was to be put in fear for one's own safety or the safety of a loved one. Was he putting his son on the very track that he'd fought so hard to get off?

"Honestly, I don't really know. I think it has something to do with a case I've been working on."

Ked just sat there, looking more tense by the minute.

"Why were you even in Quebec City in the first place?"

"I was there trying to find Lonnie's remains."

His son looked crestfallen now. "Lonnie Rhodes? The guy who used to look after me when I was a kid?"

"Yes. We — *I* — found his remains. He died there."

Why was it so hard for him to say Lonnie committed suicide?

"How?"

"He fell from a tower. He killed himself, Ked. I'm sorry to tell you that. It happened a long time ago, only we didn't know about it until recently. That's why I went to Quebec, to bring him back."

Ked nodded. Dan hated spilling it all out to him like this.

A memory flashed. One afternoon, when Ked was four or five, they'd been out in the backyard when a fierce squawking caught their attention. Turning, they watched a hawk lift off from the roof with a squirrel clutched in its claws. The bird flew to the top of a nearby tree and proceeded to tear the rodent apart. Dan saw the realization dawn in his son's face: something that had been alive was suddenly gone in seconds. It was his first encounter with violent death. The only thing worse than knowing was not knowing, Dan told himself.

"Why? Why did Lonnie kill himself?"

"He wasn't well emotionally. He may have been schizophrenic. We're not really sure."

"And now his mother's dying in the hospital?"

Dan nodded. "Yes, in all likelihood."

"This is what you were trying to tell me the other day, isn't it? When you said things happen to people and you can't always do something about it."

"Yes. It is."

"And that's why you do what you do? To try to change things for people? To make things better for them?"

Dan was grateful Ked had made the association, though he wouldn't have described his work in such terms.

"I do what I do to help people get answers. Sometimes. I don't always get answers. And when I do, it's not always enough, but that's what I try to do for them, yes."

Ralph moaned and rolled onto his side, as though some secret had finally been revealed and a great weight lifted at having things out in the open.

"So who beat you up?"

"I don't know for sure, but I'm pretty sure it was nothing to do with Lonnie or Domingo. It has to do with a case I'm working on. That's all I know. Some people don't want me doing what I'm doing, because they don't want certain information to come out. I'm trying to find someone who may have that information."

"Why did they follow you to Quebec?"

That was what Dan had been asking himself all the way back home. Why would they follow him to Quebec? Should he state the obvious, that it was just an easy way to get rid of him, by following him away from home where he'd be vulnerable and in need of protection? Because that was the only likely explanation why they would track him out of town when he was looking for the remains of a dead boy.

"I don't really know, Ked. But it means they're serious about wanting me to stop doing what I've been doing."

"And will you stop now?"

Dan heard the fear in his son's voice, but he resolved not to lie to him.

"No." He paused. "Listen, I want you to go and stay with your mother for a few days."

Dan saw the flash in Ked's eyes.

"I know you hate it when I say that. I'm sorry."

"Why? Why do I have to go?"

Just — to avoid complications."

"Why?"

"I just told you."

"You didn't tell me anything. Are you staying here?"

"I'll stay here, yes."

Ked stood. "Then I'm staying."

"No, Ked —"

"Dad, I'm staying. I mean it!"

"It might not be safe for you. You need to leave. Just for a few days till I know everything is safe."

"Then who looks after you?"

"I'll have police security. They'll be outside in a car."

His son loomed over him. When had he grown so big?

"Do you think I'm going to be able to sleep at Mom's place knowing you're here alone in the house?"

Somehow, Dan didn't know when, his son had become an adult. Sooner or later, he was going to have to accept and deal with it. He knew his home was secure — strong locks on the doors and windows, an armed circuit that sent alerts whenever a breach was noted. No one could get in without triggering an alarm at the security division's head office, which was monitored twenty-four-seven. He was safe. But then that was probably what Yuri Malevski had believed at one time.

Dan stared up at his son. There was no getting around him. The time had come when his son could say "no" to him and hold his ground. That wasn't a surprise: Dan had raised Ked to think about what was good for himself as well as others. Tonight he was doing both, knowing they were inextricably intertwined. Ked could not go to his mother's and at the same time also not worry about his father. Nor would Dan have felt any different in his shoes. But the fact was they now had the assurance of an armed guard at their residence. If they went to Kendra's house or to a hotel, they would not even have that, and it might bring danger to her. It seemed as though the choice had been made for them.

"All right," Dan said slowly, hoping he was doing the right thing. "We'll stay here together, you and me."

Ked sighed with relief.

"I don't know what time the guard will be coming, so for now we have to remain vigilant," Dan told him.

"I can do that."

Dan had visions of his son sitting armed at a window, keeping watch over the yard hour after hour till the morning light.

"No tough-guy shenanigans. We don't have guns to protect ourselves. This isn't TV and we are not Americans. No vigilante antics, no crazy stuff. Just listen and keep alert. Is that clear?"

"Yes."

"When we go to bed, we'll both be upstairs. All the doors and window are locked. The alarm is on. If you hear anything at all, you call 911 immediately. Then you call me. I'll keep my cellphone on all night, sitting right beside me."

"Don't worry, I will. Good night."

Dan heard the latch click into place. In fact, he realized with a smile, he could have done a lot worse for a personal bodyguard.

Twenty-Two

Rare Flowers

The plant was on the kitchen table when Dan got up in the morning. He opened a palm-sized envelope and read the card: *I'm sorry.* Then underneath: *Hank, xo.* As apologies went, it was neither original nor comprehensive, but Dan could tell Hank was genuinely sorry by the simple fact that he'd sent it. Still, it would do nothing to change his mind about seeing him again.

He looked over at Ked, who stood wrestling with a spatula, transferring pancakes from frying pan to plate.

"Good night's sleep?"

"Yeah, Dad. All good. You?"

"Yes, thanks. I take it this showed up this morning?" Dan said, with a nod at the brightly wrapped offering.

"Special delivery." Ked said. "I signed for it. The guy wasn't going to leave it on the porch. He said it was too expensive."

Dan looked at the flower; it was an orchid of some sort. The leaves were a deep, waxy green, the stems laden with violet blossoms dropping downward. Fleshy roots gripped the potting material like fingers poking through soil and groping hesitantly at the world around them.

"I saw the name on the delivery slip. Who's Hank?"

Dan smiled. It was like Ked to keep track of his amorous pursuits, even when Dan tried to keep them to himself.

"A nice guy who meant well, but not a contender, as they say."

Ked hesitated. "Well, I hope you keep the orchid at least. It's nice."

Dan turned over the instructions, noting that his new acquisition required select environmental conditions, liking it neither too hot nor too cold. *Goldilocks would approve*, he mused. This particular plant, it said, was known as *C. Purity coerulea*. The irony wasn't lost on him. Hank might be sorry, but he was still cheeky.

"Let's see how green my thumb is at keeping it alive," he said at last. "Sounds like orchids are fussy about their environment."

"I can lend you my sling psychrometer to measure the humidity."

Ked pointed to the paraphernalia splayed out on the sideboard. It looked like a complicated child's toy.

"Is it finished?"

"I stayed up all night working on it."

Dan noted the dark circles under his son's eyes with a mixture of amusement and fatherly concern. Nothing he wouldn't have done at that age. His raised eyebrows said Ked was supposed to have been sleeping, but that under the circumstances perhaps the behavioural lapse would be overlooked.

"Watch this," Ked said excitedly.

He gripped the psychrometer at the base and twirled it overhead. A pair of arms lifted and whirled like helicopter blades. After a minute he stopped and placed it on the table.

"Now we check it."

He pointed to two thermometers encased in glass.

"The first one is dry," he said. "It measures the actual room temperature. The second is wrapped in a wet cloth. It calculates the temperature as the water evaporates, so that should be cooler. Now we take the two numbers …" He leaned over a numeric table in a textbook. "… then we do a calculation and *voilá*! We have the relative humidity of the atmosphere. In this room, it's 22.3 percent."

He looked up expectantly. "Are you impressed?"

"Of course," Dan said. "Everything you do impresses me."

"Cool. I can never tell from looking at your face. You don't show much emotion."

"Well, I am very impressed. And I wish you luck in the science fair."

Ked looked at the flower. "I don't know if this guy is going to be happy here. The card says orchids like a humidity level between 40 and 80 percent. We could get a humidifier, but at that level it might peel the paint off the walls. What we really need is a greenhouse."

Dan thought of the moisture-laden atmosphere in Yuri Malevski's lush, indoor garden. "I don't know if one plant translates into a greenhouse, but I'll keep it in mind."

"Actually, I did a bit of research," Ked continued. "If we put a few flowers together on a tray covered with pebbles and then pour water onto it, it produces a micro-climate that keeps the humidity levels higher. They sell orchids at Loblaw's. I could get a few more."

Dan gave his son a curious glance.

"You know, to make the house a bit greener." Ked put a plate mounded with pancakes on the table. "To make it feel more homey. Or something."

"Okay by me," Dan said, reaching for a fork.

"Good?" Ked asked.

"You bet."

Pancakes were a shared culinary passion dating from Ked's childhood, when Dan made them as a Saturday-morning treat. Now he was getting them served to him in return. He wondered how far Ked would take the campaign to look out for his well-being. From making sure he didn't spend the night alone, through negotiating the reckless passage of his romantic interests and seeing his nutrition was looked after, his son had Dan's best interests at heart.

He checked his watch: he just had time for a second look at Lionel's file before meeting Lydia Johnston. Coffee in the village appealed to him.

"I have to go soon. I'd like us both to leave together. I can drive you to school, if you like. That way I won't have to worry about you while I'm out."

Ked's expression said he concurred. While his father's face might not show much emotion, Ked's did, and clearly this openness was a good thing as far as he was concerned.

"I'm ready any time you are."

The Second Cup was dead, but that was just as well, as far as Dan was concerned. No noise was good noise. He sat in one of the stuffed armchairs in front of the gas fire, spreading his coffee and paperwork on the table before him.

He struggled with his fold-up reading glasses, the latest encumbrance in his fight against mortality. Untangled at last, he set them on his nose then went through the accounts methodically, stopping to note Lionel's penciled *!!!*'s in the margins directing him to hidden errors, strange codes, and numbers made to look like something other than what they were. Wormholes where the dollars trickled away unseen by any but the most observant. Dan felt as if he were filching a corpse's secrets, hauling Yuri Malevski and his dark secrets back from the grave.

Half an hour later, he scooped up the papers and stuffed them into his briefcase. He'd just stepped out into the sunlight, blinking away the brightness, when a half-familiar face passed by.

"Excuse me," Dan called out.

"Yes?" came the throaty reply.

There was nothing pretty about it: heavy eyelids, coarse skin, the mouth downturned at the edges. Instead, there was a commanding gaze and black eyes set slightly too far apart, pitiless as a hawk alert for prey from a thousand feet up. All the features were over-pronounced, like a burlesque queen in full makeup, as though the proper distance for viewing this face would always be from a stage. The scent of frangipani at midnight was the only hint of femininity.

"Are you Jan?"

Dan wondered what life must be like on the street for a transgendered person. Being gay was hard enough when it came to dealing with the world at large, but this was a notch above.

"I think so. And you would be?"

"Dan Sharp. I'm a private investigator."

Jan's expression turned from surly disregard to one of interest.

"Really? A private dick. I didn't think they existed outside of the movies."

"I exist. Have you got a moment to talk?"

"About what?"

"Yuri Malevski."

"Well, let's see. Did you make an appointment? Hmm? I don't believe so. I'm on my way to the Hassle-Free Clinic at the moment." Jan paused and leaned against the wall with all the poise of a first-class hooker. "The sexual health centre? Apparently they want to counsel me not to go around spreading filthy diseases. Not that I would."

"I was wondering what you could tell me about your relationship with Yuri."

"I don't have one. He's dead."

"But you used to know him."

"That was a long time ago. Before he decided he didn't need friends. Permanently." Jan gave an impatient shrug. "Yuri was all right. He was just too temperamental for his own good. We got along for a while and then one day we didn't. There's nothing to tell."

"What did you disagree about?"

"He thought I made a pass at his boyfriend." Jan's eyes rolled dismissively. "I didn't, if you're wondering."

"Did you like Santiago?"

"Not by a long shot. But I don't speak ill of the dead."

"You heard then."

Jan shrugged again. "What can I say? Word gets around."

Two skateboarders in ragged jeans and T-shirts zoomed past, the pace of life on the street revving up.

"What about a kid named Ziggy? He was living at Yuri's place and might have sold drugs out of the Saddle and Bridle."

"Sure. Tell me something I don't know."

"So it's true?"

"That Ziggy sold drugs or that he lived with Yuri?"

"Either. Both."

"Then 'yes' to both, as far as I know. Though I don't think Ziggy is what you'd call a big-time drug dealer. He sells the odd joint. He used to be a heroin user, but he quit last I heard."

"Do you think drugs had anything to do with Yuri's murder?"

Jan snorted. "There may have been drugs going through that home, but Yuri's murder wasn't about drugs."

Dan watched the expressions flitting across Jan's features, the face no doubt reshaped and rebuilt. How much would have been impossible to say. Charles had been right in saying it would be difficult to make a snap judgment about gender.

Jan caught the look.

"You're wondering whether I am or not? Well, don't get yourself all bothered about pronouns and such. I am a full-blooded woman. You wanna feel my boobies to make sure?"

The question was followed by the same throaty cackle Dan had heard the first time he saw Jan on the street.

"It's all right. I'll take your word for it. So it wasn't about drugs. What was it about then?"

"You better look closer to home, baby. That's all I can tell you."

"The Lockie House, I assume you mean. You used to work there, didn't you?"

"A lot of people worked there. I was one of them."

"Do you know the security code for the house?"

"I used to, but not lately. Not for a long time before Yuri was killed, if that's what you're implying. I couldn't remember it now to save my life."

"Do you know who else had it?"

Jan sighed. "As I said, look closer to home."

Something occurred to Dan. "Do you know a guy called the P-Man?"

"You mean Pig?"

"So you know him?"

"I *knew* him. Sure. He's quite the piece of work for a straight guy. He was a regular at the Lockie House, once upon a time."

"Really? I got the distinct impression he didn't like Yuri Malevski."

"He did and then he didn't. Just like me."

"Why?"

Jan smiled. "It could have something to do with the night a bunch of drag queens got him so drunk he passed out. When he woke up, he wasn't wearing anything except a lot of lipstick kisses all over his body. And I mean *all* over. He never spoke to Yuri after that."

"Is he what you meant when you said to look closer to home?"

Jan shrugged. "Oh, baby — you look pretty smart, for a dick. You'll figure it out."

Dan felt a flash of annoyance. "If you know anything relevant, you should go to the police before they come to you. Otherwise, you can be charged with withholding information."

Jan brushed a length of hair over a shoulder. "Do you think I should turn myself into the police? I could do with a new set of head shots."

"You should tell them whatever you know."

"I don't *know* anything. It's all street talk. I'm just telling you — look closer to home. I think I heard that in a movie."

"What movie?"

"The one with the bell tower and the bridge. Somebody jumps. I can't remember the name of it."

Dan felt a jolt at the mention of jumping. "Who jumps?"

"Some blond chick."

"And what would I find if I looked closer to home?"

Jan shrugged. "I surely don't know, baby. You should watch that movie and you might figure it out. You know somebody had to clean up that mess."

Jan turned and sashayed down the sidewalk, hips sawing back and forth with as much conviction as Mae West exiting on a famous one-liner.

Twenty-Three

Post-Op

Inside police headquarters, Dan had barely waited a minute before he was ushered into Inspector Johnston's office. She was friendly but businesslike as she offered him a seat.

"Thanks for coming in. It's been busy since you were gone. As you no doubt know, I met one of your ex-clients, quite by coincidence as it turns out."

"Yes, I heard. You asked Lionel to identify a body."

She flashed him one of her rare smiles. "His business card was discovered on the body. When I heard his name, I recognized it thanks to you. The chief already knew it from the investigation." She paused. "We think the suicide could be an admission of guilt on the ex-boyfriend's part. If he killed Malevski, whether it was accidental or premeditated, then the grief may have hit him harder than he expected."

"Then you're convinced his death was suicide?"

"Young man jumps off a bridge in the dead of night with no witnesses?" Only her raised eyebrows said she might leave room for skepticism. "Until we have reason to believe otherwise."

"So the fall was what killed him? No traces of Rohypnol or anything suggesting he might have been drugged and pushed over?"

"The fall definitely killed him. Rohypnol doesn't stay in the body long, but toxicology reports for both Rohypnol and alcohol were negative."

They stared one another down for a second.

"I find it suspicious that a suspect in the case dies before he can be found and questioned," Dan said. "Particularly since Santiago was the one in charge of handing protection money over to corrupt cops."

She sighed. "Me, too. But for now, I don't have a lot to go on. Is there anything you can tell me?"

"I don't have much to add, but I just had an encounter with a transwoman named Jan — sort of a fixture in the gay village. I don't have any contact info. Jan knew Yuri and suggested I should look closer to home if I want to know who killed him."

"Any idea what that means?"

Dan shook his head. "None, though I had a strange encounter with a next-door neighbour who calls himself Pig."

"Charming. I'll look into it. Anything else?"

"Apparently it could have something to do with a movie about a bridge and a bell tower."

She rolled her eyes. "Let's not make this harder than it has to be. Tell me about Quebec again."

Dan outlined briefly what occurred, how he'd been pursued by two men waiting outside his hotel, had grabbed one of them, then tackled a third before changing hotels.

"Did you report the incident to the police there?"

"No. I saw no point. As far as I can tell, it had nothing to do with why I went to Quebec. These guys were professionals."

She gave him a wry look. "Not so professional you couldn't outfight them."

"True. Was there anything to report from your security detail on my home last night?"

She shook her head. "Nothing. I had a patrol in place not long after midnight. There was nothing suspicious from then until the time you left in the morning. I have someone on your house now and we'll keep him there for the time being. You'll get ample warning should we decide to curtail the operation, in case you want to hire someone privately."

"Thanks for that. I appreciated your getting there on such quick notice."

She considered this for a moment. "The reason we were able to move so quickly on assigning you protection was that we had already considered it a possibility. In fact, we thought there was a chance you might be a target …"

Dan's eyebrows shot up.

"… so we granted you emergency clearance."

He managed a rueful smile. "Nice, but I could have done with a little security in Quebec."

"You did have. We had a man tailing you there."

Dan's smile faded.

Lydia nodded. "Nothing official, of course. We don't interfere in Quebec police operations. This was a private request from the chief, completely off the books." She gave him a knowing look. "As he told me, you did him one hell of a favour once."

She picked up her phone, all the while watching Dan's face.

"Send him in please," she said into the receiver.

The office door opened. For a second, Dan barely felt a jolt on finding himself face to face with the hirsute stalker he'd encountered in Quebec City. Then it hit him square in the stomach. He turned to Johnston. She'd set him up, after convincing him to believe her. He felt the betrayal. She was still talking, but the words scarcely registered. Something about "… one of ours … thought it was time you two met … best to clear this up before we go any further."

A hand extended. Dan stood and blinked.

"You gave me a hell of a wallop," the man said.

He was still trying to make sense of things, to glean some meaning in the confusion of words. Lydia was telling him that Sergeant Nick Trposki wasn't really on the take, but only pretending to be in order to gain inside information, officer to officer.

Their hands met over the desk. Dan felt the prickle of sweat running between his pectorals.

"So, please," Lydia was saying. "Don't keep slugging our best officers and your security contingent."

Dan shook his head. "This is why you couldn't tell me."

"That's right. And of course it goes without saying that this is completely in confidence. You'll probably be seeing Sergeant Trposki around from time to time.

Try not to act surprised." She turned to her colleague. "Thank you, Sergeant. That will be all."

Dan watched as he went out the door.

Lydia turned to him. "The chief has asked me to fill you in on the case, if you'd like to hear it."

Dan nodded and sat down again. "Please."

"We've been going over Yuri Malevski's phone records. We were able to determine that he made at least one call of twenty-three seconds duration in the days prior to his death. That call was relayed by satellite over the west coast of Mexico."

Dan nodded. "Lionel — my ex-client — mentioned getting a call from his boss while he was in Puerto Vallarta."

"Yes, it was to his number. Do you know what they talked about?"

"I don't think they spoke. Yuri left a message to confirm their meeting on Lionel's return. Yuri's cell was full when Lionel called back, so he left a message on Yuri's home phone saying he would be back in time for the meeting."

Inspector Johnston nodded. "That jibes with what we know. We found his reply on an answering machine in the home. There were a few other messages with it. One was from a florist about a delivery. We wondered if that was code for drugs."

Dan laughed. "Not very subtle if it was, but it was probably legit. He had a greenhouse."

"The day after the call to Mexico, Malevski used his cell to text a number we still haven't been able to trace. It was one of those disposable mobile phones, paid for by cash in Chinatown. Whoever had it seems to have tossed it since."

"What was the text?"

"A series of four numbers. At first we thought it was an account reference number, but now we think it was his entry code. He changed it the week of his murder. We're assuming it's because he was worried about something. We don't know exactly how many people had it, but presumably only a handful at best."

"So if Yuri changed his entry code and sent the new numbers to someone not long before he was killed, he might inadvertently have set up his own murder."

"At the moment, that's our theory. It could have been the owner of that phone." She caught his expression. "Do you know who it might have gone to?"

"In fact, I might. There's a kid named Ziggy who's staying in a cubbyhole on the third floor of the Malevski mansion —"

"We know about the kid. So far we've haven't been able to talk to him. We thought he'd done a runner, but I don't think anyone knew about the cubbyhole. Do you think he's our killer?"

Dan scratched his head. "I'm not sure. For one thing, I don't think he would have stuck around after the murder if he killed Yuri. For another, I went through his diary when he wasn't there."

He caught Lydia's look.

"Oh! Didn't I tell you I went to the house and looked around?"

"Not to my knowledge, no."

"Okay, so I went to the house and looked around. Lionel gave me the code. From what I could tell, you guys were finished with the place."

She tapped a pencil on her desk. "It's still a crime scene, Dan."

"I'll remember that next time." He grinned. "Don't worry — I didn't touch anything."

"Except a diary we probably should be having a good look at."

"Yeah — I wondered why you hadn't. Anyway, according to the diary, Ziggy was locked out by Yuri for using hard drugs the week of the murder. I know the people Ziggy stayed with while he was away. That part checks out."

"But it was Ziggy who Yuri texted the new code to?"

"No. He accidentally saw the code on Yuri's cell."

"Then he must have seen Yuri."

"I'm not sure. He said he went back to apologize, but never got the chance."

She looked annoyed. "Well, where's the phone? We don't have it. It wasn't in the house. All we have are the phone records."

"Maybe Yuri left it at the bar."

"We checked. It's not there. So if your boy didn't see Yuri, how did he get back in the house?

"He said he sneaked in when the cleaning lady arrived."

"Cleaning lady! What cleaning lady?" Lydia made a show of mock-pulling her hair. "Let's go over this again."

Dan told her what he knew.

"So you're saying Yuri was killed by a cleaning lady? Wouldn't Ziggy have seen or heard something, if he was there? Or were they in on it together?"

"That I can't say. You'll have to ask him."

Lydia sat back. "You've certainly been busy. The chief's away today, but I'll pass this along when he returns."

Dan considered what she'd told him. "How much time elapsed between Yuri sending the text and being killed?"

"I'm sure you know forensics is a bit iffy when it comes to pinpointing time of death. It's an imperfect science, impossible to narrow anything down to minutes. Hours maybe, but even that's dicey. Sometimes when the body is so decomposed you can't even narrow it down to specific days or weeks. Malevski's body was discovered Saturday. The coroner placed his death within days, but whether that means two, three, or, at a long shot, stretching it to four days is anybody's guess."

"So he makes a phone call on Tuesday, sends a text on Wednesday, and then fails to show up for a meeting on Saturday, by which time he's dead."

She nodded. "That's what we know."

"We also know that between sending the text and finding his body, the house was visited by Ziggy and a cleaning lady. What about the code? Can you tell when it was used?"

She checked the papers in front of her. "The log shows it was used once on Tuesday, once on Wednesday, and then again on Thursday. It wasn't used again until we entered the house on Saturday and discovered the body."

"Tuesday and Wednesday might simply have been Yuri coming and going. Thursday could have been the cleaning lady and the boy sneaking back in. Ziggy told me he came to apologize, but never saw Yuri again. If he's telling the truth, it sounds to me like Wednesday or Thursday are your best bets for the murder."

"That jibes with what the coroner said. After the body was discovered, we disabled the alarm for convenience. Once we were finished our investigation we told your accountant he could reset it."

Dan smiled. "Yes, he reset it to the old code. He told me he has a habit of dotting *i*'s and crossing *t*'s. He also said Yuri changed the code from time to time to discourage entry by people he'd given the code to and then wished he hadn't."

"We're still hoping to find his phone. It might be interesting to see what messages are on it. Sometimes these things only make sense after everything is put together."

"When I see Ziggy again, I'll ask him about it. I'll also tell him to call you and answer whatever questions you might have." He paused. "No guarantees, but I'll try. He seems to trust me."

"Great. Thanks for doing our job for us."

Dan hadn't seen Domingo since leaving for Quebec. He called her cell several times, but there was no answer and he hadn't left a message to tell her about Lonnie. News like that needed to be delivered in person. He made his way to the hospital now, feeling the weight of doom he carried and wondering whether she'd be strong enough today to bear it.

In the corridor, two spectral-looking men sat at opposites ends of a bench, both dressed in blue hospital gowns. They looked like bookends, oblivious to one another as much as to the rest of the ward bustling around them. For some, the world went by far too fast; for others it barely moved.

Domingo wasn't in her room. Dan thought she might be out wandering the halls or perhaps was being taken around in her wheelchair by Adele.

He went to the front desk to ask.

"Are you family, love?" the clerk asked in a soft Irish brogue.

Dan hesitated a fraction of a second then said, "Yes, I'm her brother."

She eyed him skeptically. "Is that a fact now?"

"Half-brother," he amended.

"And you weren't informed that her condition had changed?"

He felt his heartbeat skip. "I just got back to town," he said, truthfully. "I was in Quebec."

"Well, your half-sister had a fall. She was operated on for an embolism two days ago. She's in the ICU." She nodded to a corridor. "You'll find gowns and masks outside the door. Make sure you're wearing them and drop them in the bin outside her door when you leave. No exceptions: no mask and gown, no entry."

"Got it," Dan said. "Thanks."

"You're welcome."

He found Domingo alone in the room. Her face was outlined in the light coming from the window. There was a big teddy bear beside a heart-shaped card from Adele on the table. Dan sat and took her hand in his. Her breathing was relaxed, but she didn't wake. No one else came in while he waited. After an hour, he got up and left.

Twenty-Four

Clean

Dan made his way back to the Lockie House, glancing around the yard as he entered. The spring rains had caused the gardens nearly to double in size since his first visit. There were no creepy neighbours watching his every move today, but no doubt the P-Man was not far off. He made a mental note to ask Lydia if he'd been on the list of people questioned in the aftermath of the killing.

Inside, the late-morning light lent the interior an air of repose, despite the fact that Yuri Malevski had been murdered there and now his former lover, Santiago Suárez, was dead as well. Malevski may have died at his lover's hands, making Santiago's death a belated murder-suicide, if it was in fact suicide. As well, one of Dan's oldest friends lay in a hospital with her life running out, dreaming of trains. For the present, at least, Dan Sharp felt himself very much in the land of the living — last he'd checked.

In the sitting room, the silver candelabra had been removed from the piano top, leaving a faint ring in the dust. The portrait of the endlessly suffering Christ now lay on its back, staring vacantly at the ceiling. It seemed someone was pilfering from Yuri Malevski's estate. Dan thought he knew who.

Upstairs, he peered into the master bedroom. It looked the same as the last time he'd been there. He glanced at Santiago's amateurish portrait of his lover. Yuri's eyes seemed to glare in the dim light. Maybe he was angry about the intrusion.

"Tell me your secrets," Dan demanded. "And I'm not talking about the drugs and the orgies. That's tame. I want to know about the guns and especially the money. Where were you sending it and why?"

The portrait failed to respond.

"In time, I'll find out. I guarantee it."

Look closer to home, Jan had said, sounding like a modern-day harpy playing Cassandra. *Well, here I am*, Dan thought. *What exactly is there to find?* A movie with a bridge and a bell tower. More melodrama or obvious truth? There'd been a death — either suicide or murder — from a bridge, but so far there was no bell tower in sight. Then again, who was to say the house didn't once have one?

Down the hall, he knocked on the hollow panel. No response. It opened at his touch. At first he thought the diary was missing, then he saw a corner peeking out from under the futon. He flipped it open. Ziggy had written in it the day of their encounter: *Met a nice guy today. He's older, sexy as hell, but he already told me he isn't into relationships. Or at least not with me. Typical. The younger guys think I'm a jerk and the older guys think I'm too much work. (Hey, that rhymes!) Too complicated, I guess. Still, he offered to help me sort out my shit. Thinks he can help me with my problems. Ha! I doubt it. I'm too fucked up, but I like him so it won't hurt to talk. Maybe I'll try to seduce him again.*

Hardly a ringing endorsement, Dan thought, but it was something.

A day later, Ziggy's spirits plummeted: *Don't know why I bother. I have no idea what I'll do when I have to leave here. Yuri was the last good thing that happened to me. Why even keep trying when every day feels like lead skies? I'd rather be dead.*

Though he was inclined to dismiss it as teenage angst, Dan was concerned all the same. This time Ziggy didn't surprise him by showing up out of nowhere, but sooner or later their paths would cross again. When that happened, he'd be prepared.

He turned to a later entry, made while he was away in Quebec: *Guess who called? He wants to meet at the Beaver!*

Not me, Dan thought. *Who else would he be so excited about meeting?*

He flipped back to the February entries. According to the dates, Ziggy followed the cleaning lady back into the house on a Thursday, as Dan had guessed. By Saturday, Yuri was dead. Did that mean one of them was the killer or had someone else been there?

Dan went downstairs. He needed to find the cleaner. Where better to look than the kitchen? The outside of the fridge yielded a few sticky notes and a handful of photos evoking enough madness and mayhem to populate an entire Pride float. They included a garish assortment of hustlers, drag queens, musclemen on steroids, several shots of Yuri, and a face Dan recognized as the P-Man's, looking very jolly indeed. Obviously, the picture had been taken in the days before his encounter with a gaggle of randy DQs. But then again, according to Donny, the world of late had become a morass of fluid sexuality. Still, there was nothing that looked like a phone number.

Next, Dan pawed through papers and letters stacked on the kitchen counter. Inside a drawer, a messy assortment of bills and flyers dominated. There was little of interest until he came to a single sheet of note paper with a flowery frill around the edges: a record of payments under the words *Irma — home* and a phone number.

"Gotcha!"

He dialled.

"Hello, is that Irma?"

"Who is it, please?"

The Bela Lugosi accent Ziggy had described.

"Just a person with a very dirty house. A friend gave me your number. He said you were reasonably priced."

"Yes, I am cleaner. What you need?"

"Just a little light housework. We can work on a cash basis, if you prefer."

The words came quickly. "Yes, is good. Where, please?"

He gave her the address as he checked his watch. "This afternoon? Two o'clock?"

"Yes. I am coming."

She hung up. Now all he needed was to go home and wait.

The woman who arrived at his door was small and neat. Plaid skirt and pink blouse. Dove-grey hair. Hardly a killer, but then again, you never knew. Hadn't Ziggy said she was a religious fanatic? Sometimes that was all it took.

She gave him a tentative smile and held out a gloved hand. "I am Irma."

They shook.

"Hello, Irma. I'm Dan."

He watched as she entered and sized up the room. Her face showed approval: this was the home of someone who took pride in his possessions and kept them in good order.

Her eyes lit up when she saw the teak table. "Is nice," she said, running a finger along the grain. She turned back to him. "I am good worker, very clean. Never steal."

"Glad to hear it," Dan said. "I approve of honesty."

She frowned, as though he'd made fun of her. "I am good woman," she assured him. "Where is wacuum?"

Dan showed her to the pantry. She smiled when she saw the Dyson. Undoubtedly a reliable brand. She pulled out a mop and bucket.

Dan left her and went to his office. From time to time, the sounds of cleaning reached his ears. After an hour, she called up to say she'd finished. She waited while he examined her handiwork, the miracles she'd wrought with a vacuum and a few household cleaners. Everything gleamed.

"I leave windows open for fresh," she said. "Upstairs now?"

"Later," he said. "Irma, I know you worked for a man named Yuri Malevski."

A hand flew to her mouth.

"Don't be frightened," Dan said, though the words had little effect. "I just want to ask you a few questions."

"Please — I am afraid!"

He indicated a chair. "Please sit."

She slumped into the seat, rigid with fear.

"You worked at his house in Parkdale?"

She stared at him a few seconds then nodded.

"Was the alarm always on?"

"Alarm?"

"Security system."

She nodded again. "Yes."

"Was there any other way into the house? Any way to get in without tripping the alarm?"

She shook her head. Tears welled in her eyes.

Dan knelt beside her and spoke softly. "I am not with the police. I'm not with Immigration. Do you understand?'

She removed a Kleenex from her sleeve and dabbed at her eyes.

"Yes, thank you." She grasped his arm. Her grip was surprisingly strong. "I don't want to sent back."

"Please tell me about the house."

She looked off, as though seeing it from a distance. "Is much evil. So much drugs and sex. Now murder. So terrible!"

"I understand. That's not why I'm asking these questions. I just want to know about the security system."

"There is no other way inside. Mr. Malevski has code. Numbers code."

"I know about the code. You punch in four numbers and the light turns from red to green."

"Yes, is always code."

"And Yuri texted you a new code whenever he changed it?"

"Yes, before I am coming."

"Did you ever give the code to anyone else?"

She clutched her breast in a portrait of shocked indignation. "Never! I never give this —!"

"It's okay. I just wondered. What about this boy, Santiago Suárez? Do you know him?"

"Yes." She managed a smile. "He is nice boy."

Dan toyed with telling her that Santiago killed himself, but she already looked too frightened. "He had the code?"

"Yes. Is living in house. Nice boy. Very clean."

"When did you last see him there?"

Her face took on its worried cast again. "He is not coming to house after they are fighting."

"Santiago and Mr. Malevski?"

"Yes."

"Did you know about the boy who lived in the small space under the eaves?"

She nodded again.

"His name is Ziggy?"

"Yes. This is correct."

"Did they fight? Did Mr. Malevski hurt Ziggy?" He

raised his fists. Irma started in fright. "I'm sorry, I won't hurt you. Can I make you some tea?"

"Please, I must go now."

She made a move to rise from the chair.

Dan held up his hands. "Not yet. Please."

She sank back.

He waited till she was calm, reading her body language like a wild animal's. "The boy, Ziggy. Is he a good boy?"

"He is ..." She trailed off, as though words had escaped her.

"Different?" Dan suggested.

She touched her head. "Yes. Here."

"Do you think Ziggy killed Yuri? Mr. Malevski?"

Irma winced. She knew something, Dan felt, but how to get her to say it? *You better look closer to home, baby.* What exactly did that mean?

"Yes," she said at last.

"Why? Why would he do that?"

"Sometimes ..." She looked away, as though trying to find a place to disappear, to get away from this madman who had trapped her with his questions. "Sometimes we suffer. Love is hard. God's love is hard!"

God's love! Dan thought of the pamphlets she left on the piano, the ones Ziggy said Yuri laughed about.

"Always God is testing us," she said.

"You cleaned the house on a Thursday?"

"Yes, Thursday always is my cleaning day."

"Thursday always is your cleaning day," he repeated. He named a date. "And that was the last time you were there. Is that correct?"

"Yes. I think so is true."

"Did you see Mr. Malevski that day?"

A quick shake of the head. "No. Upstairs bedroom is locked. Maybe he is sleep."

"So you let yourself into the house with the new code he texted you?"

"Yes, on day before, but front door is locked two times. I must go to back."

Dan's brows knit. "Two times? You mean double-locked?"

"Yes. Always I come and go in front doors, but this time is locked."

He recalled Lydia's comment that the door had been locked from inside. Yuri texted the new code on Wednesday, but before Irma arrived on Thursday someone double-locked the doors. Why? Had Yuri been trying to keep someone out? Or was it something more? *God's love!*

What if Ziggy had lied? He could already have been there when Irma arrived. Perhaps Yuri had met him and let him in. Dan considered: a boy kills an older man who showed him kindness then locks the house up tight. Not simply to hide the death, but out of consideration for the man he loved. He thought of Yuri lying in bed, all dressed up. *Almost as if he was going somewhere*, Lydia had said. Killers often professed to love their victims, dressing them in special clothing and laying them out in poses suggestive of peace and repose, as though a final act of grace had been granted them in death. An immolation, a final dignity, as though to say, "I killed you because I loved you." More than a fetishization, it was an act of veneration: *I loved you enough to kill you. Consider the benefits: you can never grow old, never get sick or suffer pain, never again be abused by anyone, including me. I have granted you immortality. I have given you a clean slate. Nothing can besmirch or dirty you ever again. Thanks to me, you are perfect.* For someone a little off in his thinking — someone like Ziggy — it might make sense.

Irma sniffled.

"What about the week before?" Dan said. "The previous Thursday?"

Her mouth broke into a relieved smile, as though sending her back to that earlier time was a pleasanter memory. A better place to go.

"Yes, always I clean Mr. Malevski house Thursday."

"Was Mr. Malevski there then?"

"Yes, is there."

"And everything was okay?" Dan pressed. "On the previous Thursday?"

"No." Her brow furrowed at the memory. "Is arguing!"

"With who? Santiago?"

"No. Is coming lawyer."

She pinched her mouth with her fingers, as though to stop the words, fearful of the outcome.

"A lawyer came to the house? Charles?"

"Yes. Is angry. Much shouting."

"Mr. Malevski was shouting?"

"No. Lawyer is shouting to Mr. Malevski. Then I turn on wacuum not to hear. When I am finished, lawyer is gone."

After Irma left, more than well paid for her efforts, Dan called Lydia for an update and to give her Irma's number.

"Go easy on her," he said. "She's an illegal. She's very panicky."

"She'll have to adjust. So will I. The chief just asked me to be a part of the investigation team."

She let that one sink in.

"Congratulations."

"I hope so. What about the boy? Did you get anywhere with him?"

"No, he wasn't there. He mentioned a hangout in his last text. I'll drop by and see if I can locate him." Dan paused. "By the way, did the investigating officers interview a dicey-looking neighbour who goes by the name of Pig or the P-Man? He definitely wasn't a fan of Yuri Malevski. I mentioned him earlier, but thought I should ask again. You never know."

He could hear her pawing through the papers in front of her.

"Presumably," she replied, "he has a real name. Which house was it?"

"One door up from the Lockie House going north. Should be easy to figure out."

"I'll look into it, thanks."

Dan considered mentioning what he'd learned about Charles, but wasn't prepared to drop him into it just yet. "By the way," he continued. "I think I know where Yuri Malevski's phone went. Try all the pawn shops in the west end."

"You're amazing. Keep me posted."

The Beaver was a small, dark pub on Queen Street West.

It suited a Goth mentality, Dan decided. That afternoon, however, it was pretty much deserted. The bartender didn't remember anyone named Ziggy, but he pointed to a young waiter making the rounds in an all-black outfit. The waiter confirmed that he knew Ziggy and remembered the last time he was in. It was about a week earlier. He'd been with an older man.

"Could you describe the man?" Dan asked, wishing he had a photograph of Charles to show.

"Not really," the boy said. "Average-looking white guy. He was pretty nondescript. I only remember him because he paid with a Palladium credit card. Never saw one before. I could probably look up his name for you."

"It's okay," Dan said. "Thanks."

Twenty-Five

Stable Boy

Charles had had an argument with Yuri Malevski a week before the bar owner was murdered, but hadn't mentioned a thing about it. Now he was hanging out in counter-culture bars with teenage drug peddlers he claimed not to remember. But then he was a lawyer, just doing what lawyers do. Dan needed to catch him alone, away from Lionel. Lionel said Charles spent his afternoons at the stable. Dan thought about stopping off in the middle of a run, making it look as though he just happened to be passing by, which would seem ridiculous under other circumstances. Then again, why not just show up and see what Charles was like when caught off guard?

He drove to the riding academy then followed the footpath to a paddock on the crest of a hill. Two riders thundered past as he made his way toward a white stable. A pair of Canada jays squabbled in a copse of gnarled branches outside the entrance. Inside, a dun-coloured gelding flicked its ears and looked him over before turning away.

A young man in his early twenties was pulling on a black-and-white-chequered sweater as Dan arrived. He reminded Dan of Ziggy, but minus the make-up. Attractive, with a pouty soap-opera smile and long blond hair. His zipper was down, but he seemed not to have noticed. He gave Dan an appraising look, as though lining up another prospect for later in the day.

"I'm looking for Charles," Dan said.

The boy nodded to the back of the stables. "Down there."

Charles frowned when Dan walked in.

"The kid out front said you were in here," Dan told him.

"My stable hand," Charles said. "Should I be surprised to see you? I thought our business was concluded."

He gripped a saddle and swung it from the counter where he'd been cleaning it to a mount on the wall. The smell of manure and hay mingled in the air, a curious combination that made Dan nostalgic for all the barns he'd never explored back in his youth.

"Sorry for dropping in unexpectedly. I wanted to talk to you alone," Dan said.

"Have you reconsidered my offer?"

"No, not exactly."

A palomino munched happily on its nosebag of oats, shifting positions noisily. A hoof rang out against concrete. On the wall, a curb bit gleamed in a shaft of light.

"Nice hobby, by the way."

Charles glanced at him. "I wasn't born rich, if that's what you're suggesting. I had to earn this. It pisses me off when people tell me they think money is dirty."

"I don't object to money," Dan said. "Though I often object to the values of people who think money is important. I grew up poor and overcame it, but ours is probably the last generation that could do that. My son is growing up in a world where he might not be able to afford the education he deserves. His peers may never be able to buy homes. Greed is the problem, not the economy. As the experts have been telling us for decades, we can afford to feed the entire world. We just don't."

"Nice speech. Sad to say, I don't really care. But in case there are any doubts, I do care about my husband's safety."

"Then I hope you show it by hiring someone to look out for him properly."

Charles gave him a curt glance. "Is that what you came here to tell me?"

"Lionel wants Yuri's killer found. I worry he might do something to put himself in jeopardy if he thinks it would help make that happen. That's why he needs protection."

"Have you got any names for me?"

Dan held out a small square of paper. "Here are two who come highly recommended."

Charles tucked it in his pocket.

"Thanks."

He picked up a rake and began dragging dirty straw out of an empty stall, his powerful body throwing more force into the action than seemed necessary. When he was done, he tossed an armful of clean straw onto the floor. So much for having a stable boy, Dan thought.

"There have been two deaths so far," Dan continued. "First Yuri's and now Santiago's. On top of that, I was attacked in Quebec. Are you willing to risk a third death, and possibly a fourth?"

Charles stopped and stared. "A fourth? Whose?"

"Yours. Don't kid yourself. Lionel may be the only one directly connected with Yuri's bar, but these people won't hesitate to put you out of the picture if they think you pose any sort of threat to them."

Charles's expression was incredulous. "For the record, I don't believe Santiago was murdered, despite what Lionel may think. I don't contradict him because he needs to believe it for whatever reason, but the facts clearly indicate it was a suicide. Even the police agree." A suspicious look crossed his face. "Are you saying you think it was murder, too?"

"Until we have any reason to believe otherwise, I wouldn't entirely discount it."

Charles threw his hands up in the air, startling the palomino, who snorted and stomped. "I'm a lawyer, Dan. I look at things from every angle. Then I ask questions and calculate the odds on whether something happened one way or another, and I try to prove it. That's what lawyers do. It's not about morality or justice. To me, it seems a simple cut-and-dried case: Santiago Suárez killed Yuri Malevski and then committed suicide out of grief or shame."

"Maybe," Dan said. "One thing that stands out for me in all of this is the front door of Malevski's house.

It was double-locked from inside. If you're committing a murder, wouldn't you just leave and not worry about the doors? Someone was bound to find him sooner or later. And it's not as if Santiago needed time to leave the country, since we now know he stuck around. Unfortunately for him."

Charles shrugged impatiently. "Then maybe it was a hustler or a drug user or even this kid Ziggy everyone keeps talking about."

"The one you had sex with? It says so in his diary."

Charles whirled on him. "Fuck off, why don't you? Why are you even here? You said you're not interested in pursuing the case any further, so drop it."

"I'll take that as an admission of guilt. He got pretty depressed over it, too, in case you have any compassion. He's a lost kid and you were fucking with him. But if you're not interested in him, then why did you get his hopes up by taking him out again last week?"

Charles stared him down. "The reason I went out with Ziggy was to try to explain nicely why we couldn't have an affair. And yes, I thought I owed him at least that much. Which brings us back to Santiago. Whether the murder was an accident or a crime of passion doesn't matter, though I will happily accept it wasn't premeditated, if you like. But this cock-eyed theory that the police killed first Yuri Malevski and then Santiago is beginning to wear a bit thin. And I, for one, would like a little closure on this case so that Lionel and I can get on with our lives. It's over."

"And you're willing to risk both your lives to prove it?"

Charles's lip curled. "Give me a break. If someone wanted us dead, we would already be dead."

"I hope you're right," Dan said. "But I still worry about it."

A floorboard creaked behind them. The boy had slipped quietly back inside. Dan turned and saw he'd discovered his wayward zipper at last. Charles took him by the arm and they stepped outside.

Dan glanced around. In the corner, a large wooden feed box was secured with a metal clasp. He pushed the clasp through the hoop and flipped open the lid. No feed inside, just a thick tarp with dark stains on one edge. Dan's mind went into overdrive: they were close to Overlea Bridge. What if Charles killed Santiago and kept his body here until he could dispose of it? Lionel had said Charles knew how to make money disappear. Perhaps he'd done just that and Santiago found out about it, becoming a threat. It was melodramatic, but that didn't make it any less plausible. Certainly no less plausible than thinking Ziggy killed Yuri Malevski out of love. Dan recalled Donny's suggestion that the police killed Yuri over unpaid protection money. Maybe he should take out a Netflix subscription, too. He'd be in good company. He closed the lid and slid the hasp back.

Footsteps approached. Charles returned. "Thank you again for the names. I'll look into it, but I doubt it's necessary now. If we needed protection from anyone, it was Santiago. I didn't really know him, but he had a motive. He was hoping Yuri would marry him for citizenship. When that didn't happen, they argued. I think that's what's behind it."

"What did you and Yuri argue about the week before his death?"

Charles stared without replying.

"You were at his house the week before he died, having a very loud argument with him."

"Who told you that?"

"A first-hand witness. Very credible, from what I could tell."

The lawyer's eyes bored through him. Dan held his gaze.

"I went there to tell Yuri I didn't like the things he was making Lionel do. The payoffs, the money he had to hide. I may have raised my voice, but I certainly didn't do anything to harm him. Anyway, I was in Mexico when he died. Lionel left that evening and I joined him two days later."

"Lucky for you."

"Yes, it is lucky for me," Charles said. "I didn't know you'd joined the prosecution for Yuri's murder, but then you are friends with the chief of police." He checked his watch. "I have to go. Is this ridiculous inquisition over?"

"Thanks for answering my questions," Dan said.

Back in the car, Dan considered the possibilities buzzing around in his head. From the start, Charles had pointed to Santiago as being the likeliest choice for Yuri's killer. According to Lionel, Charles wanted the police to pin the murder on him and be done with it. And of course it had been Charles who first brought Dan in to find Santiago.

Charles and Yuri had argued not long before Yuri's death, but he only had Charles's word for what caused the argument. Despite being in Mexico at the time, he could still in some way have been responsible for what happened to the bar owner. Maybe that was what Santiago knew. And where did Ziggy fit in? Charles and his Palladium credit cards would surely seem impressive to someone like Ziggy, a messed-up young man who could scarcely conceive of his own future. Ziggy was no fan of Santiago, according to his diary. Had he ever been to the stables? What had they really discussed that night at the Beaver? It would have been at most a day or two before Santiago's body was found.

Dan's mind was on fire. He pulled out his cell and dialled Lydia Johnston's number. She answered right away.

He launched in without a preamble. "This may be a strange question: did the coroner's report mention anything about horse hair on the body retrieved from below the Overlea Bridge?"

"It is a strange question, but coming from you, Dan, I'm not so sure it isn't relevant in some weird way that you haven't shared with me yet. Should I ask why you want to know?"

"Just a tangent I'm following. I saw a movie on Netflix the other night. There was a body in a box in a stable."

"Is this the same movie with the bell tower?"

"Different one."

She laughed. "Okay, I'll indulge you. Let me get back to you on it."

Dan put his car in gear and drove out of the park. Sunset was breaking on the underbelly of clouds. A streak of blood seemed to be spreading over the river.

Twenty-Six

Bloodless

Dan woke to a chilled house. Winter was over, but it had left a stark reminder it would be back. With a flick of the thermostat, the furnace chugged into life. In the kitchen, he was greeted with a sorry sight: Hank's floral apology had lost all its blossoms. Two naked stems extended from the pot. The leaves were still waxy and resilient looking, but the petals had fallen to the floor in soft, pale clumps like the bloodless brides of Dracula.

Ralph glanced up from his basket. He wasn't wearing his guilty look, the one that said he'd done something wrong. Clearly, he hadn't been up early eating flowers and spitting them on the floor. With a shock, Dan saw the open window behind the pot. He reached over to shut it, cutting off the stream of frigid air as his mind leapt at the implications: someone had broken into the house while he was asleep upstairs.

He looked around, but nothing seemed awry. Ralph had doubtless slept in his basket all night. No alarm had sounded. Then he remembered: Irma had left the window open to give the house a breath of fresh air. That was all. Nothing to panic over. No doubt she would have closed it later, but he'd terrified her with his questions about Yuri Malevski. He wanted to kick himself for his stupidity. With a police guard outside his house, he'd gone to bed leaving his place vulnerable and exposed. At least he'd talked Ked into staying with his mother.

It was just seven, but his answering machine yielded a message from Inspector Johnston. Yes, her officers had spoken with a neighbour of Yuri Malevski who answered to the name of P-Man. He had, despite his weird moniker, seemed an ordinary Joe to them. And Dan's assumption, based on whatever movie, had been wrong. There were no traces of horsehair on either the victim or his clothes. Dan felt deflated. Perhaps it really was just a simple suicide and Charles had been correct all along in assuming Santiago killed himself out of a combination of guilt and grief.

He looked in the mirror with displeasure at his lined, unshaven face. He needed to get a grip before the day got totally out of hand. Coffee brewed as the house warmed. The phone rang. It was Kendra.

"Hey, how are things on the sunny side of town?" he asked.

Lately, he preferred to keep things light between them, conscious of the need to disarm her fears before they worked themselves into a serious concern. These days he was treading carefully on all fronts.

"We're fine. Ked's gone off to school. Something about a big science project coming up." She paused. "He told me a little about what's been happening. I have to say you scored big points by letting him stay with you the other night. I just hope you knew what you were doing."

"Not to worry, we were safe," Dan told her. "But the truth is, he didn't give me a choice. There was no way I could dissuade him. In any case, we were armed to the teeth, cops on the doorstep, the whole nine yards."

Kendra said nothing.

"You know I wouldn't do anything to jeopardize Ked's life."

"What about yours?"

"I'm doing my best," he said, knowing there was scant reassurance in the statement even if it were true.

"Dan, we're worried for you. Please don't treat us like idiots."

"I don't," he said softly. "Believe me, I don't."

He had Donny on the phone.

"What movie has a bridge and a bell tower?"

"Category?"

"Thriller, I think."

There was barely a pause.

"*Vertigo*, 1958. Kim Novak and Jimmy Stewart."

"Hitchcock?"

"Of course!"

"Never saw it."

Donny snorted. "Barbarian. It was voted one of the forty greatest movies of all time."

"Oh, really? For the record? I hate Hitchcock. I feel the psychology is unsound."

"Unsound?" Donny spluttered.

"It's not like real life.

"Of course not. It's a movie!"

"Well, it's unbelievable," Dan insisted.

"What about *Psycho*?"

"Leave Norman Bates alone. He's okay."

"Fine. Nevertheless, the movie you want is *Vertigo*."

Dan paused to regroup his thoughts. "Does someone die falling from a bridge?"

"No, from a bell tower. The same woman who tries to kill herself by jumping into the water beneath the Golden Gate Bridge in San Francisco."

"Suicide heaven," Dan mused.

"You got it."

"Was it a murder?"

"No. The first time it was faked. The real death at the end is an accident."

"Hmm. I'm not sure this fits the scenario. The one I'm looking for has a suicide from a bridge and a murder inside a house."

"Yuri Malevski's?"

"I can't keep anything from you." Dan paused. "What connects the two deaths in the film?"

"Love and regret."

"Well, the theme works. Anything to do with immigration?"

"Not at all. A man kills his wife, then hires Kim Novak to replace her and fake her suicide. Since she's supposed to be dead, she has to disappear. All's good till bumbling Jimmy Stewart comes onto the scene. He finds Novak, only she says she's someone else. Trouble ensues. She returns to the scene of the fake suicide and climbs the bell tower just as she realizes she's in love with Jimmy. Alas, this time she falls to her death for real."

"And the moral of this quaint tale?"

"If you're afraid of heights, stay off the roof."

"An apt precept."

"Who got you onto this kick?"

"A transie named Jan."

"Ah, yes. A stalwart figure in the ghetto. Jan was once part of Yuri's in-crowd till rumours spread that she had one of his delivery boys busted for drug peddling. Seems he'd been her boyfriend, but he jilted Jan for a newer, prettier face on the block."

"Is that fact or just ghetto lore?"

"The latter, probably. Why? What have you heard?"

"From Jan comes the tale that Yuri thought Jan was coming on to Santiago, who as we know was prone to deploying his charms on others."

"Huh. So what do I know? They're a sordid bunch." Donny paused. "Are you all right? You're sounding a little jittery and obsessive."

"I'm okay. It's been weird. I almost had sex with a nineteen-year-old the other day."

"Almost?"

"He was stoned. I turned him down. He came on to me, I feel I should add."

"Congratulations."

"For turning him down or for being propositioned by someone half my age?"

"Either. Both. Many wouldn't have let that deter them."

"It just felt weird. It was Ziggy, by the way."

"Deploying his charms, as you said. Yes, he likes older men. He tried it on with me, too. I had zero interest, though I have no qualms about shagging a younger man. You have to remember it's not the same for us queers. Two men are on common ground, even if their experience levels are unequal. We're a different tribe from the straight world. It's like native justice. They want their own set of values recognized. Why shouldn't we?"

"Well, maybe. But I read his diary and saw in black and white that he's depressed and confused. I wouldn't want to add to that."

"Because you care about these things, Danny. It's what makes you the difficult-wonderful person you are. You do the work of saints and angels every day and don't think twice about it."

"I'm hardly a saint. My life is far too messy."

"Ah, but that's where you're wrong. Saints are made, not born. Mother Theresa came from a wealthy family and had to cast it off. Same with Gautama Buddha. Mandela was jailed for conspiracy to commit acts of violence against the state. He went to prison, got squeezed like carbon into a diamond before he became a saint. It doesn't just happen. Sainthood is thrust on you."

"Okay. In the meantime, I've got a killer to track down and a movie to watch." Dan paused. "You know, I miss all these cultural conversations with you trying to convince me that black-and-white films are inherently superior to colour —"

"They are."

"— or that some quirky, obscure jazz musician was the unheralded genius of his age."

"Lennie Tristano. I'll pencil you in for some art therapy."

"Thanks, I'd appreciate it, but I don't want to take away from your time with Prabin."

"We're not joined at the hip. At least not yet."

No cigarettes had joined the conversation, Dan noted after hanging up.

Dan called the hospital to ask about Domingo. He was connected with the front desk. The voice hesitated. Dan recognized the Irish nurse's accent immediately.

"This is her half-bother," he said. "I talked to you yesterday."

She sounded relieved for a moment. "Oh, yes. I remember you." The pause told him. "I'm sorry. Your sister died early this morning."

For a moment, he couldn't speak. The blood drained from his face; his feet felt unsteady. He wondered if her train had come at last, and, if so, was she glad or disappointed with its long-awaited arrival. Dan had an urge to put the phone down and walk out of the house and never come back.

"Are you all right?" the nurse asked.

"Uh, yes. I'm … I'm all right," he said.

"I'm sorry to tell you over the phone, but as you're a relative we're allowed to do that."

"Yes, thank you. Very kind."

Dan stood and paced. He didn't want Ked to see him in this state. He put on his jacket, grabbed his keys, and left. The car seemed to steer itself of its own accord, down to the lakeshore near Cherry Beach. Something inside him wanted space, broad vistas. Here the sky arched bleakly overhead. The snow had melted, but ice lingered along the shore like the vestiges of a vanished world. He sat and stared across the water till numbness replaced the shock.

What had he told Ked? That you could understand life's problems intellectually, but you could never fully prepare yourself emotionally. A good lesson. It had been a long time since he'd shed tears, but he felt a great emptiness knowing this ball of joyous energy and goodwill had gone out of the world. Maybe the only consolation for Domingo's death was in not knowing her son had predeceased her after losing the battle for his mental well-being.

Dan thought of his own genetic heritage, the legacy of two alcoholics. Both had died early, his mother when he was just four. Nothing could have brought her back, but there were times when he wondered whether his life would have been any better had she lived. She'd been more of a good-time girl than a silent abuser like his father; her wrongdoing lay in the neglect of her son. But between the two of them, what chance did he have? Dark side or light, the odds were against him. Dan, too, loved alcohol, but he loved his son more. So it might be true after all that love could save you, as long as one outweighed the other.

The loss Dan felt as a boy had eventually been sup-planted by rage, overwhelming him with paroxysms of feeling. He'd had his moments of smashing things in anger, staving in the side of a filing cabinet at work and once, in a private moment of drunken grief and rage after being dumped by a partner, he'd grabbed a ball-peen hammer as it flashed through his mind to hit himself senseless, though he'd checked the urge. Rage was a glaring red eye in the darkness, a fury coming at you from out of nowhere. It exploded when you least expected it, and got bigger and more menacing when you tried to repress it. The last thing Dan ever wanted was for his son to have to live with it, but in his drinking years it had been there until Ked told him to stop. *Stop drinking, Dad.* And he had. So far, he had.

He'd looked into the darkness and lived to tell the tale. The rage had largely dissipated on discovering the circumstances of his mother's early death, a dismal tale of drunkenness and betrayal, but now and then it returned with a vengeance, startling even him and making him drift off in the middle of conversations, averting his gaze to avoid eye contact with people he despised, where once he would have stared them down. From waking sweating from traumatic nightmares through to anxious nights where sleep never came, all he knew was that his subconscious was at war with itself. Despair had been a keynote for many years; now it was an undercurrent running through everything he did, a battle he'd been fighting for years.

What had Donny said? That he was a saint. Not true, Dan thought. Rather, he was a shepherd keeping track of wayward sheep. To him, his life seemed unremarkable, or nearly so. He'd spent the first half as a lost boy, the second half finding others who got lost, as if it were a given that loss should be at the core of his existence. But if he got lost, who would come looking for him? Ked, of course. Donny, too. Yes, and Kendra. So, three people. That wasn't bad. Some people had no one.

After a while, he turned the car around and headed for the ghetto. He'd spent many afternoons there knocking back a few in the days when he used to drink. Domingo had joined him from time to time. She never encouraged his excesses, though. In fact, he recalled how she once told him in a gently reproving tone that he needed to put fatherhood above his indulgences. She was right, of course, though at the time he thought she was overreacting.

Getting drunk wasn't his intention. He simply wanted to forget, if only for an hour. He also didn't want to risk seeing Hank, so he went to Crews & Tangos, twin bars housed in a gaudy old mansion on Church Street. The place had a reputation for being a lesbian hangout. All the better, he thought, as he was less likely to have to fend off hopeful men thinking he might be the answer to their problems, if only for an afternoon.

He ordered a Scotch, barely registering the bartender's queries as to whether he wanted it neat or on the rocks. A glass of yellow liquor — the drinker's fool's gold — was set in front of him and the bartender left him to his ponderings. Not everyone came in to socialize.

He turned his attention to the alcohol. It reminded him of all the long days and nights of one-too-many. The first went down without leaving a mark. The second barely registered. He was standing on the edge of no man's land. Carelessness took over for an instant and he ordered a third, feeling its long, slow burn as he swallowed.

It occurred to him that he should hand over his keys now rather than take a chance later. He'd just pulled them from his pocket when the bartender leaned down to him and nodded to the far corner of the room.

"A friend over there says he'd like to join you."

Dan looked over and saw Sergeant Trposki watching him. He nodded.

The cop came and sat next to him, dressed in jeans and a black T-shirt. He looked different from when Dan had seen him at police headquarters. He wasn't sure why, but it was more than that he'd been in uniform then and was in mufti now.

"Bad day?" Trposki ventured, with a nod to the empty glass.

"You could say that."

"I used to think maybe there wasn't any other kind." Trposki said. "By the way, I didn't follow you here. I was just finishing up with a date when I saw you come in."

That was the difference, Dan thought. He looked sheepish, as though he'd rather not be seen in a bar.

The bartender came by.

"Soda water, please," Trposki said.

"Not a drinker?" Dan asked.

"I've had my regulation drink for the day." The cop nodded ironically. "I'm a drinker when I choose. I prefer straight rye, doesn't matter how old it is. But lately I've learned to hold back. Too many mornings after the blackout the night before."

"You had a problem?"

"Still do. I just control it better. I knew it was a bad

idea having a blind date in a bar, but it didn't work out for more reasons than that."

Dan sighed and pushed his glass aside. He called to the bartender. "Make that two soda waters."

Trposki extended a hand. "I'm Nick, by the way. Please don't call me Officer Trposki in public."

"Nick it is. And I'm still Dan."

They shook.

"There were days I used to drink until I thought my blood must be almost pure alcohol," Nick told him. "Did you ever get like that?"

Dan nodded. "Pretty much for years. Can't say I'm proud of it."

"What made you stop?"

"My son. I knew I had to be a better dad."

Nick's face clouded over. "Mine made me start. My boy died when he was five. Leukemia."

"I'm really sorry to hear," Dan said. "That has to be about as rough as it gets."

"It was. And I needed to forget. One day about ten years into it, I had a realization that not only had I lost my son, but I was also in the process of throwing my own life away, as if that could somehow bring him back."

The bartender set two glasses on the counter. Icy cool, with lime wedges and straws.

Nick lifted his glass and drank. "When I saw you in action in Quebec," he said, "I thought, 'There's one tough son of a bitch.' But you're not all tough guy, are you? You've got some soft spots. Your son, for one, and probably you bleed for your clients as well, trying to deliver the goods to stop their pain."

Dan nodded. "I still feel things. How about you? Are you a cop for the love of the job? Making the world a better place and that sort of thing?"

Trposki gave him an assessing look. "I am, in fact. Bet you didn't think cops were like that anymore."

"I've known a few."

"That's how I got to know Lydia Johnston. I liked her rep, so I asked to work with her. When she told me about the anti-corruption detail, I said I knew a bar owner who was being hit up regularly."

Dan's gaze focused on Nick. "You knew Yuri?"

"From way back. Another lifetime. We went to school together in Macedonia."

"No kidding!"

"No shit. When my folks moved to Canada, we lost touch. Then a few years ago I heard he was owner of the Saddle. We had a good laugh to know we both turned out gay and in Toronto. Me a cop and him a bar owner. When he told me about the payouts, I told Lydia and she got the ball rolling." He stared off for a moment. "I was real burned when he got killed, let me tell you."

"I hope you figure out who killed him," Dan said simply.

"I will."

Conversation faltered. The sad, doomed voice of Amy Winehouse, a fellow addict, took over the airwaves. The bartender looked over with no real expectations. They weren't big spenders, but they were his only customers.

"You single?" Nick asked after a moment. "I only ask because you likely wouldn't be drinking alone if you were. That's probably another weak spot."

"Guilty as charged. I just don't want to drink at home where Ked could find me."

"Ked?"

"My son, Kedrick. It's Old English. His mother's Syrian. Don't ask. It all manages to work out somehow. Unlike the rest of my life. The romance, especially."

Nick smiled. "Heavy drinking and relationships usually don't mix. Or if they do, you're doubly in trouble for having someone to encourage you. I only had one keeper among all my boyfriends. Best man I ever met, but alcohol got the better of me."

"Stay friends?"

"Nah, it was beyond repair." Nick shrugged. "My fault. No self-deprecation there. I destroyed it. Thought I was the tough guy. Couldn't bear to see myself through his eyes, so I tried to prove I was right. He couldn't stand me afterwards."

"That's rough." Dan looked at his face. "How's your jaw, by the way."

Nick laughed, reached up and worked his lower jawbone back and forth. "A bit tender. It was a good workout, though. You?"

"Still a bit sore. That flip caught me by surprise. You're good."

"I keep in practice. Works on boyfriends, too." He winked. "Okay, time for me to scram."

Nick stood and handed Dan a business card. "Any late-night urges you want to resist badly enough, call me. I'm usually up howling at the moon."

Dan's lips curved into a smile, his first that day.

Twenty-Seven

Breaking Glass

Dan was surprised when he heard Adele's message informing him of the arrangements for Domingo's funeral. He'd expected to have to scour the newspapers for information. She couldn't have disliked him that much or else she'd softened with age. He'd called to offer his condolences and inform her of Lonnie's fate, arranging for the delivery of his ashes and suggesting a double service. She was stoic about it. Like Domingo, she'd accepted the probability years before, but the logistics of combining funerals must have given her pause, compounding her misery.

By the morning of the funeral, Dan still hadn't heard from Ziggy since his text in Le Drague. There'd been a lot of water under the bridge since then. Maybe it was time to have another chat with the Goth-loving kid in light of what he now knew. A nagging feeling told Dan he should be wary of meeting him in private, but he'd deal with it when the time came.

He checked his watch: it was a little before 10:00 a.m. The funeral was at two. If he got dressed first, he could swing by Parkdale, have a chat with him and get back downtown in time for the service. He sent a text: *Hey! In your neighbourhood. Coming over now.*

There was someone on the stoop when he pulled up outside the Lockie House. For a second, Dan thought it was Ziggy, but this guy was heavier and dressed in the nondescript brown jacket of delivery drivers. Two potted plants sat at his feet.

He turned when Dan approached. Attractive. Nice build, dark hair. This was one of Yuri's special deliveries of rare flowers, no doubt.

"Are those for Yuri Malevski?" Dan asked.

The man watched him curiously. "Yes."

"I don't know if anyone's home."

"Okay, thanks." He stooped and picked up the plants. Orchids.

"If you want, you can leave them with me" Dan suggested. "I'll make sure they get inside."

The man shrugged. "I'll come back."

It's okay, Dan thought. *I wouldn't trust me either, buddy.*

"I don't know when you'll be able to deliver them," Dan said.

"No worries," the man said, turning and walking down the drive. "They're too expensive to leave."

Dan scratched his head. That was what the delivery man had told Ked on bringing Hank's gift to the house. He tapped in the numbers, but the light stayed red. Someone had changed the code. His knocks resounded inwardly, but there was no reply. Maybe Ziggy was inside. He stepped back and looked at the house with a twinge of foreboding. His mind flashed on a passage in Ziggy's diary: *I'd rather be dead.* It was disconcerting, especially combined with the boy's bravado in declaring he would simply lock the doors and "unplug" himself.

Dan went around the house banging on each window, but it was futile. He tossed a clump of earth against the porthole in Ziggy's bedroom. It burst open and showered him with dirt. There was no response, no pale face at the glass.

He went back to the front door and tried the code again, thinking he might have entered the numbers incorrectly. Still red. He pulled out his cell and dialled Lionel, but the call went straight to voicemail. He found the couple's home number. Charles answered.

"It's Dan. Dan Sharp. I need the new code to Yuri Malevski's house. It's important."

"Sorry, what?"

"The entry code. It's been changed. I think Ziggy might have done something to himself. He could be inside."

Charles hesitated. Dan felt his anger building.

"Come on, Charles. What's the code?"

"Dan, I —"

"The number, damn it! You must know the code."

Charles sounded dumbfounded. "I don't have the code. I've never had it!"

"He could be dying!"

"Dan, I don't know the code," he insisted. "Let me ask Lionel."

Dan heard a terse conversation in the background. After a long wait, a groggy-sounding Lionel came on the line. More sleeping pills, Dan thought. Charles's influence.

"Hi, Dan. What's the problem?"

"I'm at Yuri Malevski's. It may be nothing, but I'm worried that Ziggy might have tried to kill himself. I want to go in and check."

"You think he tried to kill himself? Why?"

"Just something I read in his diary. The code's been changed. If you have the new code, please tell me."

"No, I didn't change it."

Dan pounded a fist against the door and heard it shudder within.

"Do you have any idea who else might have done it?"

"Maybe someone at the bar. I could make a call ..."

"It'll be too late. I'll call you back."

He glanced over at the fence dividing Yuri Malevski's property from his neighbour's. Now would be a good time for the P-Man to make one of his unwanted appearances, but there was no sign of him.

He looked around. The greenhouse windows glinted ominously in the morning sun. He hung up and dialled Inspector Johnston's number. She answered.

"It's Dan Sharp. I'm breaking into the Malevski mansion," he spouted at her. "I can't wait for emergency services."

"I assume you have a good reason," she said calmly.

"Damn good," he said, picking up the end of a hose and smashing a pane of glass. "I think there's a kid in there who may be trying to kill himself."

"I'll send someone right over."

He was upstairs in Ziggy's room when he heard the sirens. He got back down in time to let the emergency crew in as the first of three vehicles arrived. Dan looked at them sheepishly.

"I was wrong," he told them. "I thought there was a suicide in progress in here."

The faces staring back at him were curious, not judgmental.

"Did you receive a call from someone in distress, sir?" an attendant asked.

"No, I jumped to a wrong conclusion based on a … a disturbing diary entry. Someone changed the entry code and I thought it was to keep me out."

Fifteen minutes later, Lydia Johnston joined the gathering. Dan led her upstairs to the hidden room and the diary. It lay face-down on the pillow where Dan had last seen it.

"Okay," she said, after reading the passage where Ziggy stated his wish to die.

"Okay?" Dan asked.

"I understand your concern. I would have done the same." She gave him a long, hard look. "What made you panic?"

Dan shook his head. For a moment, he couldn't remember.

"There was a delivery guy here when I arrived. Yuri used to give out the code when he had plants coming, but it was changed. It triggered something in me."

"So who changed it?" Lydia asked.

"I have no idea," Dan said. "I called Lionel, but he didn't know it had been changed, either."

They went back downstairs. Lydia busied herself with the EMS drivers. Dan went into the greenhouse. The air was humid, as it had been on his other visits. He thought of Ked's sling psychrometer as he looked over the orchids. Only two appeared to be thriving. The rest had died. *Odd*, he thought. He reached up and pulled out a tag, jotting the Latin name in his notebook.

Once a through search for Ziggy had been made in the house, Dan headed to Radio City. This time the concierge wouldn't allow him in until he phoned up to be sure Dan was welcome, though "welcome" wasn't exactly the word Dan would have used. Unexpected, certainly, but not welcome.

Charles opened the door. "You have a lot of nerve coming here."

"I came to apologize," Dan told him.

"Apology accepted," Charles said coldly. He paused. "How's Ziggy?"

"Good of you to ask. He wasn't inside the house. I'm still not certain he's okay. I wondered if you might have any idea where he is."

"No," Charles said. "I wouldn't worry. He'll turn up. He always does."

Dan saw a pair of expensive-looking bags sitting at the end of the couch. Charles caught his glance.

"We're taking a short trip," he said. "Up north for a few days to a wilderness retreat. We thought it easier than hiring someone to look after us here in the city."

Dan envisaged a smart little log cabin in Killarney, the park's famous pink quartz throwing off a quiet glow in the sunset. He heard footsteps. The bedroom door opened. Lionel stood there, dishevelled, in a bathrobe. He caught Dan's eye and quickly shook his head. Was it anger at his continued invasiveness in their lives that Dan saw there, or was it fear?

"A trip would be smart," Dan said, though in the back of his mind there was something vaguely unsettling about the idea of Lionel being alone in the wilderness with Charles. He envisaged a canoe tipping in white-water rapids, news reports of an accidental drowning. Maybe a fall from the steep cliffs of Manitoulin. No one to hear, no one to see.

Charles checked his watch. "You'll excuse us. We've got a plane to catch in a few hours. Neither of us expects to see you again."

"No, I ..."

"Goodbye."

Twenty-Eight

What Remains

Dan had a funeral to attend. Passing the Saddle and Bridle on the way, he wasn't surprised to see a For Sale sign in its windows. The world was rapidly moving on, while he dawdled and wasted time on a matter his rational mind had told him was better left to the police in the first place.

The afternoon was sombre, with precisely the sort of weather befitting a funeral. As if knowing that, April showers began beading down against the thump of his wipers, dragging long lines across the windshield like some slow, sinister form of water torture. He barely made it to the church on time.

If Dan ever chose to attend a religious institution, it would be the progressive Metropolitan Community Church in leafy Riverdale. It had been on the front lines in the fight against AIDS discrimination and later hosted the world's first legal same-sex marriage. He approved of the church's activities, if not of religion's many wars of flesh and spirit.

The MCC was also known for its musical performances, hosting an outstanding choir and guest artists. They were said to throw a rocking good party, too. It was no surprise Domingo had chosen it for her service. The service would be less an oration than a celebration of her life and loves.

As Dan entered, he saw two urns placed near the altar. One for Domingo, he presumed, and the other Lonnie's. The teddy bear from the hospital sat between them.

Domingo's brothers and sisters were there, as well as a few young nieces and nephews. They seemed oddly subdued, as though in the presence of God they'd submitted to a higher power. Domingo had told Dan how her fellow islanders embraced religion with a fervour that often included a strong dose of homophobia. When gays were dying by the bucketful during the AIDS crisis, the righteous wound themselves into a frenzy proclaiming that God had avenged himself on the sinners. But no one ever said God had avenged himself on the money-launderers when 9-11 happened, Dan thought. He recalled Irma's pamphlets, her declaration that God's love could be hard. *Yes*, he thought. *God's love is hard as hell, but better not to point fingers till after you're dead.*

On the far side of the church, seated in uneasy proximity, were the other righteous, a handful of hardcore lesbians seemingly willing to fight over the remains. They kept to themselves for the most part, shooting occasional watchful glances over at Domingo's family. For the moment, there appeared to be a détente between the warring factions.

Dan made his way to Adele to extend his condolences. "She loved you very much," he said simply. "Right to the very end."

"Not enough to let me have my way." Her expression was stony. She nodded to where Domingo's family were clustered. "Look at them. They despise us. I can't believe they came."

"They're behaving," Dan said. "I doubt they would make a scene in a church."

Adele sighed. "They're only here because Domingo made me promise to let them come."

"Of course. She was a peacemaker. That's why she asked you to let them come to the funeral. Who knows? Maybe there's one small girl here today who will see you and think that her auntie's friend was a nice lady, and maybe grow up less afraid of being a lesbian because of what she witnesses here today."

Adele's mouth was down-turned. "That's a bit optimistic, isn't it?"

"You can't change people overnight," Dan said. "We can wish it were otherwise, but it isn't so."

She stared at him, struggling with her feelings. Dan wondered if his words had angered her. Instead, her expression softened.

"You're right," she said. "That's what Domingo would have said. Thanks."

Dan took a seat in the middle ground, among what he thought of as the non-religious and non-politically motivated. From the corner of his eye, he saw Donny and Prabin enter, holding hands as they passed down the aisle and sat behind the lesbians. A few of Domingo's relatives took note of this pairing of black and brown seating themselves on the wrong side. What were they thinking? Dan wondered. The Bible had prohibitions on almost everything, including the intermarrying of races. Something to frown on for every occasion. No joy left unpunished.

At that moment, the minister began. This man was also a peacemaker, Dan knew, though he had a reputation for being a firebrand when necessary. You don't get to conduct the world's first same-sex marriage without a fight.

"Death is a profound force that can divide people," he began solemnly, looking from one side of the church to the other. He smiled. "Or it can bring them together."

Dan glanced around at the two minorities, both facing discrimination from the world at large. They should have had much in common, but they fought one another instead. If Domingo had been there, she'd be offering an ironic commentary on the combative elements brought together by this service in her honour. Perhaps death really was the only common meeting ground.

The minister's words buzzed overhead as he described Domingo's upbringing in her native Caribbean. Despite having shunned her, her family seemed pleased by this recognition that she'd been one of theirs. He then went on to say how she'd found a new home and family in a community reviled by many. The rainbow, he said, symbolized God's love for all creatures, while declaring that the persecution faced by the LGBT community today was no different from that of early Christians. Dan heard a murmur among the family, whether in dissent or recognition of the truth of his words wasn't clear. The pastor continued, captivating them with his voice and sermon. If all religious leaders were so engaging and inclusive, Dan thought, they might be worth listening to now and again.

A buzz alerted him to an incoming text. He pulled out his cell. While some were being buried, life was quietly going on outside the church's walls. Lydia had texted to say Yuri's phone had been found in a pawn shop. *Fingerprints check out as Suárez's,* she added. Dan experienced a brief curiosity as to what messages had been left on it, then forgot again as the service continued.

The minister raised his arms and Dan stood with the others. For a moment, he felt something like pride: pride in his city, pride in his community, pride in his country. All these disparate tribes coming together to celebrate the life of a woman born in a land and culture so different from his own. Yet here they were, in an openly gay church, commemorating their faith together in a place that represented every nation, even to the point of allowing all who came there to reshape and colour the fabric of the land.

"Let not your heart be troubled: ye believe in God, believe also in me," intoned the minister.

Dan glanced at the heads bowed in prayer. He envied the untroubled faith of this man who extolled such brave words and the believers who calmly accepted them, even if he could not.

"In my Father's house are many mansions: if it were not so, I would have told you."

A fervent *Amen!* rang out. Dan considered Yuri Malevski's mansion. It too had been a place for all, even the outcasts: drug users, immigrants, transsexuals. It was a dream Malevski had believed in to the point of helping even those who sometimes despised him. He thought of Irma, who thought his life an abomination, even while he paid her bills and calmly accepted her censure. So too with Yuri's young lover, also from another culture, whom he accepted under his roof where they once planned a future together.

"I go to prepare a place for you ..."

And then there was the odd boy, Ziggy, who also relied on Yuri's hospitality. Yuri had ministered to each of them, in his own way. He opened his doors and welcomed them all.

"And if I go and prepare a place for you, I will come again, and receive you unto myself; that where I am, there ye may be also."

The minister's sleeves billowed as his words echoed around the sanctuary: *"And if I go and prepare a place for you, I will come again ..."*

Dan was on his feet even before he fully understood. Heads turned in curiosity as he made his way down the aisle and along the creaky wooden floors, banging knees, and trying desperately not to run until he was finally outside and bolting down the stairs to the street.

He had his cell in his hand and heard the line ringing.

I will come again ...

She answered. Dan listened to her impatiently, waiting for her to finish.

Look closer to home, baby.

"We found it. It took a lot of looking, but you were right, Dan."

"Good, good!" He told her what he knew.

What movie has a bridge and a bell tower?

She listened carefully. "So you're saying Santiago was there, too? In the house?"

The first death was faked ...

"Yes, that's what I'm saying! But earlier."

"I don't understand. Who brought the phone to the pawn shop? Santiago's fingerprints were all over it."

"And nobody else's?"

"No, not even ..." She was already with him. "... Yuri Malevski's!"

Dan's words fell out in a jumble, describing his encounter with the illegal immigrant who cleaned houses, of her passion for Christ, her intense dislike of Yuri Malevski. She had been there.

"Those weren't Santiago's fingerprints."

"Then whose were they? Are you saying the cleaner stole the phone?"

"No, listen. I think we're missing the boat here."

He told her his theory. A missing phone, a missing candelabra, a missing immigrant. Even the missing fingerprints. Not what was there, but what wasn't. She was harder to convince this time after his blunder at the mansion that morning, but she was willing to consider it.

"Can you prove it?" she asked.

"Give me half an hour."

Twenty-Nine

Orchids

She started at the sound of his voice. "Please, no! I cannot!"

"Irma, you must help. What would Jesus have done?" Dan blurted out before she could hang up. "Would he have turned his back on the sinner?"

He knew she wouldn't turn him down.

"I'll come to you."

He scribbled her address on a napkin and dashed to his car before she could change her mind. She'd been there, Dan realized. She was a witness to something, even if she didn't know it. He himself didn't know precisely what he was looking for, just that beneath the surface of a very clean house lay a clue that would help him unravel the mystery.

When he'd checked the weather, he saw it had snowed the previous evening and well into the night. The month had been terrifically cold, the temperature hitting a low of minus eighteen-point-three. Nothing unusual for February, but he thought the snow was the telling detail.

Yes, she said, watching him nervously. No one had been in or out of the house when she arrived that morning. No footsteps trod through the snow from either the back or front door. The drive hadn't been shovelled. Anyone coming or going would have left a trail. It was impossible to cover the tracks. Ziggy hadn't lied when he said he hadn't been in the house before she got there. Donny had told him Ziggy stayed on his couch that week, even if he was a little cloudy on the precise dates. It didn't matter, really, because no one could pinpoint exactly when Yuri had died. Still, that wasn't it.

No. What he was seeking lay elsewhere.

Dan glanced around the minuscule apartment. It was neat and clean, pretty much as he'd expected. It was also barren. A poverty house with crosses adorning the walls in every room. The only true decorations were a couple of framed prints and several orchids just opening into bloom.

"Nice flowers," Dan said, hoping to put her at ease.

"Yes, thank you. From son."

She was far warier this time. Her dark eyes followed him, reading every gesture. Words could be made to say anything, all stories were half fiction, anyway, but a person's movements did not lie.

"You said the house was very clean when you arrived."

"Yes," she said hesitantly.

"As though no one had been there for some time?"

"Yes."

Because in all likelihood no one had been there, Dan thought. *No one living, at any rate.* He saw the dawning, the realization in her eyes. She'd seen something.

"He is —"

"He is what, Irma?"

"He is still there!"

Curiosity turned to fear. Her eyes darted around the room, like a trapped bird looking for a window.

"Who?"

A hand rose to cover her mouth.

"Jesus!"

She uttered the name with quiet vehemence. For a second, Dan thought she was cursing. Or worse, losing her mind. She'd be hopeless as a witness. *Who did you see?* the prosecutor would ask. *Jesus!* she would respond, staring out at the court like a madwoman. He needed to bring her back to sanity for a few more minutes, until he'd finished questioning her.

"Mr. Malevski doesn't take away," she said.

"Take away what?"

"Every week I leave pamphlet, every week he put in garbage. Wicked man. But this is same pamphlet I leave on table one week before. Why he doesn't throw out?"

Dan shook his head. "You're saying you left a religious pamphlet and Mr. Malevski didn't move it or pick it up from the previous week?"

She nodded fearfully. "Yes!"

"So when you got there, the house was the same as it had been when you cleaned the week before?"

"Yes! Except kitchen. I wipe …"

Someone had to clean up that mess.

"You wiped up the blood?" he asked.

A sob escaped her. She nodded.

"Tell me what you found when you arrived."

She sat silently for a moment, collecting herself. "House is very clean, except kitchen. But greenhouse is not normal."

Dan turned to her. "The greenhouse?"

"Flowers are dead. I wacuum. So many on floor."

Dan nodded, thinking of Hank's peace offering. "They all died, didn't they?"

"Maybe one, two is okay ..."

Dan thought of what he'd learned on the Internet. There was such an amazing variety of orchids. They were like immigrants, of every race and colour, brought from shore to shore by travellers, traders, and buyers. Ziggy had told him how much some of them cost. Dan hadn't believed it until he read it online. One particular plant had sold for two hundred thousand dollars. Most of them lost their flowers when exposed to cold, but others — a handful — actually thrived, one or two varieties out of thousands. Yuri had owned several such orchids.

"Was it cold when you arrived? In the house?"

He already knew the answer.

"Yes, is freezing. Like refrigerator."

Sensitive to temperature, humidity and light, the orchids had suffered with the lowering of the thermostat. But not all.

He thought back: Lionel left for Mexico on the third, but Charles had stayed behind, joining him two days later. What had Lionel said of Charles? That he was afraid of him. That Charles had experience making money disappear into foreign accounts. He thought of the sleeping pills Charles insisted Lionel take to relax. Another piece of the puzzle fell into place: Dan suddenly knew who Santiago's other boyfriend was. Charles had known, too.

Irma waited until Dan asked everything he needed to know. There wasn't much time left. On his way out, a photograph caught his eye. Irma, looking much the same as she did right now, only smiling and with a handsome young man at her side, his arm thrown over her shoulder.

"Son?" he asked.

She hesitated. "Yes."

"A good-looking boy."

"Thank you."

"Family is important," Dan said.

She smiled.

Thirty

The Unravelling

Dan knew he had to move fast. At least one life was at stake. There was no sense going back to the Lockie House. The code had been changed and he thought he knew by whom. It wasn't necessary to break in to confirm anything. Even if his theory proved correct, as he was sure it would, there were limits to what the police would accept. He'd simply have to prove to Inspector Johnston what he knew to be true.

He pulled out his phone as he turned his car around. Johnston was with him now. She agreed he had a point. A big point. And he was closer to Radio City than she was.

"I can get there first," he said.

"Be careful!"

Charles and Lionel were just crossing the lobby, bags in hand, when Dan arrived.

Fury rose on Charles's face. "I told you to leave us alone!"

"Please, Charles!" Lionel grabbed his husband's arm to quiet him. "Dan? What's this all about?"

Dan gave him a rueful look. "It's about …" He shook his head. "It's about orchids."

"What?"

"Yeah, it's about orchids."

"What are you talking about?" Charles demanded.

Lionel quieted him again and said softly, "I don't understand."

Dan took a breath. "To understand, you have to work backwards. A man is killed in his own home and the door is double locked. Makes you wonder why. Why go to the bother of locking a door when you know someone's going to find the body eventually? The easy answer is, to give the killer plenty of get-away time. Sure, why not? It's the likeliest reason, but in this case it wasn't the real reason because nobody was trying to get away. Then I thought maybe it was a sign of veneration. Of love, even. It fit Ziggy's story. Maybe Santiago's, too. He and Yuri had been together long enough. In any case, either of them could have done it. It might have been an accident and the killer later sealed up the place like some kind of shrine. But that wasn't it, either."

"How do you know?" Charles asked.

"Because this murder was meticulously planned. The only thing that didn't fit was the timing."

Dan saw the first cruiser pull up outside the building. Inspector Johnston got out and drew her gun. A second cruiser nosed into place behind it. Two more officers leapt out and followed.

Dan kept talking. "So I asked myself, what if the death didn't occur when it was supposed to? What if it occurred earlier than we were led to believe? Once I asked that question, things started falling into place. Except in that case, why would someone break into the dead man's house to use his cell phone?"

Lionel shook his head, a crease puckering his brow.

"You would only do it if you wanted to make it look like the cell's owner was still alive. Someone used Yuri Malevski's phone to make a call to Mexico and to text an entry code to a house cleaner."

Lionel shook his head. "You mean it wasn't Yuri who called me?"

Dan shook his head. "No. It was someone else."

"But who?" Lionel asked. "It was Yuri's voice on the message."

"Or a recording of Yuri's voice."

"Oh."

Dan nodded. "Who else was around to use Yuri's phone? You and Charles were in Mexico. The cleaning lady was just a cleaning lady who'd been set up to further the plot along, so I didn't think it was her. A transsexual named Jan used to frequent the house, but no one had seen Jan for some time, so once again it was unlikely. There was even a weird neighbour with a grudge, plus a supposedly crooked cop thrown into the scenario to confuse things. And, unbeknownst to nearly everybody, a strange boy named Ziggy lived under the eaves in Yuri's house. He confessed to me he'd extracted the entry code texted to the cleaning lady from Yuri's cellphone. A very sweet lady in possession of some extremely valuable orchids, by the way."

Dan saw Inspector Johnston standing at the back of the lobby listening to him.

"At first I wasn't so sure about Ziggy, but I quickly realized he was more of a neurotic than a psychotic. Killer? Nah, I don't think so. So who else was there?"

Dan let the question hang in the air. He turned his gaze on Charles. "You left late to meet Lionel in Mexico, didn't you?"

Charles suddenly looked bewildered, dropping the lawyer's bravado.

"I had a case to close. I made arrangements to meet with Lionel two days later. It was a Saturday. The airline will have a record. I told you this already."

"True," Dan said. "I don't doubt what you say. But somebody made a call and sent a text. Then the phone disappeared. I don't think that was part of the plan. It showed up this morning in a pawn shop with the fingerprints of the suicide victim who jumped from Overlea Bridge, by the way. Though it's beginning to look as though that wasn't really a suicide after all," Dan said.

"I knew it wasn't," Lionel said, turning to Charles. "Didn't I tell you?"

Dan continued. "But the question remains: why make a call and send a text? Why? To frame someone for the murder and cover up for the missing money that had been siphoned from the bar. Someone wanted to make it look as though Yuri was still alive, when in fact he'd been dead since the third of February." He turned his gaze on Charles. "Probably not long after your argument with him."

"I didn't kill Yuri!"

Dan watched him. "I believe you now, but for a while I thought you had. Still, there was that call and the text from Yuri's phone. They had to have been made by someone else, since Yuri was no longer alive."

Everyone stared at Dan.

"But how do you know?" Charles ventured.

"The orchids."

"What orchids? What are you talking about?"

"You know, I couldn't figure it out. Here's a man who is supposedly crazy about orchids with a greenhouse full of dead plants. He'd paid a lot of money for those plants. They should have had flowers on them. They should have been alive. But most of them were already dead when a cleaner arrived and vacuumed the petals off the floor. That was a Thursday. Yuri's body was discovered two days later, on Saturday. The coroner's report said he'd been dead for two or three days at most, but in fact he was dead well before that. The house was nearly freezing for a week. The thermostat had been turned down to keep the body from decomposing. That's why the doors were double-locked, to keep anyone with the code from entering and turning it back up until a few days before your return from Mexico by a cleaning woman who always cleaned house on Thursday."

"Then who made the call and sent the text?" Lionel asked.

"Your lover."

Lionel looked to his husband. "But Charles was with me by the time I got the call. Besides, he changed his plans for business reasons at the last minute. His boss insisted. It wasn't anything he planned."

"Yes," Charles broke in. "I changed them for business."

"Nevertheless, Charles came later. He met you two days into your vacation in Mexico, as you both pointed out. It would have given him ample time to do the deed before turning down the thermostat and heading off to Mexico. As I say, he *might* have done it, but Charles didn't have the code to Yuri's house. In fact, he told me himself he never had the code."

"Then how could he have made the call or sent a text?" Lionel asked. "You just said —!"

"I didn't say your husband made them. I said your lover did. The same person I saw standing on the stoop when I arrived at Malevski's house this morning. I thought I saw a delivery man trying to get into the house with an old code, but in fact he had just changed it after removing some very expensive orchids from the greenhouse. It was Santiago."

Lionel shook his head. "But Santiago's dead!"

"No, he's not."

"Then who —?"

"A boy who had already threatened suicide. Ziggy was pale as a ghost, even under all that make-up. Didn't you notice the discrepancies on the body you identified as Santiago's?"

Lionel looked bewildered. "His face was damaged badly. I … I told you, he didn't look right. He was all swollen up!"

"Yes, and Ziggy told me Charles said he looked like Santiago's younger brother. True, they looked a bit alike, but they were essentially different in obvious ways. Santiago has olive skin where Ziggy's is pale. Santiago was hairy, while Ziggy was smooth." Dan held Lionel's gaze. "Ziggy told me he got the new code from Yuri's phone. He would have had to pick it up to read it. Then later he sold it to a pawn shop, along with a few other items. That was a problem. They weren't Santiago's fingerprints on the phone, they were Ziggy's. As his lover, you would have known you were identifying the wrong corpse. I saw Santiago's picture about an hour ago, in fact, so I have a pretty good idea where the police will find him. He seems to have found an adopted mother. She keeps his picture beside the orchids he gave her for safekeeping."

Charles set his suitcase on the floor and looked at Lionel. The anger had been replaced by fear and uncertainty.

"Why?"

"Why?" Lionel looked away. "Why were you running around with that stupid little boy in girl's clothes? And all those other scum you picked up, thinking I would never find out? You made me sign that prenuptial agreement, virtually locking me into marriage. Is that your idea of fair — tying me down and making me risk all my savings if I left you?"

"That wasn't the purpose ..." Charles started to say. "I was protecting us. I was just doing what lawyers do."

"Protecting us?" Lionel spat at him. "And I was just doing what accountants do, balancing the accounts and tidying up your dirty little affairs all over the city. Santiago is twice the man you are."

From the corner of his eye, Dan saw Inspector Lydia Johnston move quietly toward Lionel.

Epilogue

Home

Dan was just edging up to the curb when his phone rang.

"Hey, Dad!"

Ked's voice nearly leapt out of the phone at him.

"Hey! What's up?"

"I won!" He waited a beat. "The science contest! I won with my sling psychrometer!"

Dan laughed. "That's amazing!"

"Old world technology," Ked said. "It's still the best."

"So are you going to give up your cellphone and revert to tin cans tied together with strings?"

"That's *too* old world for me. It probably even predates you." There was a pause. "This will really help with scholarships."

"Great! I guess that'll make it easier for you to move away from Toronto when you go to school."

"I guess." There was a longer pause. "You really want me to move away?"

"I want you to see what the rest of the world looks like. You have to leave home to do that. But it doesn't mean you can't come home again whenever you want." He paused to consider. "How does Elizabeth feel about this?"

"She thinks I should go, too."

"Then there's your answer." Dan put the car in park and turned off the ignition. "I'm truly thrilled for your win, but I just arrived somewhere and I need to do something. Can we talk about this later? Maybe over a little celebration?"

"Sure." Hesitance crept into Ked's voice. "I'm busy tonight, though. Elizabeth and I are going out. Sorry."

"No worries. We'll arrange something."

Dan got out of his car and stood looking up at the house that had relinquished nearly all of its secrets to him. For a moment, he wondered about the future owners, then decided he'd let them discover the secret panel on their own.

He punched in the four numbers of the entry code, gratified to see red turn to green once again. Still welcome, after all. He was beginning to feel like part of the family. Maybe that was Yuri Malevski's influence, creating a place where everyone could be at home.

Most of the plants had been removed from the greenhouse. The few that remained were dead or too large to be moved easily. He hoped whoever took them knew their worth. Or maybe not. Why not just let them be plants, with no special price tag attached to them? *Let them be appreciated for their beauty*, he thought.

Dan bounded up the stairs to the third floor and pushed on the panel. It swung open. He looked around the tiny space. The diary was gone — police evidence. The fingerprints on it had confirmed what he'd already known, that it was Ziggy who was pushed from Overlea Bridge.

He nudged the curtains aside and looked out on Yuri Malevski's lush garden. Who knew, but the fruit trees and flowers might have dated to the time of its construction, back when it was just becoming known as the Lockie House. It was a pleasant thought, all that stretching back into antiquity.

It was a cozy hiding spot. Dan could have benefited from something like this as a boy escaping his father's drunken aggression. He lay on the futon and stared at the beams overhead. Three words were scribbled in chalk on the wood: *Ziggy was here!* He felt a lump in his throat.

Just then, his cell buzzed. It was Donny.

"Are you still angry with me?" Donny asked.

"Angry with you? Why?"

"For introducing you to them and getting you mixed up in that sordid tale."

"Not your fault. You couldn't have known. And no, I'm not angry with you."

"Thank god. Prabin told me I was imagining it, but I've had nothing but sleepless nights ever since."

"In fact," Dan said, "if I'd listened to you in the first place, I might have been further ahead. You made the whole thing sound like a bad TV drama, and in fact that was what it was. I need to learn to think in clichés if I'm going to be more successful. It really was all about the protection money, but not because of the police. It was Lionel and his Cuban boyfriend scheming to steal from Yuri and have a life of luxury."

"So who did the killing?"

"I thought you were above asking such sordid questions."

"Humour me this one time."

"Ziggy felt protective of Yuri, so he told Yuri about Santiago's affair with Lionel after he saw them together. It wasn't long before Yuri threw Santiago out. I think that was when Yuri discovered the missing money. His private file showed they'd been siphoning it out of the bar for months. When Yuri confronted Santiago, he killed him in his kitchen. With Lionel's help, they made it look like Yuri died while Lionel was in Mexico and Santiago was off with the girlfriend at Jane and Finch. Lionel had an old recording of Yuri's monthly meeting reminder. Santiago played it back to him over the phone while he was away."

"When did you catch on?"

"It took a while. There were so many things telling me I was wrong, particularly the coroner's report on the timing of the death. But once I reconsidered that in light of their affair, everything made sense. Lionel even made threatening calls to Santiago's girlfriend to warn her off. He would probably have married Santiago himself if he hadn't already been married to Charles. A divorce would have cost him dearly. I first began to suspect Lionel because he tried too hard to convince me it was Charles, when he should have been protecting him. It would have been all too convenient for them if Charles had been convicted of Yuri's murder."

"Hmmm ..." Donny said meditatively.

"I blame myself for Ziggy's death," Dan said, running his fingers across the lettering overhead. "I don't think anyone knew he was in the house till I mentioned it. The decision to make it look as though Santiago committed suicide figured neatly into their plans. Santiago lured Ziggy to the bridge, saying Charles wanted to meet him, only Charles wasn't there when he arrived. Lionel planted his card on Ziggy to make sure he would be asked to identify the body. Being an illegal, there was no record of fingerprints or family to come looking for Santiago when he disappeared. Ziggy was perfect."

"How long will you beat yourself up for that one?"

"How long have you got? I feel culpable. That won't change."

"But in reality, Ziggy started the ball rolling by telling Yuri about Santiago and Lionel. With or without you, it would have come back to him once they knew. And you have to remember you saved Charles's life, at least."

"I suspect the trip up north would have resulted in another fatality, made to seem accidental. Lionel hated that Charles was able to lord it over him once he'd signed the prenuptial and then went all over town having affairs. I was wrong about Charles, though. He may have ordinary human flaws, but he wasn't the cesspool of immorality I thought he was."

"Glad to hear. So does this mean I can stop worrying about you for the time being?"

"Why would you worry about me?"

"Oh, I don't know — getting beaten up in Quebec didn't exactly quell my fears."

"A couple of thugs hired by some renegade cops, nothing more. Lydia thinks she knows who to pressure for an answer. I doubt I'll be looking over my shoulder for that one the rest of my life."

"I just wish you'd stop taking chances. By the way, where are you?"

"Yuri Malevski's mansion."

Donny sucked in his breath. "Okay — I don't even want to know."

"It's all right. I wouldn't tell if you tortured me."

"That sets my alarm bells ringing."

"Don't worry your pretty little head about it. Besides, you know what they say: wild horses couldn't drag it out of me."

A match flared on the other end.

"Question," Dan said.

"Shoot."

"If you were single and knew a very sexy cop who was also single, would you date him?"

"If I were me, sure. If I were you? Definitely not."

"Why?"

"Because he's a cop and you're a private eye. Isn't that a little like dating the enemy?"

"Kind of. It's okay, I just wondered. I'll talk to you later."

"Wait!"

"What?"

"If you do date him, will there be coercion?"

Dan smiled. "If there is, it'll be willing."

"Then it won't be coercion. But in any case, take pictures."

Dan was seated at his kitchen table. He glanced up at the cupboards that once held his alcohol. What would they hold when Ked went away to school in the fall?

He pulled out Nick Trposki's card, pushing Hank's orchid aside as he reached for his cell. The cop answered right away. There was a pause when Dan identified himself.

"I'm not in a bar, if that's what you're thinking," Dan said. "I'm not calling you to rescue me."

"Glad to hear. How can I help?"

"Do you ever think about the future?"

"Is this a trick question?"

"Not really. I'd like to know."

"All right. Then, yes. Sometimes."

"That's it?"

There was a laugh. "Okay, here's what it is. Mostly it depresses me to think about the future. I can barely stand to think about tomorrow let alone the distant future, but every once in a while I think about what I'll be doing a year from now and whether I'll be with anyone in another five. How's that for a true confession?"

"Pretty good," Dan said. "I've got one, too. I don't want to grow old alone. Especially since I've come to the realization that I can't live with alcohol in the house. Imagine that — a grown man who can't trust himself."

Nick gave a begrudging laugh. "I hear you."

"Some days I think the solution is to live *with* somebody. But then I think about it and I don't like what it says about my independence."

"Giving it up, you mean?"

"Yeah, that. At times I want to be with someone, but at other time I don't want to be crowded out."

Nick waited. "So why are you telling me all this? Are you asking me out or something?"

"Yes, I am officially asking you to go out on a date with me. No commitments, apart from dinner. What do you think?"

"I'd be willing to consider it."

Dan laughed. "That's it? Just willing to consider it?"

"It would have to be a decent place. I may be a cop, but I still like good restaurants with nice atmosphere and top-quality food."

"How about Italian to start?"

Nick laughed again. "When?"

"I think we should begin tonight. No use waiting. I don't know about you, but I'm already forty. I'm pretty sure neither of us is getting any younger."

"I agree," Nick said. "I'm not far behind you in years."

"Tell you what. I just got home. I'm going to take a shower. Then I am going to make a reservation for two somewhere in the city. I'll call and tell you where."

"Sounds good."

Dan waited a beat. "By the way, you know how you told me your last lover was the best guy you ever met?"

"Yeah?"

"Well, that's not me. I'm more thorn than rose."

Nick laughed. "I never said I was perfect either. But he wasn't really all that perfect, to tell the truth. You know the thing that pissed me off most about him?"

"What?"

"When he wanted out of the relationship, he was so angry he just moved away. He never even called to say goodbye."

Dan thought about this for a moment. "Don't worry, I wouldn't do that. I always say goodbye."

Acknowledgements

Thanks to Red Cruz, Mark Round, Luba Goy, David Tronetti, Keith Garebian, Sheila McCarthy, Geordie Johnson, Phil Bedard and Larry Lalonde, Tim Leonard, the staff of The One in the Only Café, John Scythes (current owner of the Lockie House), Shannon Whibbs, and the good folks at Dundurn who give me a reason to keep doing what I do. A tip of the hat to Scott and Ken of the Crystal Method for the groovy late-night vibes that kept me up writing way past my bedtime. Thanks also to you, the readers, who write to tell me how much you enjoy Dan and his world!

DUNDURN

VISIT US AT

Dundurn.com
@dundurnpress
Facebook.com/dundurnpress
Pinterest.com/dundurnpress